Cries in the Night

A Lowcountry Ghost Story

LORI ROBERTS

Cries in the Night

A Lowcountry Ghost Story

LORI ROBERTS

Crecelius Haus Publishing

Copyright 2020 by Lori Roberts

All Rights Reserved.

No part of this book may be reproduced in any form or by any electronic or mechanical means, including information storage and retrieval systems, without written permission from the author, except for the brief quotations in a book review.

Cover Design by Dennis Collins

Library of Congress Cataloging-in-Publication Data

Roberts, Lori.
Cries in the night : a Lowcountry ghost story / by Lori Roberts. pages cm
ISBN 978-1-7322492-3-3 (trade pbk.) -- ISBN 978-1-7322492-4-0 (e-pub)
1. Haunted houses--Fiction. 2. Charleston (S.C.)--Fiction. I. Title.

Library of Congress Control Number: 2020905603

AUTHOR'S NOTE:

For information about permission to reproduce selections from this book write to:

Permissions
Crecelius Haus Publishing LLC
31 Sir William Drive
Bedford, IN 47421

Dedication

To Pa~ I love you more.

In memory of Revis Crecelius and Jerald Roberts.

For~ Haden, Hadley, Gibson, Iyla, Nash, Lydia,

Griffin, Adalyn, and Amelia

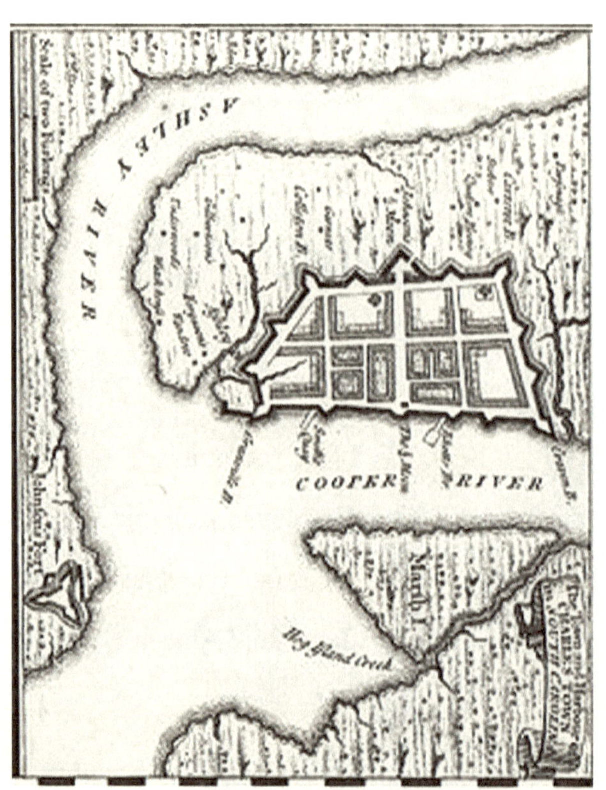

Charleston, SC 1733

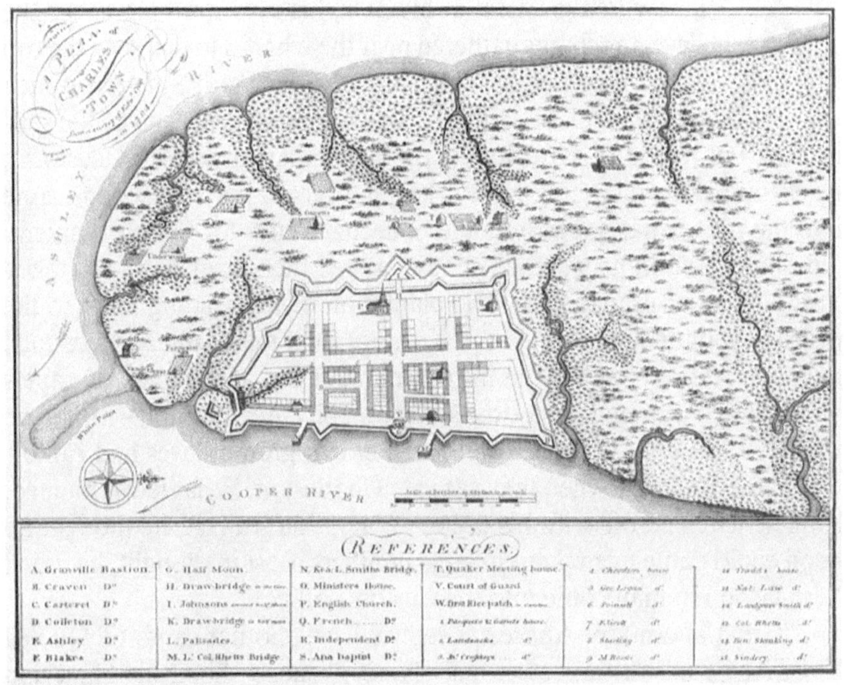

Charleston, SC 1809

Prologue

Charleston, South Carolina – 1799

Andrew Pettigrew sat at his desk, his eyes straining to see the slave merchants gathered near the wharf. He had seen the trio keeping company with Sally, the McCrady's tavern wench who had taken a shine to him. He needed a touch of the spirits now, but he didn't dare partake on the job. As inspector of customs, he examined the incoming vessels, keeping account of what goods came into the port, what goods left, and collected duties for the government. On this afternoon he watched ebony-colored men from Barbados taken from the vessel in manacles. The plantation owner leading them to the pens to await auction was Alston Keating, local rice planter and council member. Andrew sat back in his chair and glared at the mess of papers on his desk. Although he saw the slaves enter by the thousands, he had no use for slaves now. Most of John Halston Pettigrew's slaves had run off to join the Redcoats when they came to Charleston. What few remained, bankers had sold off with his father's plantation. In fact, he thought no good could come from them in large numbers. Lost in thought, he didn't hear Jacob Hinman come into the Customs office.

"Good afternoon, Andrew. I see we have another cargo of Guinea boys. Any rum on the vessel, per chance?" Jacob shook his hand and pulled up a chair to talk trade. He sank into the chair opposite Andrew's desk and began to pare his fingernails with his knife.

Andrew had begun holding back a barrel of fine Caribbean rum as well as other items that could be stored and resold for profit, and Jacob arranged the sales. Andrew didn't like the quandary he found himself in, but thought it best to keep his end of the bargain. The two friends had made an agreement that came about from tragic circumstances.

"No rum today." Andrew hoped the two kegs wedged beneath the large mahogany desk would go unnoticed. "I'm awaiting the arrival of a sloop from the Indies later in the week." He swallowed the bile rising in his throat, not liking the spot he was in.

Following the war with the British, dozens of planters in the area had fallen on hard times. Andrew's father witnessed the British army lay waste to his plantation, and watched his rice fields and indigo set afire. Jacob Hinman's father's plantation had suffered a similar fate.

As his father's only surviving son, Andrew would have inherited Cypress Hall and 150 slaves one day. After the devastation of the farm, Mr. Pettigrew died leaving the estate to his son. A few years later, Andrew found a wealthy planter from Savannah who bought the plantation and restored it to its former glory. He wanted nothing more of the plantation life and to leave behind forever the memories of his mother and sister dying of yellow fever.

In 1789 Andrew had come to Charleston to buy a lot and build a new home in town. After receiving his money from the sale of his farm, Andrew and his boyhood friend, Jacob Hinman, visited McCrady's to partake of spirits and wenches. As dawn broke early the next morning, Andrew woke up face down on Unity Alley, a bloody knife next to his hand.

"Comin' around, are ye? You stabbed that scrawny sailor." Jacob helped his friend sit up and slipped the knife inside Andrew's coat pocket. He pointed to a body lying on the other side of the alley.

"His mate attacked me, but the cur ran when he saw his friend lying dead on the street," Jacob said.

Andrew shook his head in disbelief.

"Never you mind. You're secret is safe with me." Jacob patted his friend on the back, not looking him in the eye.

Andrew had no memory of them carrying the lifeless body to the wharf and dumping him in the river, which the crew of The Leander found the next morning.

Andrew's deed had been kept secret by Jacob, for a high price. He grew tired of Jacob's weekly visits to the Custom's house, demanding rum and gold coins.

Andrew worked hard for this important job as Customs Inspector, and he couldn't allow Jacob Hinman to ruin his life.

Jacob slammed out of his office without a word.

After his shift ended, Andrew walked the same route home, looking forward to his ritual of tucking his take from the day's inspection into his hidden safe near the fireplace. It made the loss of the family plantation less painful, but Jacob's blackmailing loomed in the back of his mind, spoiling what little satisfaction the loot gave him.

Chapter 1

Charleston, 2013

Carly Tabor didn't like Charleston's humidity. It took twice as long to straighten her shoulder length hair, not to mention the increased amount of anti-frizz gel she used on a regular basis. She had lived in the Rocky Mountains for the past seven years, and humidity wasn't a problem there. She considered herself a Charlestonian since resigning from her television position and selling her home. Her husband, Dr. Austin Tabor, accepted a position at the Medical University Hospital in Charleston. Carly hoped she'd find work in the future, but for now, she wanted to supervise the renovations of their home.

When they'd visited the city earlier in the spring, Austin heard of this "diamond-in-the- rough" from one of the hospital surgeons. The doctor had bought the house on King Street when the market was down but with his wife's death, he wanted to get rid of it. A few years prior, a home on historic King Street sold for more than three million dollars. Austin and Carly purchased their gem from the doctor for just under a million dollars. For a good neurosurgeon, the house was affordable, but they'd need to budget for a few years until Austin established himself in the medical community.

Carly wanted to start a family before they got any older. She was thirty-one, and Austin, thirty-nine. As soon as renovations ended, they'd start planning their family. She hoped that supervising the renovations would occupy her mind, so she didn't brood too much about it.

Carly surveyed their bare apartment. Even though the apartments were past their prime, they had good bones. In a few months, they'd leave their temporary quarters. The place resembled a frat-house rather than a neurosurgeon's home. They had stored their belongings while living in the apartment. It was sparse, and she missed their "things," but their new house would be done by the first week in June. In the meantime the apartment was only a couple blocks from the hospital, and since Austin's surgery schedule had been heavy with late shifts it worked out fine.

Carly hadn't heard him early that morning when he collapsed asleep on the sofa. She watched him sleep and thought about how much she admired his soft-spoken manner with older patients. He always included a reassuring pat on the hand or hug before leaving their room. She knew he'd be a loving father. She smiled at the thought of the child she wished for, hoping she'd be pregnant as soon as they settled into their new house.

Carly finished her second cup of coffee watching Austin sprawled out and exhausted on the overstuffed sofa. She felt sure the dark green faux suede sofa had been a flea market find by a previous resident. She sighed. In another month they'd be out of there.

The next morning Austin rubbed the sleep from his eyes. "Hey hon, you wouldn't mind if I skip the shopping trip with you and Elise, would you?"

"It's okay. We're going to the antique shops and you'd just be bored."

Carly looked forward to her shopping trip, a girls' day out, with Elise Ravanel, their realtor.

Austin sat up hearing her text alert announcing that Elise had arrived.

Carly stepped out of the bedroom to answer, giving him a quick kiss as she rushed out the door.

Elise drove them in her Volkswagen bug. Carly wondered why a successful real estate agent drove buyers in such a small car, until she saw her maneuver through some tight spots. Carly rolled down her window, breathing in the fragrances in the air.

"There's the shop I told you about earlier." Elise pointed up the street, parallel parking in front of a row of shops. "I think you might find a few nice pieces to put in the house."

Other than Elise, Carly didn't know anyone else in Charleston, except for the few doctors' wives that Austin had introduced her to. Being younger and not of their social circle, Carly didn't feel she'd be invited to lunch anytime soon, even though they'd been courteous. Carly wasn't interested in playing Bridge or serving on countless committees.

Several hours later, Elise had driven Carly to four antique shops in the downtown area and one north of town in Mt. Pleasant. Her purchases included two navy barrel back antique chairs for the receiving room, an oil lamp, and a small child's metal rocking horse that had belonged to a family from near Mt. Pleasant. Dating from the mid-1850s, the much-loved toy was faded and missing its string, and the previous owner's had left old photos of it in an album that she also bought. She'd overspent her budget but justified her purchase because she felt drawn to the toy horse.

"Want me to drive you over to look at your new house, or have you had enough for one day?" Elise opened the door for Carly to place her purchases on the back seat.

"If you don't mind, I'd like to go back and get my car. I need to stop by the contractor's office to make sure the workers start first thing tomorrow. Thanks so much for touring me around."

Carly met the owner, at the entrance just as they both arrived at the Trevenour Office Building.

"Hi, I'm Carly Tabor and I'm here to see Rich." She noted that the building carried his last name.

"I'm Rich. Great to meet you. Let's go inside." He opened the door for her.

"I wanted to check on the workers for tomorrow at my home on King Street." Carly stepped inside moving sideways so he could enter and lead the way.

"Sure, I remember talking to you last week. Come on back, and I'll see who's scheduled. I'll be there as well to get things going."

Carly surveyed the office. She smiled at the thought of Austin swinging a hammer. He knew nothing about construction matters, so she had been grateful when Elise recommended Trevenour Building and Renovation. As a realtor, Elise cultivated the best vendor list in Charleston. Carly had done her homework too. She found only good reviews on the Better Business Bureau's website.

"Looks like Steve, Dan, and Chase will be the head crew for you. All good guys, so I know you're in good hands," He smiled.

Carly thanked Rich and left the office. She decided to have a look at their dream house without Elise along and imagine the possibilities, so she headed that direction, dodging through tourists, mule-drawn carriages, and the always heavy traffic.

Driving along in her Range Rover, she thought about her lifestyle changes. She'd moved from her family farm twelve years earlier to attend the University of Kansas. There, while working at a nearby gym, she met Austin, a resident at the local hospital. After a year-long courtship, the two married. Austin took a position at a hospital in Denver, and they purchased a home in a gated community. With this latest move to a coastal town, she felt like a stranger but excited to try a new adventure.

Pulling the car up to the front of their King Street house, she unlocked the wrought iron gate to their property and drove into a small brick covered area. A nine foot brick wall surrounded the property on three sides. She particularly admired the double piazzas and the rest of the house faced towards the Battery, a famous defensive seawall and promenade used during the Civil War. Although Carly hadn't had a chance to read up on its history, she enjoyed imagining what it looked like when it was first built. She'd gleaned bits and pieces of its history from Elise. As she unlocked the door and walked inside, the musty smell of a closed-up, old house in the summer heat of Charleston assaulted her nose. When she saw once again the partial renovation in progress, Carly sighed.

The previous owner, Dr. Howard Hutchinson, who had purchased the house ten years before, had started with the most urgent renovations so he and his wife could move in. He updated the wiring and electrical issues first, including a leak in the roof. Dr. Hutchinson and his wife had researched how to restore the house without damaging its historical features. However, during the renovation, Mrs. Hutchinson was diagnosed with an aggressive cancer, and within just a few months, she had died. The grieving doctor moved back to his condo, leaving the house vacant for several years, until finally deciding to sell the house at a loss.

When Carly and Austin viewed it, they fell in love with the possibilities. Thankfully, Austin's father helped with the down payment, they made an offer and the house was theirs.

Carly doubted the house could ever be as nice as it once was—a gem among the lovely houses along King Street. But she planned to update one floor at a time, completing their bedroom and bath on the second floor first and then update the bathroom downstairs. She and Austin considered painting and making cosmetic changes to the front rooms downstairs a priority too. Remodeling the kitchen could wait until later since the Hutchinson's had partially renovated it. They'd finish the attic room on the third floor last.

The house had three bedrooms and two baths, besides the master bedroom and its adjoining bathroom. As Carly walked up the curved stairway, she skimmed her hand along the cherry wood railing. When she reached the second floor, her footsteps echoed through the empty house. She shivered. It felt cooler upstairs than it had downstairs. She wondered why? The house had been closed and the summer temperature outside had reached the upper 80's. Had it been insulated better than they thought? She returned her focus to the task at hand, noting the good condition of the heart of pine floorboards throughout the first and second floors. They only needed a good polishing and buffing. The three bedrooms and baths needed updates and new window treatments. She stopped and looked into the bedroom that would become a nursery. She made a trip back down to the car, retrieved the small rocking horse and placed it in the middle of the mantle. Perfect. She smiled and wondered about the children who had once played with the toy.

A loud boom like a gunshot brought her thoughts back to the present. Goosebumps rose on her arms, and she held her breath. Carly slowly stepped into the hallway, glancing around for the cause of the noise.

"Hello? Anybody there?" No answer. Carly admonished herself for getting scared and made herself walk down the stairs to investigate. She inched her way, while chewing her bottom lip, past the living room and dining room, looking for anything out of place. She saw nothing that may have fallen. Entering the kitchen, she scanned the room and noticed the small wooden door leading to the cellar. It was ajar. She frowned, knowing it was closed when she'd come inside.

As she touched the door handle, she pulled away. The cold handle startled her. She opened it gingerly and was surprised by a rush of cold air puffing into her face. She jumped back and yelped. Then Carly felt the air return to a normal humid cellar temperature. She shook her head, not sure what had happened, but now—even more curious. She took a deep breath and flipped the light switch inside the door. Nothing happened—no light shined down the dark stairs. "Darn, the electricity won't be turned on until later today." Saying it aloud felt silly, but somehow the normalcy comforted her. What was going on here?

When she and Austin had walked through the house with the realtor, Carly had been preoccupied with the upstairs, and didn't inspect the cellar with Austin. She didn't like cellars and was afraid of spiders and centipedes, so she closed the door. No reason to get disgusted by what was likely a filthy cellar. She decided her investigation of the cellar door and what was behind it could wait until tomorrow when it was daylight, and the electricity was turned on. As she locked up the front door, Carly noticed her goosebumps had returned and she rubbed her arms. With one last look backwards, she quickly got into her car, locked the entry gate behind her, and drove home. Her heart only returned to its normal rhythm when she entered their apartment and locked the door behind her.

Chapter 2

As Carly finished her Starbuck's coffee, the doorbell rang. She checked her watch—seven—the construction workers had shown up right on time. The electric company inspector was already out back finishing his inspection of their work from the day before. Carly was thankful they'd turned on the power when they finished yesterday.

"Welcome to our historic house." She greeted the construction crew one by one as they entered.

Next the electrical inspector gave word that he'd approved the work. Progress had finally begun and she couldn't be happier.

Listening to the activity as the men got to work, her eyes went wide as she remembered the home ovulation kit she'd left on the bathroom counter earlier that morning. "Oh my gosh!" She dashed down the hall to retrieve it. Stuffing the unopened package in her purse, she admitted to herself that she wouldn't conceive this month anyway, with Austin working so many long hours. She took a breath and reasoned with herself. There's always next month to worry about that issue, and she'd need to focus on the house renovation project anyway.

Carly jumped when she heard another sudden boom. Had one of the workers dropped something? What if they were hurt? She scanned the hallway but saw nothing. She listened. Where exactly had the noise come from? She couldn't tell. It seemed to come from all directions. Had anyone else even heard it? No one else seemed concerned about the noise. The crew had split into two groups. One worked in the receiving room downstairs and the other in the upstairs bathroom. She went to check on the workers in the receiving room. She liked calling it by its historical name. These day's people called it a front room or parlor. The workers were busy stripping the faded wallpaper off the walls as if nothing had happened.

Frowning, she looked around the downstairs again but heard no more loud noises. Had she had too much caffeine this morning? Was she imaging things? Was she letting the stress of the home project get the better of her? Could it have been the air conditioner about to go on the fritz? She hoped not. Summertime in Charleston meant hot, humid weather.

The following morning, Carly greeted the crew again at the house. She wanted to stay out of their way, so she stayed in the kitchen unpacking boxes of basic kitchen items and small appliances.

While she worked, Carly thought about the little apartment they'd rented and how claustrophobic it made her feel. She hoped the crew would finish by the end of the month. She couldn't wait to move their furniture into the house.

After a week into the renovations, troubles plaguing the downstairs crew worried Carly. The unusual problems all happened in the receiving room. Tools had gone missing. The baseboards should have been removed intact but broke in several pieces—they'd need to be replaced with new ones. The foreman had difficulty finding the same style baseboards. They no longer manufactured that type. Would they meet their deadline?

"Mrs. Tabor, I don't know how to tell you this…but something weird is going on in your house." Dan shook his head. "Well, I know this sounds crazy, but earlier today, I could have sworn that my hammer flew towards me like … well, kinda like a missile." Dan's face reddened and he scuffed his work boot on the floor.

"What? Are you joking?" Carly almost dropped her handbag." Are you alright?"

"Yes. I'm fine, but I'm afraid it damaged the recently painted crown molding." Dan's eyes didn't meet hers, and he studied the wood floor like it was classic literature.

Carly didn't like hearing about odd things happening in her dream home.

Dan continued, "The crew is complaining about strange noises in the house, mostly a loud banging. Look … I realize it's an old house and all—"

"Yes, but …"

"An older house might have creaks from settling, but flying hammers aren't normal at all. In fact, they're downright dangerous." He gave her a hard stare directly in the eye.

"I'm so sorry. I don't know what to think. I can't understand what's happening myself. I haven't experienced anything being thrown, but I have heard a noise or two." Carly wrung her hands and looked down at her feet. What could she say that would make everything right?

The other men in the crew hurried and packed up their tools and arranged their drop cloths for the next day. Carly watched them leave with their tool boxes and noticed that one nervous worker with a facial tic looked back at the room and tripped over his own feet. A co-worker grabbed an arm and kept him from going down.

"Don't worry, Mrs. Tabor, we'll be back tomorrow to finish this room and then the downstairs is done. In a couple more weeks, we'll be done with the upstairs. I hope you're happy with the job so far." Dan stuck his hands in his pockets.

"Very happy. It all looks great so far. I don't know what went on with the hammer, but I'm really sorry. Thanks for hanging in there with us." Carly walked him to the door.

The burly man took off his cap and wiped the sweat from his forehead. "I've never had tools moving around the room right in front of my eyes before. We work on a lot of old houses, but this is the first time I've had the hair on my neck stand up, that's for sure."

Carly closed the door and went back into the hallway, she felt a coldness wrap around her. "Who's there?" She felt a presence. Someone or some *thing* was there with her. She tried to ignore her feelings. She went to inspect the newly painted receiving room. She entered the room and a deep voice moaned. "Who's there?" Carly asked again. She dashed back out into the hallway and looked up the stairway to the second floor. Nothing. Was she being paranoid? Had she heard anything? She ran to the kitchen. No mistake—she felt a cold strong presence again. The voice came from the hallway, clear and strong. "Get out of this house!"

In a second, Carly ran to the counter, grabbed her purse and bolted out the door. She didn't take time to lock up. She didn't care. She didn't look back at the house until she started her car. Her hand shook so much, she had trouble fitting the key into the ignition and locking her doors. Their lovely home looked just the same as before, but it wasn't the same. She couldn't think of anything except to obey that angry voice telling her to leave. As she careened out of the driveway, her heart pounded like a hammer in her throat.

After having a glass of wine to settle her nerves, Carly accepted the fact that she'd better tell Austin about the odd happenings in the house. She worried that he'd laugh and think it was nothing, but she decided to tell him all.

Hoping Austin would be in good spirits, Carly brought it up during dinner. "Today, Dan wanted to talk to me about some weird things going on in the house." Austin stopped, mid-chew, putting his garlic bread back on the plate. "Weird? What kind of weird?"

"Well, this sounds crazy, but while Dan worked in the receiving room, his hammer picked itself up and, um, well, it kinda flew across the room. To make matters worse, it landed right on the brand new crown molding." Carly reached for her wine glass and took a sip. "And today, when I came back into the house, there was someone in there with me." The sentence took on a different meaning than Carly intended.

"You saw someone?" Carly had his undivided attention.

Carly let out her breath in a rush. "No, but I felt someone was there. Then, he shouted for me to get out!"

"You know I don't like guns, but would you feel better carrying one?" Austin placed both hands on the table.

His serious gesture helped her feel better. "I don't know. Maybe I just need some rest. Besides, I don't think a gun would do much good." She tried to joke, but her throat tightened. "I can't very well shoot something I can't see."

"I don't feel right leaving you alone in the house. This puts me in a tight spot. You know my workload is crazy now. Can you get someone to be there with you?"

"I don't know. I can try."

"Do that." Austin took a drink of wine and picked up his fork.

An uneasy silence accompanied the rest of the meal.

Carly didn't want to impose on anyone, so she only stayed at the house while the work crew was there. She left at the end of the day when they did. The next two weeks, the house project passed without any odd happenings. In the evenings, Carly kept busy packing what little they had in the apartment, and Austin continued with long hours at the hospital.

When he had a few minutes to spare, Austin went with Carly to inspect the work. They were impressed with the speed and quality of the workmanship. They'd soon finish, and their dream home would be ready for their own belongings.

By the end of July, Carly had new window treatments in place and the furniture had been delivered that she had purchased and placed in storage. A gift from Austin's parents, the antique receiving room settee, chairs, and tables went well with the rest of her decor. There were plenty of auctions and antique shops from which she could find suitable pieces to place throughout the house. The antique shop in Mt. Pleasant had arranged for the chairs to be delivered that she had purchased earlier in the month. Now her house was becoming a home.

Carly walked into the hallway of the second floor, surveying the work that had been completed, giving it her silent approval. She opened the door to the future nursery, the sunlight bathing her face as she entered the room. The sunny yellow color seemed brighter than usual on this morning. She liked how the white marble on the mantle of the fireplace had been cleaned and polished to its former splendor. She hadn't had time to dwell on starting a family during the renovation, but now that work was completed, perhaps she and Austin could give the matter their undivided attention.

She had found the perfect crib, and had even placed a few antique toys on the mantle in the so-called nursery. In the corner, an antique chifferobe, inherited from Carly's grandmother, set in the otherwise bare room. Displayed from the opened door were two Victorian christening gowns, once pristine white eyelet, now yellowed from age. Carly smiled, closing the door behind her. For a moment she'd forgotten about the strange noises she'd been hearing.

Since her first encounter with the man's voice, she started hearing other strange sounds. She told herself they were normal creaking noises heard in all old homes. Could the house still be settling after all this time? She doubted it.

One afternoon, Elise stopped by and exclaimed over the homey feeling in the long-vacant home.

"I can't believe how much a bit of work can bring a house back to life!" Elise handed her a potted geranium plant for a house-warming gift.

"Oh yes, that is an understatement." Carly chose to interpret the meaning in a different way.

"What do you mean? Is something wrong with the house?" Elise frowned.

Carly thought she shouldn't share what had happened since moving into their home but decided she needed a confidant. She didn't have other friends in town.

"Well, this house makes noises. Not just that, but things move around by themselves ..."

"Whoa, girl. What are you saying?" Elise shifted in her seat.

Carly sensed her discomfort, and tried to back pedal. "Look, maybe it's my imagination. Forget I said anything." Carly chewed on her bottom lip.

"Well, there have been rumors about the house. I've never experienced anything when showing the house, but I've heard about sounds coming from the walls." Elise gave her a sympathetic pat on the shoulder.

Carly's heart started racing.

Elise continued, "A friend of mine inspected the house, and said she heard knocking sounds in the kitchen, and thought she saw someone in the hallway. It scared her pretty bad." Elise sat up at the edge of her seat.

"You're telling me this house has a ghost? I don't believe in that stuff. Dead is dead, you know?" She didn't divulge hearing the man's voice telling her to get out of the house.

"You're right. I'm sorry I said anything." She watched Carly frown. "Your house is charming, and like all old houses, has typical old age sounds. No ghosts!" She stood up. "I'd better go. Just wanted to drop off the plant." She gave Carly a hug and the two walked to the door. "Enjoy your beautiful new home."

Carly walked her out.

Chapter 3

Carly met Austin for dinner at their favorite restaurant, The Noisy Oyster.

"I love the festive Caribbean atmosphere this place gives off. We haven't had any fun in a long while." Carly tapped her foot to the island music played in the background.

She ordered a Mojito and Austin ordered an iced tea. While waiting for their drinks, they looked over the menu.

"It's nice to see you happy." Austin set the menu down. "Shall we start with some fried oysters?" He smiled at her, that special twinkle in his eyes, she'd grown to love.

"Um. I'd like that." Carly took a drink of her Mojito, giving him a sultry look as she sipped it. Maybe tonight's the night.

The waiter returned. "Have you decided what you'd like? Or will you need more time?

"I know what I want." Carly nodded at Austin. "You?"

"Yes."

Carly ordered Low Country Shrimp and Grits, and Austin the Baked Seafood Au Gratin.

Halfway through their meal, Austin said, "You don't think there's something paranormal happening, do you? I mean, we both know that's a load of crap, right?"

Carly knew she was above getting into the paranormal craze that seemed to be rampant in historic places, but this wasn't some tourist tale to bring in money—this was her home!

"Elise said that others had experienced seeing or hearing strange things in our house too, Austin." Carly set her fork down and took a drink. "I'm not saying there are ghosts in our house, but weird things have happened, and it scared me."

Austin finished chewing his fried oyster, wiping his mouth on a cloth napkin.

"Rich told me about the hammer flying across the room. I don't know what to make of that one. You're sure you don't want some sort of protection? I hate the thought of you being scared of our house."

"Well, I do love the house, and I want to live in it until we're old and gray!" She took a deep breath. "On another note, I was wondering if we can have a night in, to relax." She raised her eyebrow in a provocative gesture.

Austin took Carly's hand in his. He looked her directly in the eyes. "Well, I meant to tell you ..." He took a quick drink of his iced tea, wishing instead he was having a beer. "I promised Dr. Farris I'd come back this evening. He's performing a malignant Astrocytoma procedure at seven, and I'd like to assist him."

Was he asking for her permission? He sounded like a child.

"This is one of the youngest children I've seen this surgery performed on, and Dr. Farris is the best in the field." His look pleaded for her understanding.

"Of course it's okay, I understand, even though I have no idea what you're talking about. It's just the timing couldn't be worse." Carly's disappointment obvious in her tone.

"I promise we'll have a nice relaxing evening soon. I might even have a few new moves!" Austin's voice deepened low and sexy.

Carly's mood changed at Austin's goofy attempt at being sexy. "Oh, I want to see that, but I'd welcome any of your old moves at this point!"

After dinner they made a quick stop at Baskin Robbins and walked back through the tourist-crowded streets. They came upon and got stuck behind a large group of tourists beginning a Ghost Tour.

"I can't believe people pay money to listen to that hogwash," Austin whispered.

Carly looked at Austin and shook her head.

A short, middle-aged woman led the tour. She wore a pair of khaki Dockers and a navy blue polo shirt. A large floppy hat topped her strawberry-blonde hair, cut in a short wedge.

Carly tried to read the company's logo, stitched on the right side of her shirt but the stitching was too small. As they followed the group, Carly enjoyed eavesdropping on her script. She loved the guide's southern drawl and engaging personality. The guide detailed the history of each of the sites along the route, her group hung on each word. After following for a while, Carly and Austin moved around the group in front of St. Michael's Church.

"I think it all sounds so interesting. Who's to say there aren't spirits haunting this town?" Carly took hold of Austin's hand and glanced at his expression. "There's so much history here .... Revolutionary War all the way through the Civil War, and lots of death. I could believe that something is going on in our house. Can't you see that?"

"Sorry to disappoint, but I just don't see it." He gave her hand an affectionate squeeze.

She knew Austin didn't believe in the spirit world. He wasn't an agnostic, but his faith wasn't something he talked about. In fact, getting married in the church was the first time he'd been in a house of worship in years. They had arrived at the car park. Quiet ensued on the short drive back to their house with Carly and Austin both immersed in their own thoughts.

Austin pulled into the dark driveway. "Okay, I'm going to head back to the hospital. I don't know how long the surgery will take, so don't wait up." He bent down to kiss Carly.

She waved goodbye as he backed his car out onto the street. When the headlights no longer illuminated the driveway, the dark humid air felt heavy and foreboding to Carly.

She got the door open as fast as she could. She laid her purse and keys on the entry table and headed to the kitchen to pour herself a glass of wine. Quiet so far, she thought. She walked upstairs to the bedroom. The four poster bed had been an acquisition from an antique shop on John's Island. The coverlet, a reproduction, but still tied into the age of their home. The sight of her room calmed her nerves.

She carried her wine into the bathroom and began drawing a bath. She sprinkled her favorite bath crystals into the water, and inhaled the aromatic scent. As she undressed, she caught a glimpse of her body in the mirror. Her eyes went straight to her stomach. Although she'd been blessed with a toned body since high school, she'd gladly change her flat tummy for a baby bump. She remembered the loss of the baby she'd carried two years before. Shaking the thought from her mind, she sank into the claw-footed tub. Carly enjoyed the feel of soaking in the deep tub full of luxurious bubbles, sipping wine and letting the cares of the day float away. She sank into the warm nest, feeling her muscles relax.

Just after two in the morning, Austin slid into bed beside her. He pulled the covers up over her shoulders and put the remote back on the night table. Soon, he too slept.

The alarm clock beside the bed gave off a blue glow illuminating the dark bedroom. Carly woke, and rolled over to see the time display 3:40 a.m. Austin laid sleeping beside her. Rolling back over, she pulled the cover up to her shoulders. Listening to Austin's shallow breathing soothed her. She had been drifting back to sleep when she heard some-one crying. She sat upright, straining to hear where it came from.

Not wanting to wake Austin, she slid out of bed and walked into the pitch black hallway. She couldn't see her hand in front of her face. She tiptoed along, following the sound of the crying. She made a mental note to place a nightlight in the hallway. She felt her way along the wall to the stairs. The crying grew louder.

Had Austin left the television on downstairs? She made her way back to their bedroom, searching inside the bedside table for the small flashlight she kept there. While it wasn't much of a weapon, she found it helpful when she had to go downstairs at night.

Carly tiptoed back to the stairs, listening for the sound. She heard weeping again. Was it coming from the receiving room? When she reached the bottom of the stairs, she shone the flashlight all around the first floor. She spotted the television, quiet, hidden inside its wooden armoire. She walked to the front door, peering out the peep hole. She couldn't see a thing. All quiet. The crying had stopped. She shone the flashlight into the receiving room. Quiet there too.

Carly was about to give up her search and chalk it up to a bad dream, when she heard banging coming from the kitchen. She felt her way in the dark, shining the light from one wall to the other. A blast of cold air emanated from the kitchen, settling into the marrow of her bones. She shivered and shined the light in straight ahead. The cellar door was ajar—again. The banging noise echoed up the stairs from below. She reached for the doorknob to close it. But just as her fingers closed around the icy knob, the door ripped from her grasp slamming on its own.

Carly's loud scream reverberated through the quiet house. Startled and terrified, she turned and ran from the kitchen. Her heart thumping in her chest. As she rounded the hall, she bumped into a solid form. She shrieked again.

"What in the world are you doing down here screaming bloody murder?" Austin took hold of her shoulders, pulled her to him, hugging her.

She sobbed. "I h-heard someone crying. I-I came downstairs." She pulled away to get the words out. "I mean, I think, I heard someone crying. I swear. I thought maybe you'd left the television on."

Carly took a shallow breath, returning to normal. "When I got downstairs, the crying stopped, but then a banging sound came from the kitchen—no—the cellar. I saw it, the door—open. When I reached for the doorknob to close it, it felt like someone pulled it out my hand and slammed it shut!" She shuddered.

"I heard the door slam and you scream when I reached the bottom of the stairs." He looked around the hallway. "Come with me into the kitchen."

Carly followed him. No cold air assaulted her.

"Stay here, and hand me the flashlight." He grabbed a rolling pin from the counter, and inched open the cellar door. He flipped on the light. Damp warm air rushed upstairs.

Austin started down the stairs, but hearing her footsteps, he turned, "There's no banging sound down here. No sound at all." He squinted up at her through the dim light. "Let's go back to bed now."

"What's happening? Why am I the only one hearing this?" She didn't understand. What was happening in their house? The banging and crying. It's not normal.

Austin turned off the cellar light and closed the door behind him. He put the rolling pin back and turned on the flashlight.

"I know what I heard. You said you heard the door slam too, and I didn't do that!" Carly crossed her arms in a self-hug.

"I admit I heard the door slam. It's an old house, maybe there's drafty air getting in somehow. Let's go." He put his arm around Carly and steered her to the stairs.

The two went back upstairs to bed.

"Since we're awake, we might as well try out some of those moves I was talking about earlier." He kicked their bedroom door shut, taking her into his arms. He kissed her gently on the mouth.

She tried to push the fear of what happened from her thoughts—for his sake. She let him seduce her and in time she forgot about the noise for a while.

After making love, Austin pulled Carly into the curve of his body, his arm resting across her hip. Together they slept for the next few hours.

Chapter 4

During the last week of July, Carly's parents, Curt and Paula Evans, came to visit. When Austin wasn't on call at the hospital, the foursome took in as many tourist attractions and trips to the beach as possible. Carly noticed that her mother avoided the topic of her getting pregnant, she figured her mom was being sensitive since she'd miscarried.

Carly knew her parents waited for word of another grandchild on the way. Carly's older sister, Cate, had just had her second child. Carly's brother, Conner, had three children, and her parents adored their extended family. Carly wanted another baby, but not the added pressure of being compared with her siblings.

"So this is going to be the nursery!" Paula admired the sunny room.

"Yes, it's close to our room and located on the quiet side of the house, away from the noise of the street."

Paula smiled at her daughter. "Especially after seeing how much traffic travels up and down the street. I can't believe all the curious tourists taking photographs of your house."

Carly showed her the toy horse seated on the mantle, and the china doll from before the Civil War displayed in a child's chair, as well as a Colonial doll with a wooden face.

Her mother noticed the family heirloom placed in the corner of the room, "These are lovely," Paula pointed to the two antique christening gowns.

"Austin and I are hoping next year to have a little guy or girl in here." Carly stroked the railing on the crib.

"You know that would make us so happy. I just wish you were closer." Paula gave her a hug.

Soon, her parents' week-long visit came to an end.

"Hey, before we go, let me get a picture of you and your mom. The light is good in this room." Curt waited for them to get positioned in front of the fireplace. Carly watched as her father adjusted the lens on his ancient 35 mm camera.

"Daddy, when are you going to get a digital camera? They're so much nicer," Carly admonished.

"I like this one. No need paying money for something I don't need." He frowned, putting away his camera.

"I know you like your camera Daddy. Just a thought though, you might find that you like the 21st century." Carly gave her father a peck on the cheek.

She hadn't realized how much she had missed her parents. Life had been hectic with the renovations and adjusting to the touristy town. Carly promised her parents she'd try to come home for the holidays.

Curt carried their suitcases out to the car. Carly kissed her parents and waved goodbye as they backed their Toyota Camry out of the drive and headed for their Kansas home.

Following her parents' visit, Carly woke to the sound of someone crying every night. Austin, oblivious, slept through each episode. To avoid being awakened, Carly put ear plugs in before going to bed. When the crying noises began to echo from the cellar in the daytime, she started taking day trips to places around the city. Carly enjoyed any social engagements that she and Austin were invited to, because she had made few friends.

Early September, she met Elise at Jestine's for lunch. Carly looked forward to seeing her. A successful, pretty blonde, she was not at all pretentious. She and her husband, Jameson, made a good living. Together, they flipped houses and sold them with one of the most successful realty companies in Charleston. They had three children: Patrick, David, and Grace. Carly marveled at the energy Elise had.

"So, how are you settling in? Are you feeling more at home with the renovations completed?" Elise asked.

Carly hadn't had a good night's sleep in weeks. Still waking to the cries or banging every night. After their last conversation, she hesitated to tell Elise about the door slamming incident. She didn't want to mention the loud voice warning her to 'get out' either. "Uh … yes … we have enjoyed the house. My parents were here for a week." Carly took a sip of her ice tea. "We were in and out so much I didn't notice the odd sounds." Carly looked down at her shrimp salad.

Elise sighed. "Listen, I'm sorry if I gave you any reason to be afraid. I'm glad to know you're enjoying it—as you should." She smiled and sat back relaxing her posture.

Carly and Elise spent the rest of their lunch talking about Elise's children and their busy summer, and set the date for their next lunch. Elise returned to her office, and Carly headed down to the Market. She spent an hour browsing the displays, purchasing a pretty scarf and a pair of earrings that had the same gate pattern as the one at St. Michael's Church. She loved the sweetgrass basket ladies, and made it a ritual to stop and talk to each, often purchasing a small basket. The hand-made, unique baskets would make great Christmas gifts for her family.

Heading back down Meeting Street, she noticed the lady who had been the ghost tour guide, getting in her parked car.

"Hi!" Carly crossed the street in front of her.

The lady smiled and returned pleasantries. Carly continued down the street until reaching King Street. Outside of her home, several older ladies with their large purses and cameras stood admiring their house. Austin had finished repainting the front gate, so it looked nice in photographs.

Before she could get close enough to speak, the group moved on chattering about the next house they photographed. Carly unlocked the front door and set her purse and keys on the entry table She kicked off her flip flops and headed for the bathroom. Something out of place when she passed the receiving room caught her attention, but she didn't take time to investigate. When she finished in the bathroom, she went straight into the receiving room. Lying in the center of the floor was the rocking horse that she had placed upstairs in the future nursery. She almost stepped on it.

How in the world did you get down here? A chill ran up her arms, causing the hair to stand on end. The room grew cold as a meat locker. As she exhaled, she saw her breath. What in the world was happening? She picked up the toy horse to take back upstairs and when she reached the landing, she saw a vapor passing before her. Carly sucked in her breath, and stopped. She continued toward the nursery, weak in the knees and chilled. She hesitated, not sure she could enter the room. She took a deep breath and walked inside. She surveyed the room. No longer cold, nothing appeared out of place, she put the rocking horse back on the mantle and left, closing the door behind her.

It was then that Carly heard the familiar and mysterious banging echoing throughout the house. It got louder as she headed down the stairs.

Carly rushed into the kitchen, searching in the small drawer where she kept her notebooks and bills. She pulled out a small notepad that she had kept notes in about the house, things that had been happening she felt were not 'old house' explainable. She described what had happened since returning home from lunch with Elise. The banging continued. She did her best to ignore it. As she wrote, she caught movement out of the corner of her eye. The cellar door opened. It had been locked since Austin went into it last month to investigate. How had it opened? She remembered the fright she received when she tried closing it last time. She shivered at the thought.

Putting her fears aside, Carly grabbed a flashlight and headed to the cellar door. The banging grew louder, deafening her. She flipped on the light and descended the wooden stairs to the semi-darkness below. The flashlight was insurance in case the lights went out, or if she needed it for protection. It might come in handy as a weapon.

Chapter 5

The dank smell assailed Carly's nostrils. Her ears strained to hear where the noise came from. The deafening noise got softer. She studied the dimly lit cellar. The stone floor had begun to crumble. In some areas, the original dirt floor showed through. It reminded her of being in a dungeon. She rubbed her arms to create warmth. The dampness sent a chill from her arms to the back of her neck. Her breathing quickened in apprehension but she forced herself to investigate.

Carly took note of the odds and ends that the previous owners had failed to remove. She shone her light into a box filled with old door locks and hinges. Another box contained a rotary telephone and pots and pans. She didn't see anything that could cause the constant noise. To the left of the stairs she spotted the newer heating system Dr. Hutchinson had installed. It would come in handy during the winter months. Even though she felt clammy, the cellar itself was dry.

Carly saw that the cellar stopped directly under the bathroom above. Was the rest of the house on ground level? Maybe the sounds came from a sewer gas build-up under the street?

She found a wall that didn't match the original and felt along it. The stone and mortar used in the original walls didn't match the brick and mortar that lined the eastern wall of the cellar. Perhaps Elise or the doctor who once owned the house would know something about it. The noise had stopped. Carly shook her head. "I must be losing my mind."

She started for the stairs and once again felt the sudden drop in temperature. She exhaled and her breath became visible. The apparition of a man stood between her and the stairs. She shook uncontrollably, a scream caught in her throat. His form appeared transparent at first, then became solid. He wore a long black coat and a three point hat, his eyes stared dark and hollow.

"Get away from me!" Carly felt frozen in place. She forced her feet to move towards the stairs. She held her arms over her head, flashlight still in her hand. As she moved, the apparition faded away. It was then that the crying began. She ran up the stairs, latching the door behind her. Weak in the knees, she leaned against the counter. She took several deep breaths trying to calm herself. Her eyes darted around the kitchen. She needed something to calm her nerves. She took a bottle of wine from the pantry. Her hands shook, splashing some wine on the counter as she poured a good amount into the glass.

She jumped when her phone buzzed, a text message from Austin: Hon, sorry, home late. Emergency surgery, car-wreck victim. Don't wait up. Love you!

Carly collapsed onto a chair, placed her arms on the table, put her head down and cried. She felt better after that. She even enjoyed the wine. After awhile she regained control, and went over to the desk, flipped open the notebook and wrote up the encounter with the apparition in the cellar, noting the time and date.

Carly needed friends, someone she could confide in. Maybe she should find a job. She looked at the clock—only 6:30 p.m. The experience in the cellar had left her drained. Afraid to be alone in the house, she decided to drive to The Noisy Oyster. Even if she had to eat alone, at least there'd be plenty of people around and she could order another drink to calm her nerves. She grabbed her purse and keys, and rushed out the door. Carly didn't see the shadow of a woman standing in the hallway.

She sank into their favorite booth, and gazed outside at the view of the busy city market. The young waiter, Jace, had waited on them several times since they had moved to Charleston.

"How are the renovations coming along?" He asked.

"We're finished, for the time being. You'll have to come visit some time. We'd love to show it off. Bring a friend if you like.

"Great! I'll ask Len to come. He's a good friend and just happens to be the new chef."

"How's school coming along? You're getting a degree in marketing, right?"

"Yes, I'll have my degree at the end of this term."

"Where's Dr. Tabor tonight?"

"Saving lives. Bad car accident on the interstate."

"Guess I better take your order before the manager comes after me." He glanced over at the kitchen. "What can I get you to drink?"

"Glass of the house Chardonnay and a glass of water please."

"Sure, I'll be right back with that."

Jace brought her drink and took Carly's order. He kept a steady pace back and forth from the kitchen. Carly sipped on her wine and people watched out the window. One of the local Ghost Tours was starting at the building across from the restaurant. As Carly ate dinner, she watched the crowd increase and decided to play tourist and join in. She didn't look forward to going home to an empty house. Well, maybe not so empty, with its bizarre sights and sounds.

Following a group of college-aged girls, she found the entrance to Ghost Tours, Ltd, and bought her ticket. Joining the tour group, she noticed the middle-aged woman whom she'd seen earlier in the day. It looked like she'd be their guide for the evening.

At 8:00 P.M. sharp, the guide introduced herself to her tour group of fifteen.

"Hi, y'all! My name's Delaney, and I'll be your guide tonight. We'll hit some of the most haunted spots in town. We'll end our tour at the oldest location on our tour, the Provost Dungeon, where souls still linger."

Carly listened to Delaney's lilting accent—she'd never tire of the long vowels and drawn out syllables of the residents in the Low Country. She could tell that Delaney was a life-long resident. Carly liked her wholesome looks. Not exactly plump, she couldn't call her skinny either. Delaney had a pleasant round face, eyes that twinkled when she talked, and a speaking voice that commanded attention. She welcomed the guests, smiled at Carly then led the group from the alley to the first stop down the street.

The tour began at Philadelphia Alley, or Bloody Alley, as Delaney explained. Carly felt a shiver as she surveyed the narrow area enclosed with ivy blanketing the imposing walls on either side. She listened as Delaney explained it was a common site for duels.

"The most common complaints from this area is the feeling of being nudged by unseen hands." Delaney continued as the college girls laughed at everything, making jokes and getting the attention of two young men who spurred them on. Carly and a few of the couples got tired of their antics. Moving closer to the guide, they tried to keep the younger members of the group behind them. Carly took a picture with her phone as she hurried to keep up with Delaney. The street lamps cast a pale glow onto the gate of the Circular Church wrought iron gate.

"Do any of y'all know the difference between a graveyard and a cemetery?" She scanned the group with her flashlight. "Well, a graveyard has a place of worship on it, and a cemetery doesn't."

Delaney produced a photograph of a woman and passed it through the crowd. "This is a photograph of Harriet Mackey. Her parents wanted a last portrait of their daughter, who had passed away. The artist, P.R. Valet, came to paint the deceased woman during the time when there was no such thing as embalming." The sound of gagging and exaggerated groans from the young girls quieted for Delaney to continue. "The picture you're seeing shows signs of decomposition. It is said that Mr. Valet began spending hours painting Harriet in the beginning, but after a month, could only stay with his subject for ten minutes before the stench drove him away." She gave her group enough time to walk through the graves, then ushered them to the next site.

The tour was interesting to Carly, even though she already knew much about the city. The tour ended in the lower level of the Provost Dungeon, where they learned about the walled city and pirates. Carly walked down the stairs of the Custom House into the dungeon. Delaney waited for the last of her group before beginning her talk. Carly glimpsed animatronic figures placed throughout the dungeon. She snapped pictures of the prisoners dressed in colonial attire, while listening to Delaney's explanation of the hundreds of souls who died in the dungeon. "In this area, folks have been scratched, had their hair pulled, and even claimed to have the sensation of shortness of breath."

Carly walked over to the area where the prisoners were chained to the walls. As she moved back to take a photograph of the prison warden working at a desk, she felt something grab her from behind. Her breath caught in her throat, whipping around to one of the girls covering her mouth, snickering. "You almost tripped over the fake guy's leg." Carly saw the leg of the prisoner poking through the cell. "I'm sorry, I didn't see you behind me." She tried to make a joke, but the humor didn't register with the girl. She went back to join Delaney, who answered a question on Isaac Hayne, a young man led from the dungeon to his death at the gallows nearby. "Yes, Isaac passed by his sister's home on the way to be hanged, and as he passed, she called for him to return to her." She brushed a stray hair from her face. "He promised his sister he'd come back, and many think he lingers in the dungeon."

The tour came to a close outside in the dark parking area. As Carly left the building, she heard the girls scream. She turned to see one of the young men running from the window outside, having banged on the outside as the girls passed by. She had to laugh at herself for jumping. She heard Delaney snicker at their antics when she ushered the last of the group through the door.

She appreciated Delaney's jovial personality. When the tour ended, she stayed behind. "Delaney, could I ask you question?" Carly lowered her voice.

"Sure! What did you want to ask?" Delaney smiled. Carly hesitated. How should she approach the subject? Something about Delaney's sensitivity to others made Carly feel like she could help.

"You're going to think I'm crazy, but I'm not!"

Delaney looked puzzled, but waited for her to continue.

Carly wrung her hands. "I live on King Street. We just finished renovations and I think our house is haunted."

"I hadn't expected that, but ... are you wanting me to include your house on the tour?" Delaney looked amused.

"Oh, heavens no! I wanted to know if you know of someone I could speak with, someone who could tell me if what I'm experiencing is real or if I am losing my mind." Carly pulled at a strand of hair.

"Did someone tell you that I might be able to help?"

"No. I've just seen you around, leading these tours. Somehow, I just thought ..."

"No worries, you're fine. Maybe I can help you." Delaney took a step back and studied Carly.

"I'm sorry I haven't introduced myself. I'm Carly Tabor." Carly extended her hand.

"You seem genuine enough." Delaney shook Carly's hand. "I haven't eaten dinner yet, do you want to tag along? I'd love to hear more about your house."

Carly thought for a second, she'd only be alone if she went home, so she texted Austin, telling him she'd be having a late dinner with a friend. They walked to the nearby Magnolia's restaurant. Carly, not hungry, ordered a cup of coffee. While Delaney ate her shrimp and grits, Carly told Delaney about all the things she'd experienced since beginning the renovations. "As you can imagine. I haven't gotten much sleep in awhile and I'm not sure if I'm imagining things or losing my mind."

By the end of Carly's story, Delaney had finished her dinner. She dabbed her mouth with her napkin, then pushed her plate away. "Carly,

I don't know why you chose my tour, but I think I might be able to help you." Delaney took a sip of water. "You see, I'm sensitive. I used to think I was crazy too, then I just accepted it. From the time I was a little girl, I could see and hear things others couldn't. I guess you'll call me crazy now." Delaney watched Carly's reaction to her declaration.

Carly's eyes widened as she stared at Delaney. She'd never met anyone who was a medium or a ghost whisperer. Never in a million years would she have imagined having such a conversation with a stranger. Tears welled up in her eyes, but a shaky laugh escaped from her throat. "You mean, you might be able to hear them too?"

"Tell you what. I don't work tomorrow. Would you mind if I came by and just got a feel of your house, maybe get an idea of what's going on?" Delaney gave her a sympathetic smile.

Carly pulled a piece of paper from her purse and jotted down her address. "Thank you so much, Delaney. I know when I get home tonight something else is bound to happen, and right now my nerves are shot! So I'll be counting the minutes until you arrive."

Carly parted ways with Delaney in front of the restaurant. The drive back to King Street allowed Carly time to get her thoughts in order. As she parked the car, the strong smell of Confederate Jasmine blew in the open windows giving her a moment of pleasure. Bushes climbed up the brick wall along the side her property. She got out of the SUV, as Austin pulled in behind her.

"Looks like we timed that just right." Austin pulled Carly into him, giving her a kiss on the cheek.

"I didn't expect you until much later!" She pulled away.

"You're shaking. Is something wrong?"

"No. I'm … um … relieved to see you. Now I won't have to be alone in the house." She clicked the key, locking her car.

"I worry about you being worried all the time. It's taking a toll on you." Austin put his arm around her as they walked toward the front door. "Wish I could be here all the time. … Maybe in time all this nonsense with the house will settle down."

"Nonsense?" Carly pulled away, stopping at the door.

"Well, Dr. Broderick is on call, so I came home after she left recovery. I'm here now. Let's go inside and get comfortable."

Carly stopped in the doorway, fear caught in her throat.

"Has something else happened?" Austin took hold of her hand. Tugging her inside, he closed the door.

Carly exhaled, tucking her hair behind her ears. "Austin, I've heard enough banging in this house to go deaf." The pitch of her voice rose higher. "I've seen a ghost who looked like he wanted to kill me, and I've heard crying coming out of the walls. And that's just today." She stomped her foot in frustration.

"I'm sorry." He wiped his hand across his face. "It's frustrating for me too. I know I haven't been home enough lately. I haven't been much support. But all I've heard was a door slamming in the kitchen."

"You don't believe me!"

"I do, but I don't know what to make of all the things you're claiming to have seen and heard."

"I'm not claiming. I *have* seen and heard them." Carly broke down and cried.

Austin rubbed the back of his neck. "I can give you something for anxiety if you need it."

"I don't need medicine. I'm not sick." Carly sniffled. She forced herself to stop crying.

"I give up. I'm just trying to help." Austin threw his hands in the air. "What can I do, Carly?" Austin softened his voice. "I want to help. Just tell me what you want me to do."

"I need you to listen. To be supportive. To believe me." Carly watched his eyes. She saw his concern.

"Okay. Let's go upstairs, settle in and then I want you to tell me what's on your mind."

"Before we go upstairs, I have a question." Carly glanced toward the kitchen.

"Okay, go ahead and ask."

"Do you remember the realtor or Dr. Hutchinson telling you about why the cellar is only partially finished? It looks like part of it's been closed off. There's a different wall down there."

"Hmm … I don't remember anything. Maybe they had issues with the walls crumbling."

He followed Carly upstairs. She stopped, almost tripping on the rocking horse lying on the second step from the top.

"How'd this get here?" Austin bent over to pick up the antique toy.

"It was downstairs this afternoon. I put it back in the nursery before I left the house for dinner."

Austin tilted his head to the side, narrowing his eyes. "This doesn't make any sense. Someone must have been in the house." He turned his gaze back to Carly. "Are you sure you weren't interrupted before returning it to the nursery?"

She stamped her foot. "No. I put it there. I remember distinctly."

Austin put the toy back in the room and closed the door.

Carly sat on the side of the bed rubbing on her lotion. "I've made a new friend tonight. She's coming over to see the house tomorrow."

"Do you think that's wise? With all that's going on?"

Carly sat up straight, her back rigid. "You'll think it's weird, but she's a sensitive. I think she could help us."

Austin squinted at her. "Are you kidding me? You invited a stranger to our home, and she's emotional to boot?"

"Okay, stop it. She isn't emotional. Sensitives can see and hear people who are no longer living. Besides, I'm the one left here all day to deal with this, and I am the one who is going to put a stop to it. If not, we might need to think about selling the house." Carly slapped the remainder of the lotion on her feet and curled up in bed.

"We can't sell it, Carly. We're going to be here until we're old and gray, remember?"

"Well then, you had better get on board and be a little more supportive. How am I supposed to get pregnant if I am stressed out all the time? You know how much I want to have our baby, Austin."

"Do you think you have the market cornered on wanting to have a baby?" Austin turned his back to her.

The tension in the room grew heavy. Carly felt the words slice through her heart, causing a flood of tears.

"Listen, I'm sorry, honey. I shouldn't have said that. I think we're both worn out."

Carly wiped her tears, and adjusted the bedcover. "Let's get some sleep before the house starts banging and crying again. I'm wearing my mask tonight. I don't want to see anymore ghosts." She pulled the pink velvet sleep mask over her eyes, turned towards the wall, and sighed. "Goodnight."

Chapter 6

Carly slept through Austin getting up and going for his morning run. When she awoke, the sun streamed in the tall bedroom windows. She put on her robe and walked downstairs, feeling well-rested after a good night's sleep. She assumed Austin had gone to work early since he wasn't at the kitchen table having coffee and reading the morning paper. The mantle clock showed 8:20. "Oh well." She shrugged. "Guess he didn't want to wake me to say goodbye." She smiled, realizing she had talked out loud. Was she going to be one of those people who talk to themselves?

By the time Carly finished breakfast, showering, and dressing, she directed her attention to Delaney's visit. She had four hours until Delaney Warrick arrived. No doubt Austin thought the whole thing was a bad idea. At least he'd be at the hospital when she showed up.

She spent the morning making lasagna and preparing a salad. Shortly before noon, she set the small table in the kitchen, enjoying the pleasant aroma given off by the baking lasagna. A few minutes before noon, the doorbell rang.

Carly opened the door. "Hi, Delaney. Welcome to our home." She ushered her in. She noted that Delaney looked quite different than she had the night before. She had curly hair, applied makeup and wore a purple maxi dress with wedge heels. She looked younger.

"Carly, you have a beautiful home." Delaney surveyed the open floor plan.

Carly smiled. "Thank you. We've done a lot of updates in the last two months, but we have a ways to go yet."

In the kitchen, Delaney headed to the counter.

"Can I help you carry something?" Carly put out her hands.

"No thanks." Delaney pulled out a bottle of Chardonnay and placed it on the counter.

Carly's eyes lit up with pleasure. "Thanks for the wine. I love Chardonnay!"

Carly served the lasagna and salad, then filled their glasses with wine.

"This looks scrumptious." Delaney lifted her wine glass. "Cheers."

During the meal, Carly shared details about her life growing up in Kansas, about meeting Austin in college and their eventual marriage. "When Austin found out about the position here, I put my career as a journalist and reporter on hold." She noticed Delaney glancing around the room, not making eye contact.

Delaney looked down at the napkin twisted around her finger. "I lost my husband two years ago last month. He passed a couple of months after his 50th birthday."

"Oh, I'm so sorry. I can't imagine how horrible that must have been."

Delaney dabbed the napkin around her eyes. "I still don't understand. He was the picture of health one day, and the next, dead from a massive heart attack." Delaney took another napkin, blowing her nose again. "Thank heavens Mark planned for the "what ifs." He owned his own insurance business for years, so he had plenty of life insurance. I'm grateful that he cared enough to make sure I'd be okay, but it's just not the same without him."

"Of course it isn't. I couldn't imagine how I'd feel if I lost my husband." Carly poured a little more wine in her glass.

Delaney explained that she worked as a dental hygienist. She made her own flexible schedule. The Ghost Tour job she'd acquired because she hated being home alone during the evenings. She also spoke about her son, Jarrod, and his studying to become a pharmacist at the College of Charleston.

After they finished eating, Delaney helped clear the table.

Carly rinsed the lunch plates and flatware, leaving them in the sink to wash later. Then she turned her attention to Delaney and the main reason for her visit. "Can I show you around? Maybe you can tell me if you see or hear anything unusual."

"If you don't mind, I'd like to walk through the house on my own. It's best if I sense what's going on without any distractions."

"Whatever makes you most comfortable. I'll just wait here." Carly turned back to the sink and began washing dishes.

Delaney headed from the hallway to the receiving room. Before her eyes, the room turned from bright to gloomy, taking on the appearance of a room furnished in Colonial times. A flickering flame cast an eerie shadow against the opposite wall. She sensed fear and sadness in the room, however, no ghosts revealed themselves. She rubbed her arms where goosebumps had risen, then she walked to the stairway. Before she had taken the first step, a wisp of smoke fluttered past her. She breathed the scent of sulfur. "Who's here? What are you trying to tell us?" No answer came to her.

Looking up the stairwell, she saw a young woman wearing a dark red dress with white apron, neckline cut low in the Colonial style, standing at the top of the stairs. She watched as the mysterious women vanished before her eyes.

"You saw it too?" Carly had come up behind Delaney.

"Yes. I'd like to walk upstairs. Go ahead and follow me up if you'd like."

Carly followed Delaney up the stairs.

When the two reached the second floor, Delaney went straight to the nursery. She walked to the mantle where the toy horse and china doll sat.

"I bought that sweet horse at a shop in Mount Pleasant. I picked up the dolls at various antique shops back in Denver. The strange thing is … I find the horse in other rooms and I'm not moving it."

Delaney picked up the metal horse then set it back on the mantel.

"I have a photo album that came with the horse. It belonged to a family who lived on a plantation near Mount Pleasant. Would you like to see it?" Carly watched her look around the room.

"Yes. Maybe relaxing my focus, the lady spirit will show herself."

Carly opened a drawer in the chifferobe. She removed the tissue paper protecting the old photo album. Handing the small leather album to Delaney, she watched the medium turn the pages.

Delaney's eyes widened with delight." Many of these are *carte de visite* photographs, as well as daguerreotypes and tin types."

"What does *carte de visite* mean?" Carly ran a finger alongside the photo of a man in 1860s attire.

"They're called visiting cards, like a post card today. They were inexpensive to print and a lot of people in the 1860s, until the first half of the twentieth century, had their pictures taken with this method."

Carly loved the pictures of the children. "I know tin types when I see them, but I'm not sure what the dark metal ones are called.

Delaney turned the page in the album. "This is an older photograph. What a find! It's called a daguerreotype. This one is about ten years older than the tin types. The chemicals used to make the image is different. Either way, what a treasure having the album with the toy horse."

"Several of them have the names written below," Carly said.

Delaney closed her eyes, "There's a woman—she comes in this room often. Have you seen her in here before?"

"Yes, I've seen her in the hallway, walking into the room, then she disappears."

"This was her room." Delaney's eyes moved with the spirit toward the window. "Are you looking for something? Can we help you?" Delaney asked the unknown apparition.

Carly got chills up her spine and on her arms. "Is … is she the one who's doing the moaning and crying that I hear?"

"I'm not sure, just yet. I'd like to take another look through the album. She might be in one of the photographs."

"That would be quite a coincidence. Finding an album and toy that came from this house. Maybe the toy horse belonged to her child?" Carly held her breath. Could it be? Could it be the strong pull I felt when I saw it at the store—like I visualized seeing it on the mantle?

Delaney leafed through the album, studying the faces. There were young men and women, all from the same family. She paid close attention to the children. "Look." She showed Carly a picture. "This looks like the same horse. Maybe this little guy is the one wanting to cause mischief."

"Oh my gosh. You're right." Carly stared at the picture, rubbing her arms.

Delaney hesitated a moment studying the picture too, then closed the album. She closed the album and handed it to Carly to wrap and put away. "I'd like to continue my tour now." She checked on the other bedrooms on the second floor and felt nothing special. Carly followed behind her staying quiet.

Back downstairs they entered the receiving room. Both felt the drop in temperature.

Delaney turned to Carly. "There's a man here. I sense that the man and woman are unable to leave. They're saying that this is *their* house."

"You mean they're actually talking to you? Why are they still here?" Carly shivered at the freezing temperature.

Delaney stared into space. "They're telling both of us to leave."

Austin flashed through Carly's mind. He'd think this was nonsense, but she now knew, she wasn't crazy because Delaney felt it too. Carly turned her gaze to the same spot that Delaney stared trying to see what she saw. She watched Delaney walk to the fireplace.

Delaney sucked in a burst of air then put her hand to her mouth. Warm air escaped causing a cloud of condensation around her. "I'm seeing blood, Carly. A lot of it. There's blood all over the floor, here." Delaney bent down, pointing to an area on the floor. "Something terrible happened in this room. I think a murder took place in your house." Delaney's face turned ashen white.

"What is it? What's wrong?" Carly rushed to Delaney's side.

"Another spirit has joined us. It happened when I mentioned *murder*."

"A murder? No. It can't be. Not in our lovely home." Carly looked about the room. A sudden chill overtook her like a ton of bricks.

Delaney shivered in the chill too. "I don't know what happened for sure, but someone died in your home."

"It's 85 degrees outside and it's freezing in here." Carly felt the coldness seep deep into her bones.

Delaney grabbed hold of Carly's hand. "The woman, can you see her? She's right in front of us." Delaney stiffened, rooting herself to the spot. "She's wearing a long gown, blood is pooling at her bare feet."

Carly strained to see.

"I believe the man died first, he's lying on the—

The banging started, interrupting Delaney. She looked at Carly, putting her finger to her lips. Within seconds, the warmth from the evening sun filtered through the window. The two women stepped closer together.

"This is the banging I told you about. It gets louder at night and after that, then the crying starts."

"Let's see if we can figure out where it's coming from." Delaney walked throughout the downstairs, looking around for the origin of the sound. She put her ear to the wall in the hallway. "It sounds like it's coming from inside the walls." Delaney put both hands on the walls feeling for a vibration.

Carly watched Delaney when they both heard someone sobbing. She felt a heaviness settle inside her chest, and her breath came in and out in bursts. "Tha … that's what wakes me up at night. You see why, I uh … can't stay here alone? I hear it during the day too." She sagged, leaning against the wall.

"I hear the crying, but it isn't coming from the woman. The man is standing beside her in the hallway, listening. I think they hear the crying too."

Carly's heart raced.

"Why won't they leave, Delaney? Ask them!" She grabbed Delaney's arm, but she let go when she felt the cool moisture emanating from her.

Delaney went back to the entry hall, speaking to herself.

The room had warmed up, so why was Delaney so cool? Carly had experienced fear many times in the house, but this time watching Delaney, she wanted to flee. She had gotten too close to something malevolent and scary. "This is freaking me out." Her eyes darted from the hallway to the kitchen.

Carly walked into the kitchen and retrieved her notebook from the counter. The sound, like the beating of a gong, increased in intensity. She leafed through the pages, reading her notes for clues.

Delaney joined her in the kitchen. "One of the things I've accepted with my gift is, I can't see everything. I know that something dreadful happened to the man and woman in this house. They're showing me, someone killed them. I believe they're responsible for the flying hammers and moving toys."

Carly grabbed two sections of her ponytail and pulled them tighter. She took a breath and leaned against the counter. "Okay, then what about the banging noises? Are they doing that too?"

Delaney frowned and looked past Carly at the walls. "No, I think that's something altogether different."

Carly put her head in her hands.

"I never expected to hear that. This is crazy. Why us?" She moved over to join Delaney at the table. "Others must have experienced this too. Why wouldn't they have said something?"

"Would *you* have mentioned it to buyers? I mean, if you were trying to sell this house?"

Carly saw her point, and that's why they'd been able to get this historic house at such a low price. Did Elise know about the house having ghosts? She did say there was a rumor about a woman being seen when she showed the house.

"What? Have you heard anything about the house having strange occurrences?" Delaney had picked up on Carly's silence.

"Let's say the signs pointed to our house having issues. We thought getting the house from the doctor wanting to downsize after the death of his wife seemed too good to be true."

Silence enveloped them as the banging stopped, and the crying trickled away.

"We'll need to work backwards. To help these people, we need to find out who they are and what happened to them." Delaney opened her own notebook and jotted a few notes. From the clothing they wear, the couple who're in the house lived in the late 1700's or early 1800's. The man is wearing short knee pants and a frock coat. The woman is wearing an expensive gown, similar to the dresses I've seen in paintings. "I saw a man dressed like that downstairs the other day. He looked evil. He scared me to death and his eyes … I think they were hollow!

Carly knew the house dated back to the late 1700's. She had deeds and ownership papers for the house, and those should chronicle the owners of the property from the early days of the colony. Those papers would be the first place to begin.

"Do you think the couple will leave if you ask them?" She fidgeted with her earring.

"I don't know if they can. Something is holding them to this house. I feel like they want you to leave or they want you to stop changing things. I don't know, I'm getting mixed feelings about what the man and woman want to tell me."

"Okay, what do you want me to do?"

"Go ahead and check the deed and any records that will give you the names and dates of others who have occupied the house."

Carly chewed on her lip. "It scares me to think I might one day see what you're seeing. At least I know I'm not crazy. Thank you for helping me understand what's going on with our house."

Delaney hugged Carly. "Don't worry, we'll figure this out. I'll find out what I can about long ago murders. Anyway, I don't think we're dealing with anything demonic. They're just lost souls."

"Thank God for that." Carly teared up, thankful for Delaney's help. "I hope I can get some sleep and find the courage to stay here long enough to see this through. I just want them to leave."

"We'll get to the bottom of it. Soon, I hope." Delaney gathered up her notebook and purse.

She watched Delaney pull out of the drive, giving the house a long look as she drove away. *I will help make this work. I will help make our home safe. Safe enough for raising a family.*

Chapter 7

Carly took the bull by the horns. She didn't like feeling afraid, but found herself leaving lights on and looking over her shoulder. She knew she'd have to find out who the ghosts were—and soon. Delaney had seen a man and woman, but were they a couple? Carly saw the filmy apparition of a woman, and the evil face of a man in the cellar. How many ghosts were there haunting her home? Her first stop, the Register Mesne Conveyance Office that records land titles, liens and other documents related to property transactions in Charleston County, to research the deeds. And second, contact the Historic Charleston Foundation for archival information and to view old news clippings.

As she pondered her next move, a waft of cold air brought her attention to the apparition of the woman standing at the fireplace, her long gown covered in crimson. Carly screamed and grabbed the afghan slung over the back of the chair, wrapping it around her like a cocoon. The sight disturbed her so that she pulled the afghan up covering her face.

Later that afternoon, Austin returned from the hospital. He found Carly in the kitchen having a glass of wine. She'd set the table for dinner of leftover lasagna.

He picked up the wine glass set by his plate and poured himself a glass of wine. "You look tired. Tough day?"

"You could say that, but at least I know I'm not crazy and I think there's hope to rid ourselves of the ghosts."

Austin looked down, not meeting her gaze. "Hon, I wanted to tell you, I'm sorry for not being more supportive about your trying to find out the causes of what you've heard and seen in the house. I can't say I believe in ghosts, but I agree that something *is* going on here."

Carly put her arms around his waist, hugging him close. The smell of his cologne comforted her. He hugged her back, kissing the top of her head.

"My meeting with Delaney went well. I've decided that I'm not going to let these apparitions or noises scare me. I'm prepared to find out all I can about what's happening here and resolve it."

Austin raised an eyebrow. Pulling her away, he studied her face.

"Tell me about your meeting. Why do you think it went well?"

"Because I found out we have at least two spirits living here. Something terrible happened here a long time ago. Two people died—murdered—in our house." She jutted her chin out and crossed her arms.

He stared at her. "You found all that out from one afternoon with the psychic? How in the world does she know this?"

"Come with me." Carly led Austin by the hand into the receiving room. She pointed to a spot in the floor, like Delaney had earlier that day. "The blood covered the floor in this area. Lots of it. The man and woman both died in this room."

Austin bent down, running his fingers along the floor. "I don't see a thing."

Carly kept her resolve. "Well, not now, because someone replaced the floor boards. But Delaney saw it, the man lying dead on the floor and the woman bleeding as well."

Austin shook his head. "I'm trying to keep an open mind, but … let's say I believe this Delaney is psychic, and she did see blood and the two people. Why are we having issues with them, or better yet, why are they having issues with us?"

"I don't know that yet. But I do believe that we're not the first ones to experience this. Elise admitted that she'd heard rumors of people seeing the woman on the stairwell."

"What do you hope to accomplish with all this psychic business?" Austin took a seat in the large Colonial chair.

"We're hoping that if we can solve the mystery of their murder, Delaney can help them cross over into the light or wherever most spirits go and they'll leave us to enjoy our home." Carly returned to the kitchen to warm the lasagna.

After dinner, Carly spent the evening at the kitchen table making a list of items to investigate at the Charleston county historical archives. She had located the property deed they received at the real estate closing and leafed through the plot information. Disappointed, she saw it only went as far back as the previous two owners.

She continued reading through the deed, not noticing the incoming call on her cell.

Austin came into the kitchen. "Avoiding someone?" he asked.

Carly looked up, recognizing the musical ringtone. "Hi, Mom! What's up?"

"Hi honey. Um … sorry to call so late, but … I thought you'd find this odd," A quick, high pitched laugh escaped Paula.

"Mom are you okay? You sound nervous."

"Oh, yes, we're fine. I … uh … picked up the pictures from our trip to Charleston. I kept forgetting to take the film out of the camera. Anyway, I finally got them developed, and it's the oddest thing!"

"What do you mean?" Carly asked.

"Remember when we went upstairs and Dad took a few pictures of us in the nursery?"

"I remember. Why?"

"Well, um, … there appears to be a little boy sitting by the fireplace. It's giving me the creeps!"

"You mean the lab mixed up your pictures with another person's or someone's kid is in your picture? I'm confused." Carly took in a quick breath. She had a feeling she knew what it meant. Delaney's going to want to know about this.

"I mean there's a boy showing up in my pictures who wasn't there when your dad took them. If I didn't know better, I'd believe a child posed in front of the fireplace. And another thing … the rocking horse is in his hand, Carly."

A chill coursed through her body.

"Mom, don't say anything to Daddy about this. He'll freak out. Could you send me the picture?"

"You don't sound surprised. What's going on down there?" Paula's tone went up an octave.

Carly debated with herself. How much should she tell her mom? "We've had some weird things going on here, but I'm okay. I'll fill you in later, we're working on straightening everything out." She took a deep breath. "Please, send me the picture and any others that look odd. I don't want you worrying."

50

"Are you sure you can't tell me now? I'm already worried."

"Mom, everything's okay. I promise." Carly's cheeks burned. She didn't like lying to her mother.

"I want you to promise to call me soon and let me know what's going on."

"I promise. Now you better go, it's late and I don't want Daddy wondering what we're going on about. I love you, Mom." Carly clicked off her phone and stared at the paperwork strewn across the kitchen table. She went to the den finding Austin, in the recliner, reading a book.

"Everything okay with the folks?" He placed a bookmark in his book, closed it and put it aside.

She sat down on the ottoman. Austin moved his feet and gazed at her, waiting.

"Mom was a bit upset."

"What's wrong?"

"Mom got her pictures back from the photo lab, the ones she took while she and Daddy were here. It sounds crazy, but she told me a little boy shows up in the pictures we took in the nursery."

He listened to Carly recount her conversation with her mother. "Carly, it sounds like the lab just photo bombed some kid in your mom's pictures. I'm sure it's something simple."

"Well, did this kid happen to have the same antique rocking horse I have in the nursery? He's holding it in the picture."

Austin had tried to remain the voice of reason throughout the noises and unexplained events that had been going on in their home. But, she could see his logical mind struggling with this latest information.

"Carly, we can't sell the house. We loved the house from the moment—"

"Don't you think I know that? We're not selling. No one, living or dead, will chase me out of our house. I love it, and it's not theirs now. I told you, I plan to find out why it's happening, and fix it."

"What if you can't? Can you live here anyway?"

Carly couldn't deny her fear.

"It scares me knowing there are things ... people in our house who died long ago. I feel like they're trying to tell us something. And before now, no one wanted to listen."

He scooted over in the chair, motioning for her to come sit beside him. He put his arm around her. "I made a promise to your dad when we got married to protect his little girl, and I'll do whatever it takes to keep my promise. And for the record, I'm proud of the way you're standing your ground on this."

Carly breathed a sigh of relief.

Chapter 8

The next morning, after Carly finished cleaning the kitchen and downstairs, she walked out on the front piazza to shake the rag rug she kept at the front door. She breathed in the fragrance of her different container flowers. Her favorite, the Confederate Jasmine, climbed up the wrought iron gate at the corner of the house, giving off the strongest scent. She smiled and said hello to several tourists walking past her house.

What had the house looked like during those early years? Were passersby friendly then, like now? She doubted they'd be tourists. Why had that couple been murdered? And now a little boy ghost also resided here in her beautiful home. How could she possibly figure all this out? Maybe there were even more spirits. What about the man she saw in the cellar? He seemed very mean. She hoped Mom would send those photographs right away. Too bad she couldn't scan and email the pictures, but she didn't know how. She wondered if she'd have to sleep with a mask over her eyes to avoid seeing ghosts for the rest of her life.

She had hoped to get through the morning with no incidents. No such luck. She started out the door to visit the historical archives and from the corner of her eye, she glimpsed the female apparition standing in the entrance of the receiving room. The sudden appearance caught Carly by surprise and she dropped her purse. This time the apparition didn't fade from view. Though frightened, she made her feet take a step in the woman's direction. The woman stared at Carly and didn't move.

"You might as well get used to me, I'm not leaving!" Carly felt foolish speaking aloud.

The woman faded away.

Was this some kind of sinister game of *Chicken*? Carly had won this round. She picked up her purse and left the house.

Carly got stuck behind a horse and carriage full of tourists, driving down King Street. She made it to the parking garage on Meeting Street and before getting out of the car, her cell phone rang. "Hello."

"Hi Carly, this is Delaney. Is this a bad time?"

She hoped to have new information before talking to Delaney.

"I'm on my way to the historical archives. Why? Did you find out something?"

"I do have something I wanted to share with you. Could we meet Friday afternoon? I have to work Friday evening on a ghost tour, but I could stop by your place earlier, say four?"

"Great! I'll see you Friday! Carly ambled through the crowded streets, chatting with the Gullah ladies selling their sweetgrass baskets, past St. Michael's Church, and finally reached the South Carolina Historical Society, on Meeting Street. The crisp white three story antebellum structure featured arched windows and tall columns facing the street. The lush lawn offered a shaded spot for patrons taking advantage of the warm autumn afternoon. She took out her notebook in preparation of meeting with the senior archivist, Kay Ann Walters. Carly flipped the pages to find her questions scribbled upon it.

She explained her situation to Ms. Walters, and that she needed to find the names of past owners of her home. She also asked to do a cross search for any hits matching the address of her home.

Ms. Walters gave Carly an overview of what papers, documents, and collections of historical papers were housed at the Charleston Historical Archives. "We keep a large selection of historical newspapers on site as well as at the *Charleston Gazette*. You'll want to visit the College of Charleston's library for their collection of historic newspapers and documents too."

"Would you have any information in the archives about a murder that happened in my house?" She felt silly asking the question.

Ms. Walter's expression changed to one of confusion. "You believe a murder happened in the house?"

Carly felt uneasy saying it aloud. "Yes, I can't be positive, but rumor has it a couple was murdered in our house."

"Well, if that's true, there might be something in the newspapers in our digital collection. You can also go to the Office of the Register of Mesne Conveyance down the street. They record land titles, liens and other documents related to property transactions in Charleston County, and although it will take awhile to find what you need, it isn't impossible."

"Thank you for your help. I'm anxious to get started!" Ms. Walters led her to a room containing the old newspaper and family historical records. Carly took a quick inventory of the space she'd be working in. The four walls, lined with volumes of records and indexes gave her a claustrophobic feeling. With no one else using the room, she'd have the space to herself.

"This section houses the oldest records of Charleston. Most of the records and documents are located on digital files online." Ms. Walters directed Carly's attention to the computers along the wall. "If you have any questions, don't hesitate to ask. Someone will assist you."

"Thank you. There's so much to learn, I'm not sure where to begin." Carly surveyed the volumes of newspapers and records.

She spent the next two hours scouring through the various volumes, none of which offered information about incidents or crimes taking place in the time period she assumed the murders took place.

Carly re-shelved the books then gathered her purse and notebook. Ms. Walters looked up from her work when Carly arrived at her desk. "It looks like I need to get better organized. I guess the first step is to find out who lived in my house, so I'll need to check for the title and abstract for the address. I'll make a trip to the Register of Mesne Conveyance. Then, I'll come back when I know what period I'm looking for. Thanks so much for your help."

Ms. Walters smiled, "Good luck with your investigation. I think the RMC might hold the records you're looking for."

Carly waited her turn at the RMC while the lady at the front desk finished with a customer on the telephone. "I'm searching for information on the original title to my house from 1790." Hearing Carly's request, Brenda Carlisle, the historian, came to the front. "Hi. If you'll follow me, I'll show you where we keep the plat books. Did you request a title search on the property?"

"Yes, my husband and I have an abstract on the house prepared by the title company. It's a history of all documents relating to the house but it only included the previous owners back to the 1960's and the survey markings for the property as well.

"Even if you have the abstract and title, since you're going back to the 1700's, you will be in here awhile. We don't provide assistance on searches." Brenda gave an apologetic shrug of her shoulders, Carly tried to remain upbeat, even with the amount of work ahead.

"I'll be back tomorrow. I want to get all of the facts organized first. I'm just thankful you have the information." Carly grimaced at the daunting task ahead of her.

Walking her to the door, Brenda reassured her. "We have records dating back to the 1600's, so I'm sure you'll find what you need."

On her way back to the parking garage, she texted Austin to ask where he'd stored the closing documents.

His return text read, "Good timing. I'm on a break. The deed and other important papers are inside the wall safe in the receiving room."

She thanked him and turned her thoughts back to the documents. She'd forgotten about the wall safe in the receiving room. She remembered Elise showing it to them when they toured the house. Later, during renovation, they instructed the construction crew to leave it uncovered when they restored the beadboard. She gulped a quick breath. Can I get to them without a scary incident?

As Carly pulled into her driveway, she noticed the postman leaving mail in the front door slot. She unlocked the heavy wooden door and stepped inside. She froze in place. Silence and cold caused panic to strike her like a venomous snake. Exhaling she watched frost escape her mouth. She clinched her teeth against her chattering from the chill. Okay, Carly. Get it together! She took a deep breath and let out a long sigh, the uneasiness subsiding.

She picked up the mail, dropping it and her purse on the hall table. She went straight to the receiving room. Located on the left side of the fireplace, hidden behind a section of wainscot paneling, she released a small spring located on the inside of the panel. The panel opened, revealing a small wood safe, eight inches square. The worn wood appeared no worse for wear.

She fumbled feeling for the slender metal skeleton key kept inside the unlocked door. Her hand shook as she attempted to insert the key in the lock. It took two tries, then once inserted, it turned easily as if new. She reached to open the safe door and stopped. She heard the front door open and close. She held her breath. Who could that be? "Hello?" Her voice shook.

Austin strolled into the room. "Sorry. Did I scare you? I finished early today and decided to spend some time with my neglected wife." He took Carly in his arms and kissed her.

Carly leaned into the embrace, hugging him tightly. "I wondered if you remembered our address." She feigned a light hearted laugh.

"Did you find what you were looking for in the safe?"

"I was just about to get the papers when I heard the door open."

"Here, I'll get them for you." Austin opened the safe revealing its contents. He reached inside and retrieved a leather satchel, handing it to her.

"I think it's neat, the original owners hid a safe in the house. What do you suppose they kept inside?"

"Uh … important papers? Jewelry? Who knows?" Austin rubbed the top of Carly's head causing her to break out in a goofy grin. "Will all this help you solve our haunted house problem?"

She rolled her eyes. "That's the plan. She placed the satchel on the hall table. "I'll look at it later. I'm starving, are you?" She headed into the kitchen, calling back to him. "How about you help me fix dinner?"

After dinner, while Austin showered, Carly relaxed in the receiving room with a glass of wine. As she padded barefoot across the cool pine floor, she grabbed the mail to read then sank down into the overstuffed wingback chair in front of the fireplace. A large envelope addressed to her in her mother's script caught her attention. Her stomach flip flopped as she pulled a note from the envelope.

Do you see the little boy in the photo? Honey, this is so bizarre. Let me know what you think. Love you, Mom.

Carly pulled the photos from the envelope. "What in the world?" She studied the two color photographs. In the first one, she and her mother stood in front of the mantel with silly grins on their faces. Her father took the second photo in case the flash didn't work. In the second photo she and her mother moved closer together, their arms around one another. A small boy sat on the floor in front of Carly, he had dark hollow eyes. His translucence made it difficult to see his features, but Carly could see that he wore a woolen cap. His breeches were knee-length, and he wore a jacket, or a large shirt. He appeared small in stature. He sat crossed legged holding the antique rocking horse that Carly had purchased. She studied his face. He looked underfed—sickly. Had this little boy lived in this house? Had he died of some terrible disease? Or, had he been murdered too?

Carly's mind whirled with possible explanations for the child showing up in the picture. If she hadn't seen it with her own eyes, she'd never believe it. She tucked the pictures in with the deed. She'd think about showing them to Austin another time.

Carly watched from the kitchen window, anxious for Delaney's visit. Right on time, Delaney pulled up to the gate and waited. Carly hurried down the brick walkway and unlocked the wrought iron gate. Delaney pulled her car onto the stone driveway.

"Hi!" Carly pushed a stray strand of hair that had fallen out of her ponytail behind her ear.

Delaney reached across the seat and grabbed a bag of sub sandwiches she'd picked up on the way over. She also picked up a small file folder that contained the information she'd located on the computer.

"Come on in, I've been looking forward to seeing you. Can I help you with that?"

Delaney handed her the bag of sandwiches.

Carly opened the door and ushered Delaney inside.

Delaney looked beyond Carly into the hallway, noting that the man and woman apparitions stood watching.

In the kitchen, Carly put the sandwiches and chips on the kitchen island. "I have iced tea or lemonade, which would you like?" She pulled two glasses out of the cabinet.

"I'd like tea—sweet if you have it."

Carly reached for the pitcher, unaware of the man standing in front of the cellar doorway. "I always have a pitcher for Austin. He's a health nut, except for his sweet tea addiction."

Delaney gazed at the apparition by the cellar door.

Carly sat the glass in front of her and turned to look at the door. She saw nothing. She handed Delaney a plate and napkin. "I have a list of sources that I'm going to check out this week, and I found the deed to our property but haven't opened it yet. Thought I'd do that today. What about you? Any luck?

Delaney took a sip of her tea. "I focused on finding what time period of clothing the spirits wore. I think I've narrowed it down.

She took a bite of her sub then took some pictures from her briefcase. "I printed these from the web. I spent a deal of time searching clothing styles that matched our two spirits. The man's frock coat and knee britches along with the woman's plunging neckline and fichu helped me pinpoint the year to the late 1700s or early 1800s. Take a look and tell me what you think."

"What's a fichu?" Delaney set her sandwich on the plate.

"It's this." She pointed to a picture of a woman wearing a light triangular scarf draped over her shoulders and fastened in front.

"It's worn for decoration or to fill in a low neckline." She handed the pictures to Carly.

Carly studied the style of dress the subjects wore in the pictures.

"I didn't get a good look at the man's breeches. I only saw him from the waist up." Carly frowned. This one does looks like the coat the man in the cellar wore."

"What about the woman? Do you remember seeing her in anything besides the gown?" Delaney pointed to the picture of the dress with the fichu. Carly shivered as she tried to remember the times the woman appeared to her. "Each time, she wore the white gown, except once I saw her in the crimson gown." Carly returned the pictures to Delaney.

"I googled Colonial dress of men and women to find these pictures. When I tried to pin point the year, I kept coming back to the late 1700s or early 1800s." Delaney shuffled the pictures and placed them inside the folder. "Did you have any luck with the names?"

"I went by the RMC today, and they have the records for land and house purchases back to the 1600's. The historical society holds papers and manuscripts, and College of Charleston has a collection of newspapers from the 1700's. I plan to go back tomorrow after I've looked over the deed."

Carly pulled a small envelope from the drawer where she kept her notebook. "This came from my mom earlier this week." She handed the envelope to Delaney.

Delaney opened the envelope and pulled out the pictures. Her reaction was immediate.

"You have another presence in the house. I knew it." She clapped her hands together, the sound echoed in the otherwise quiet kitchen.

"How did you know?" Carly gazed at the child in the picture.

"When I was here last time, I felt another presence. I wasn't sure because I couldn't see him, but this young boy must be who I sensed."

Carly shivered. "Do you think this child's connected to the toy horse I bought at the antique shop?"

"I don't know. I didn't feel anything when I held the horse." Delaney studied the picture. The boy's ghostly image stared back at her. "I don't know if he's intimidated by the other two spirits or if he's connected to the house from another time."

"Great! Now what—another mysterious presence—just what we need." Carly's shoulders drooped as she shook her head.

"It's going to be okay. Don't worry, we'll figure it out." Delaney reached across the table and patted Carly's hand.

"I know." Carly's half-hearted response came out in a whisper. She looked Delaney in the eye and smiled. "Let's eat our lunch in peace." She did her best to sound calm but her voice shook anyway.

While Delaney finished her sandwich and drank her tea, Carly noticed her glancing into the hall. Carly looked back over her shoulder trying to see what Delaney saw but saw nothing. Carly threw up her hands. "What? What are you seeing?"

"It's the woman. She's standing at the entrance to the receiving room wearing her bood-stained gown. She's sad. I'm feeling her sadness. ... Sorry ... I didn't want to bring her emotions to our lunch."

Before Carly could respond, the cellar door flew open causing both to scream. The door opened with such force it slammed against the wall.

"What in the—" Carly's throat tightened. She could barely speak.

"The woman—" Delaney stood, looking into the hallway. "The man was with her earlier. Both are gone now." She turned her attention back to Carly. The banging had started again, louder than ever. The two stared at each other, listening to noisy racket.

"I get creeped out every time I get near the cellar," Delaney shouted. She edged over to the cellar door, reaching out to flip the lights on.

Carly followed her, grabbing a flashlight. They crept down the steps. The banging grew louder, almost deafening, as they reached the bottom of the stairs.

"I feel like we're in a dungeon." Delaney surveyed the large room, noting the crumbling foundation. She searched for the source of the sound—anything that explained the loud banging. Not having any luck, she closed her eyes and waited.

Carly's chest tightened, the odd sensation felt like a heavy weight beating on her chest to the rhythm of the banging noise. It reminded her of the time she'd had pneumonia as a child. She moved up close to Delaney. It took every bit of effort for her to ask, "Do you see anything, Delaney?"

Delaney shook her head. She walked the perimeter of the room, touching the large stones that made up the foundation of the home.

Carly followed close on her heels. Delaney continued to the furthest part of the cellar, where she noticed a change in the material in which the walls were constructed. The light bulb hung from a long cord. It flickered. Delaney pulled a small flash light from her pocket and flipped it on. She pointed it at the section of wall, different from the rest.

Delaney turned and shouted to Carly. "Do you know why this wall is different from the other three?"

Carly shouted her answer, "I asked Austin about the wall. He thinks there might have been structural issues."

"I see the floor needs repairing, and most of the stones that were laid to cover the floor are different next to the odd wall." Delaney ran her hand along the wall, her eyes closed. It was then that the cellar door slammed shut, startling both women. Carly grabbed Delaney's arm. The two stood silent. The banging stopped. They stood there waiting—the cellar deathly quiet.

Carly whispered, "What's going on?"

Delaney didn't answer but started moving back toward the stair-well. Carly still gripped her arm. Delaney shined her flashlight on someone only she could see.

"Who are you? What business do you have in this house?" Her voice firm, taking a tone of authority.

At that moment, the window facing the street, which had long been nailed shut, blew open hitting the block foundation so hard, that the glass shattered onto the dirt floor below.

Carly screamed. Panic took over her actions. She let go of Delaney and raced past her toward the stairway. "I have to get out of here, Delaney." She stopped on the bottom rung and looked back over her shoulder. Delaney had not followed her.

Delaney inched her way over to the open window. She felt along the wall, her hand touching the masonry patch where a window once opened to the street. "Look, Carly. How did the window blow open? There's no way. The mason blocks were filled in from the outside."

Carly stared in disbelief as Delaney shined the light at the hole. Moving away from the window, the broken glass crunched under her feet. She followed Carly up the stairs.

Neither of them saw the man and woman standing in front of the wall, their forlorn expressions fading along with their translucence.

Carly flipped off the light to the cellar, closing the door and locking it. They took a seat at the table. Delaney looked at the photograph of the boy again.

Carly took a drink of tea then looked Delaney square in the eye. "Okay, what's going on with all the people in my house?"

Delaney licked her lips and glanced around the room. "I need to figure out if there's a connection between the boy and the adults. We know that the man and woman were murdered. The other man, he's the aggressive one and probably responsible for all the banging and slamming doors. I would venture to say that he's the apparition you saw in the cellar." She rubbed her face then took a drink. "Until I find out who the people are and why they're here, I can't help them leave. I haven't seen the boy. Have you?"

"No."

Delaney rubbed her eyes, trying to sense him. "No, that's what's so frustrating. He's clearly here, the picture doesn't lie. But maybe he's connected to the photo album and toy horse, not the house?"

"Is that even possible?" Carly went over to the hall table and re-trieved the deed and title to her home. She opened it until she came to the page that gave the history of the house.

Delaney read the note on the abstract. "Carly, it looks like you only received a sixty year title search. That takes you back to the forties. You've got your work cut out for you."

Carly didn't answer, but went to the page she wanted. "Here's the deed for Dr. Howard Hutchinson and wife, Maureen. It says they pur-chased the house in 2002 from Ross Burkhart. No mention of a wife."

"You might want to write down the names and year the house changed hands. We might need it later. Take the last name with you tomorrow when you search the deed books."

Carly put a sheet of paper in her spot and closed the deed. "I can do this later. Would you like to walk through the house again?"

Delaney stood, looking towards the receiving room. "I really feel like the room that holds the spirits here is the receiving room. All the blood tells me it was the scene of the murders. The cellar is the other place. I feel that it's where the bad spirit stays. I'm not getting anything on the boy."

Delaney stood in the hallway, staring up at the second floor. She walked up the stairs, approaching the next to the top step, she found the toy horse sitting there.

"Carly, come up here! The horse is on the step again."

Carly hurried up the stairs. "I put that horse away and closed the door."

"I think the boy is trying to let you know he's here."

Delaney walked into the nursery and placed the horse on the mantel again. "Little boy, I want to help you. But you have to help me, too. I can't see you. I can't hear you."

Carly shuddered, listening to Delaney speak to the boy's spirit. In response, it was faint, but both women heard crying.

"Little boy, I hear you crying, but I can't help if you don't let me see you."

Carly walked to the hallway. "The crying seems to be coming from within the walls." Carly clasped her arms over her chest. "Delaney, I have to get out of here. I feel like I am suffocating."

With that, Delaney stopped her conversation and hastily took Carly by the arm. "Oh my, you're clearly in distress. Let's go downstairs."

By the time they reached the last step, Carly felt faint. Delaney took her outside on the piazza, where she sat her in one of the large wooden rockers.

"Do I need to call an ambulance?" Delaney asked, flustered.

Carly finally spoke, "I don't know what came over me, Delaney. I literally couldn't breathe. I had a similar feeling downstairs in the cellar, but nothing like this. I've never had that happen before in my life!"

Delaney had seen it happen before—to herself. She had felt what the spirit wanted her to feel. It didn't happen often, in fact, it had only happened twice in her lifetime. But each time was traumatic.

"Carly, one of the spirits reached out to you. You're going to have to be careful from now on. It might be the aggressive spirit causing you to have symptoms."

"Then we have to get to the bottom of whatever is going on. I can't bring a baby into this house."

For the first time, Carly let down her guard and said what she had been feeling all along. She was under so much stress, and afraid she might never get pregnant.

Delaney put her arm around Carly, giving her a much needed hug.

"We're going to get to the bottom of this. I'll do whatever I can to help you."

Carly's breathing returned to normal and her heart beat slowed. "I guess we're done for today. I'll finish working on the names in the deed, and I'll go to the RMC tomorrow. Thank you so much, Delaney."

"You stay here for a while. Get some rest and fresh air. I'll run in and get my purse and briefcase and be out of your way in no time." In the kitchen Delaney stood listening a moment. She heard a deep male voice. He laughed. Delaney shook off the chill that the evil sound had given her. She didn't stay to hear any more.

Later that afternoon, Carly sat at the kitchen table making a list of the home's owners dating back to the year 1949. She wrote down the name Samuel Arminger and his wife, Ruby. These were the last owners on the deed, and they owned the house for only one year. They sold the house in 1950 to George and Ellen Geier. Carly noticed the length of time between owners wasn't long. The longest was six years. She found that odd, but after the events she had experienced, she could perhaps understand why people wanted out.

Austin didn't return home until seven o'clock that evening. He walked in the bedroom and found Carly sitting in the middle of the bed, with the deed and several notes spread out in front of her.

"How'd your meeting with the psychic go? See any spooks?"

Carly looked up from her notes. She gave him a cold stare and up-turned chin.

"What's wrong, Are you okay?"

"No, I'm not okay. It was the worse day yet. Delaney saw all three spirits, and we heard the little boy crying. It was awful. I couldn't breathe."

"I'm sorry. I shouldn't have joked about it." Austin sat down on the bed, pulling Carly beside him. "Let me check your pulse. Are you feeling like you can't breathe now?"

Carly's tone softened. "No, I'm okay now. But it was something I'd never felt before. It really scared me, Austin."

"I don't understand what's happening. I've been having second thoughts about keeping the house. I don't know how to help you, Carly. You know I'm having a hard time believing in ghosts, but I believe *you*. Is there anything I can do to help you?"

Carly's chin trembled. She had tears in her eyes. Knowing Austin was truly concerned buoyed her confidence. "Support me. Believe that I'm not crazy." She took hold of his hand. "Yes. I'm scared to death, but

I have to find out what happened to the people in this house. Until then we won't be able to help them find closure and peace."

Austin ran his hand through his hair. "Do you want me to get you a sedative? I'm sure you haven't slept in a while. It might do you good."

Carly didn't want to take anything. There was a small chance she could be pregnant.

"No, it's okay. I'll be okay. I just have to be careful."

That night, Carly slept in Austin's arms. She didn't hear any noises or crying.

Carly slept later than usual. When she rolled over to check the time on the bedside clock, she rubbed her eyes to make sure was seeing it correctly! Nine o'clock? She must have been wiped out! Sad, she'd missed Austin, who had already left for his rounds at the hospital, she spent longer than usual in the shower, letting the hot water massage the stiffness in her neck from sleeping so late. As she reached for the shampoo, she heard a loud boom. Should she stay put? Quickly put on her clothes? She put the shampoo back on the shelf, got out of the shower and wrapped a towel around her dripping body. She opened the door and peered cautiously into the bedroom. The house seemed eerily quiet. She had become used to odd noises and unexplained crying coming from the walls, but this was the first time she had heard this sound. It sounded like a gunshot. She quietly tiptoed to the landing between floors, looking down into the hallway below. Carly was about to step onto the final step when her foot came down on the corner of the toy horse.

Carly bent down to pick up the toy. She felt she wasn't alone. She raised up quickly, causing her to lose her balance. Grabbing the banister, she steadied herself. "Okay. I get it, little boy. You're here. But you have to do more than this if you want me to help you." Before reaching the top of the stairs with the toy, she heard another boom, causing her to jump. It was then that she smelled an acrid odor. She raced to the bottom of the stairs, darting into the hall. She followed the smell into the receiving room. Carly had grown up around guns. Her father was an avid hunter, taking both she and her older brother on an occasional deer hunt. It reminded her of the distinct smell of gun powder. She stood in the center of the room, remembering the spot where Delaney saw blood. She had even said the man and woman appeared to her with gunshot wounds. Could she be smelling gun powder from another century?

She took a deep breath and braced herself. Straightening her back, she held tightly to her towel and marched back upstairs, shaking off her nervousness and fear. She placed the toy back in the nursery and since it was already after ten, she decided to skip shampooing her hair. She got dressed, put her hair in a ponytail and headed out for a bite to eat. Before leaving, she got her keys and clutch purse, her notebook, the deed file, her sunglasses and a bottle of water, putting them in her tote bag. She'd walk the five blocks to the RMC and find a nearby café to grab breakfast. As luck would have it she found a breakfast bar on the way. She ordered a cup of coffee and an omelet. While she waited for her order, she recorded the latest ghostly experiences. After finishing breakfast, she headed to the RMC to find the previous owners and their links to the unwelcome residents inhabiting her house.

Chapter 9

arly dialed Delaney's cell phone while dodging tourists along the street and admiring the vibrant flowers and trees. She knew her friend worked several days a week as a receptionist for an orthodontist and hoped to catch her at lunch. At first she'd wondered why her ghost hunting friend would work as a receptionist, until Delaney had told her how after her husband Mark had passed away. She sold the family insurance company but wasn't content to retire. She took the receptionist position and ghost tour job to provide her spending money and keep from being lonely and bored.

"Hey, Delaney! Is it a good time to talk?" Carly put her hand over her other ear to block the street noise.

"Sure, hon. Just drivin' to White Pointe Gardens for my lunch break—perfect timing."

"Great. I'm headed to the Register of Mesne Conveyance right now." Carly raised her sunglasses to squint at the pedestrian crossing signal. "So, how far back did you get last night?"

"Can't remember all the names, but I did trace back to the 1950s. Let me park, and I'll call you right back, okay?" said Delaney.

Carly's phone rang a few minutes later. "You were lucky to find a parking spot so quickly."

"What's been going on with your house of spirits lately?"

Carly heard a chorus of bird calls so she figured Delaney must be entering the popular city park.

"Well, it's never calm anymore. Today, while showering, I heard a boom so loud, it shook the shower door.

"Oh, dear! What'd you do?"

"I froze, afraid, because it came from inside the house and sounded like my father's antique muzzleloader firing." Carly plopped down on a wooden bench in front of the RMC.

"My goodness, did you call Austin?"

"No, I didn't want to bother him. I grabbed my curling iron to use as a weapon, and then I heard a second boom. It sounded like it came from the receiving room." She lowered her voice to a whisper. "I smelled gun powder!"

"Gun powder? Isn't the receiving room the same room where I saw the blood?" Delaney asked. "We call this type of paranormal occurrence a residual hauntin' experience."

"Residual, you said? You're saying the gun powder smell and the booms have lasted two hundred years? That's pushing even my ability to buy into all this." Carly's breath began to speed up and she tried to calm herself down watching the busy street scene. "But, if it's true, do you think the two gun shots killed that man and woman we've seen?"

"I don't know, but anything's possible with the paranormal." Carly heard Delaney's voice deepen. "I don't want to scare you even more, but since we're being honest about what both of us are seeing and hearing, I smelled sulfur the first time I entered your house."

"I haven't smelled a sulfur smell, but I was so weirded out by the boom that I left home in a hurry." Carly's heart rate increased remembering the encounter and goosebumps traced her arms. She tried to calm down by watching the normal activities around her.

"You know sweetie, I do believe you're sensitive, like me, because you can hear and smell things from the past, too."

Shocked by her friend's words, Carly stood up and rubbed her arms to make the chill bumps go away. "Um … listen, I'll let you go now, but is it ok if I call later?" She pulled her purse over her shoulder. This day became more bizarre as it went on and she needed to check some facts on their house to find some reasons for these hauntings.

"Why sure, hon. I'll catch ya later."

"Thanks for listening."

She hung up her phone.

After entering the RMC building, Carly lined up at the counter to wait for research assistance.

"Hi, I'm Carly Tabor." Carly adjusted the tote bag holding the deed and title. "I stopped in earlier to search your records to find the owners of our King Street home."

"Why, of course, I remember you." An elderly lady with grey curls stepped from behind the counter and smiled. "After you left, I jotted down a list of places to search. I'm Brenda and will be glad to help."

"Thank you so much. I appreciate your help." Carly said.

She led Carly to a room lined with metal shelves filled with rows of tall plat books. "As I said earlier, I'm not allowed to help you search." Brenda handed her a note page. "But, to save you time, I've listed the different volumes to search." She pointed out the numerous books of information. "We house the largest collection of abstracts and deeds from 1680 through 1929 in the state, as well as various Charleston newspapers which are available online in the room next door."

"Thanks for your help—you're so kind." Carly sat her purse and tote bag on the cherry library table.

"And, we're fortunate to hold the John McCrady Plat Collection." Brenda pointed to a row of books with threadbare covers. "You'll want to start with the newer volumes, since you have the names back to the 1940s." Before leaving the room, she handed Carly white cotton gloves to handle the old and fragile books. "Now darlin', please don't hesitate to ask for help."

"Thank you, Brenda. I'm amazed by this collection." Carly checked her Seiko watch and noted it was already twelve-fifteen. The office closed at five, so she'd better get busy. She pulled the books off of the shelves for the appropriate dates, and located the first name, Sheldon Arminger. Checking the deed, she located the names of Sheldon and Ruby Arminger, and it stated they purchased their home from Lawrence and Margaret Russell on December 15, 1947. Continuing through the musty pages, she found Lawrence and Margaret Russell. They purchased the home from Hugh and Ann Marie Petry on May 2, 1945. She kept tracing the owners' names back to the name Robert Ellsworth, who owned the home from 1848 until 1869.

It was after five when Brenda stuck her head in the door. "We're closing shop. I forgot you're working in here. Any luck?"

"I did, thanks. I think I'll bring my friend Delaney on the next visit, and the two of us can finish in a couple hours." After helping Brenda reshelf the large volumes, Carly left for home.

She walked a different route home, enjoying a change of scenery. The trees wove a canopy over the sidewalk, providing some shade from the still bright afternoon sun. At first their historic house had held this same southern charm, but lately the house's atmosphere ruined that feeling. If only they'd known, she and Austin might not have taken on the project. But, it was her home now and she determined the spirits of the house wouldn't ruin their happy lives. She and Delaney would figure out how to get rid of them. It was their house, after all.

Unlocking the front door, she caught a glimpse of movement on the upper piazza. She squinted up to check it, but only saw the ferns swaying like the hooped skirts of southern belles. Was she becoming paranoid?

Entering the receiving room, Carly closed her eyes and tried to see the room as Delaney described it. In an instant, she felt the room's temperature drop. Her pulse rate quickened. She spun around, sensing another presence in the room. Terrified, she froze, as a man appeared near the fireplace. She stifled an urge to scream. The man became solid, while a fog wrapped tentacles around Carly's ankles. Her nose picked up the scent of wood smoke from centuries ago. She stood watching the scene.

Summoning up the last of her courage, she quavered. "Who are you? What's keeping you here?" She cowered down. The man ignored her and floated through the doorway.

What had just happened? It seemed so real, down to the smell of smoke in the room. She heard the phone ring and pushed herself up from her cowered position to answer it.

"Hey, there. Did you have any luck today at the RMC?" Delaney's voice came through normal and concrete.

"I did, but—just now I saw the ghost of that man again and smelled the smoke, too. It freaks me out, I'm not used to this." The pitch of Carly's voice rose up high.

"Calm down. Remember, they can't hurt you. And … now we know you're sensitive to these spirts in your house. That's good, you can help figure out why they've stayed and how to make them leave." She took a breath to calm herself. Delaney's voice of reason helped. "Did you finish your research today?"

"I spent the afternoon searching the plat books and found the owners back to 1848, but there's still more to trace." Carly chewed on her lips and looked into the receiving room. "I wanted to ask, would you be able to help me finish up tomorrow?"

"It happens I'm off, so let's meet there in the morning."

"Great." Carly sucked in a quick breath, still feeling unsettled.

"You're able to connect with the spirits, so they're appearing to you for a reason. We're going to figure this out together and get you peace in your beautiful home. Don't worry, okay?"

"This home means everything to Austin and me. So this is a battle, I'm not willing to lose." After agreeing to the meeting time, Carly hung up the phone. She looked into the receiving room and hallway again. Nothing seemed out of place. How was it she could love a place and hate it at the same time?

She shrugged and headed for the kitchen to start dinner. Stepping on the slate kitchen floor, her foot came down on the pointed end of the metal rocking horse. "You again?" She leaned over and picked up the metal toy. "Okay. I get it. You want my attention." Carly held out the toy horse. "If you want the toy, take it." She looked around in anticipation, waiting for something to happen. The toy didn't frighten her like the other apparitions and noises did. After a few minutes, she set it on the counter. All she could do was go through her normal routine and not have others think she's crazy.

Austin finished rounds and arrived home at seven-fifteen. He came up behind Carly in the kitchen, wrapping his arms around her, and smothered her neck with kisses. "Umm … you smell delicious. Or is that dinner?"

"I'm sure it's dinner." She turned to face him and threw her arms around his neck, sinking into his safety.

After a hug and a kiss, she made Austin sit down to rest.

"How about filling me in on your day. How was your trip to the RMC?" Austin watched her put a chicken casserole in the oven.

"Well, let's see." Carly leaned against the counter, brushing a loose hair from her face. "This morning, I heard gun shots in the receiving room during my shower. Then, I smelled gun powder, saw a man with a gunshot wound, found the toy horse twice, but I made headway on the list of people who lived here. It's sad that this is becoming a normal day for me."

"Wait—you heard a shot? Oh, hon, this house is becoming too dangerous for you to be alone." Austin started to rise from the table.

Carly motioned him to stay put. "Sounds unbelievable, but I heard it. And when I got downstairs, I smelled gun smoke. I don't know how much more I can take…" Carly twisted the hem of her shirt and wiped away a tear. I'm trying to stay strong … but …"

"Carly, I do believe you, and you're going to figure this out. We're going to figure this out." He reached around and pulled out her chair. "Come … sit down.

She sank into the chair.

"I don't understand half of what happens in our house, but I love you unconditionally and I know you're not imagining it. Did you tell Delaney?"

"Yes, and she said I'm sensitive too, like her, and that I have the ability to help in resolving the hauntings." She glanced up, meeting Austin's eyes.

"Good lord! What does that even mean?" He rubbed his forehead, raking his hand through his dark hair.

She got up from the table. "It's where something that happened in the past keeps repeating over and over." She knew this was hard for Austin's scientific mind to understand, as it had been for her. She opened the refrigerator door, retrieving the salad she'd made. "Delaney thinks I smelled the gunpowder from the shot that killed the man and woman."

"This is hard to believe." He watched Carly flinch. "But I don't doubt you. I just wish I could do something to make it all go away." Austin got up from the table, hugged her again and began setting the table. "All this stress is bad for your health. I'm concerned."

Carly kissed him in thanks. "I'm okay ... really. Delaney's a big help. She's teaching me how to deal with these spirits. Tomorrow morning we're meeting at the RMC to search the deed books. We should finish up and find the original owners, or at least the ones who may have been murdered."

"I'm glad she's here to help us. What have you got so far?" Austin poured two glasses of red wine.

"I tracked the owners back to the year 1848. I'm hoping to find the original—" A muffled sound of crying interrupted Carly. For the first time, they both heard and experienced the sound together. Austin frowned and raised his finger to his lips. She crossed the kitchen to his waiting arms.

"I hear it now. It does sound like a child, and I think it's coming from the wall." He led Carly by the hand with him as he looked into the hallway.

She pulled him back to the kitchen. "I think it's louder in here."

They stood in the center of the room. She felt the air grow cold, and saw Austin shiver too.

"Is this cold draft what happens? Maybe the HVAC is breaking down." Austin rubbed his hands up and down her arms.

"Don't think it's the heat pump, hon. This always happens before a spirit appears," Carly's voice inched higher in pitch, and she leaned into him.

"Let me check this out and we'll get to the bottom of it. There just has to be a scientific explanation. This feels too much like a scary movie and not our lives." Austin's brow wrinkled, and he kissed the top of her head.

Austin strode over to the cellar door, and grabbed the knob. The door knob started vibrating in his hand. Carly, frozen like a statue, watched Austin struggling with the door.

"Austin, please don't touch that!" Carly hid her face in her hands and screamed.

"I can't let go, Carly! What the heck?" He held on to the door knob, his arms shaking as if operating a jack hammer.

Carly darted to help him. But as soon as she reached him, the door flew open and Austin fell back with a thud. Then the door slammed shut.

"Sweetie, are you okay?" Carly crouched beside him and cradled his head in her lap.

"I'm okay. I swear someone was pulling the door from the other side." He pushed himself up on his knees. "I wasn't convinced we had ghosts until right now, because there's no other explanation."

"Austin, someone doesn't want us down there. I think it's the dark spirit." Carly helped him stand up and brushed off his clothes. "What are we going to do? This is our house, and I won't let some ghost kick us out. Delaney saw him, and he told me to 'get out' of here."

"Damn right, they won't chase us out." Austin walked back over and opened the door cautiously. Carly stood close behind him as he flipped on the cellar light. "You might as well get the hell out of our house, we aren't leaving. You hear me?" Austin stared into the empty cellar.

"Babe, let's close the door. I don't want to provoke him anymore. Let's have dinner and calm down." She took a long sip of wine and pulled out her notebook, writing the events of the toy horse and the encounter. Austin shut the door with a bang.

"Tomorrow, call Delaney and invite her back." Austin winced as he eased down into the chair. "I don't want you going to the cellar, okay? For now, let's keep the door locked."

"Okay… for now. It's no wonder our house accumulated a long list of owners." She brought the deed information over to the table.

"I'm concerned about you staying alone here while I'm at work, but we'll figure this out soon. What's this?" He glanced through the papers.

"So far, 1848-1869 is the longest anyone lived in our house." She ran her finger down the list. "Most owners sold after two or three years. I'll bet they experienced the banging and crying, and that's why they moved." She scooted her chair next to Austin.

"I don't remember Dr. Hutchinson mentioning a word about ghosts." Austin drummed his fingers on the table and sipped his wine.

Carly brought the casserole out of the oven and they began eating dinner. "Would you tell a prospective buyer, 'Hey, we're selling a haunted house, but you'll love it!'?" She raised her eyebrows and picked at her food.

"Point made, Sherlock. I have a hard time giving credence to this." He ate quickly as if normal actions would keep everything fine. "People will think we're crazy if we tell anyone."

"Delaney believes us. For now, she's our only hope. And we have each other to lean on through this. If we can survive a ghost, we can endure anything, hon." She patted his hand across the table.

For the rest of the evening, they stayed in the den, enjoying a rare evening together and cuddled on the couch. After locking the doors for the night, they climbed the stairs to the bedroom. She lit a single candle on the nightstand, the soft glow flickering like a lightning bug. They made love as if newlyweds, each taking comfort from the physical bonding. The stress from the constant haunting had affected both of them. Tonight, it brought them closer. As she slept in Austin's arms, she didn't notice that the toy horse appeared at the foot of the bed.

Carly stirred, feeling the warmth of the sun streaming through the window. She squinted at the clock and saw 7:45am.

"Austin, wake up! It's late and you've got rounds this morning at nine." She shook his arm.

Austin rolled over to check the clock with one eye still closed. "I wonder why the alarm didn't go off?" He flipped off the blanket, and they heard an object hit the wood floor.

"What on earth?" Carly peered over the side of the bed. "Wait, I left this toy downstairs last night after I almost stepped on it."

"I wish they'd leave us and our house alone. No offense, little boy!" Austin held up his hands in a mock surrender.

Carly placed the horse in the nursery. She removed the skeleton key from the mantel, locking the door behind her. By 8:15, Austin stood at the door to leave for the hospital. Carly kissed him and he held her for a long while.

"I hate to leave you here, but I can't cancel. Remember, stay out of the cellar. I'll call you later. Love you." He tightened his arms around her and she breathed in his scent.

"I'll be fine, and we'll figure this haunting out and claim back our house. Delaney will help me research the deeds and put together the puzzle pieces." She put on a bright smile to hide her fear.

After Austin pulled out of the driveway, Carly straightened up the kitchen then left to do research. Turning to close a cabinet door, she saw the open cellar door. She knew Austin had closed and latched that door last night. Trying to remain calm, she slammed the door and turned the lock. Remembering Austin's words, she grabbed her things and started out for the RMC.

Chapter 10

Carly noticed a light rain begin as she drove to the RMC office. By the time she'd parked in the deck and ran across the street, it had become a hard rain. She met Delaney at the building entrance, both laughing at the tourists running for cover from the downpour.

"The tourists look like chickens running for the coop, don't they?" Delaney wiped the raindrops off her black leather briefcase. "Rushed here, because I didn't sleep well and overslept."

"They do look like chickens." Carly giggled and gave Delaney a quick hug. "We had lots of excitement last night so we slept like babies. Fill you in later." She held open the inside door for Delaney.

Brenda, the friendly volunteer, greeted them and escorted them into the research room.

"Okay, here's where I left off yesterday." Carly shared her notes. "Robert Ellsworth bought the home in 1848, but I've found several volumes of that year."

"No problem, hon, let's get started." Delaney opened the first volume.

Ten minutes into the search, Carly found the entry documenting Robert Ellsworth buying the home from Daniel Guerard and his wife Sarah, in the year 1848. As the records moved into the early 1800s, Carly asked Brenda to help them decipher the handwriting. The two women started seeing a pattern in the length of time between owners. By lunchtime, the two worked back to the year 1800.

"Yes, I've hit pay dirt!" Carly's outburst echoed like a gunshot in the quiet room. "Caleb Smith, and his wife, Carolania, purchased the house in 1800. If the house were built in 1790, then we're almost to the original owners."

"Wonderful, hon. But, how about stopping for lunch?" Delaney sighed and looked up from her volume. "I need to rest my much older eyes."

Leaving the building, they found a bench near the entrance, and munched into the sandwiches and chips Delaney brought. Carly explained the encounter she and Austin experienced in their kitchen the previous night.

"Now that Austin's hearing and seeing first-hand the spirit activity, he'll understand what we see and hear and won't think you've lost your marbles. I do think the spirits want to communicate." Delaney tucked her striped skirt around her legs and patted Carly's hand.

"Definitely, now that he's experienced it too. Austin wants you to come back to the house." Carly sipped her diet Coke. "He's on board with trying to rid the house of ghosts."

"Hon, I'd be happy to come back. After my dream last night, I'm more confused about the spirits." Delaney closed her eyes, as if recalling the dream. "I saw two men dragging a dead body of a man, judging by his dress, to the wharf. They rolled him into the river."

"Wow, did you see their faces?" Carly's eyes widened.

"Sorry, couldn't make out faces. But, how'd you feel about gettin' help from a friend of mine? He's a paranormal investigator from the College of Charleston." Delaney lowered her voice to a whisper.

"Let's think on that; I'm not sure we're ready to go there." Carly looked down at her notepad. "But I'd like for you to come to the house and try again."

"I know, but not sure I can help. Do discuss the paranormal investigator with Austin, and let me know when you're ready." Delaney began to pack up the debris from their lunch.

"Your dream—what do you think it means? I mean, I'm getting scared to be in the house alone. We need to figure it out. " Carly picked at her sandwich, but watched her friend.

"Well, I know the appearance of the men in my dream matched that of the two male spirits I saw. I think we're getting close to finding out who the mystery couple are. I'm going to help you, so don't you worry." Delaney hugged Carly, and they picked up their picnic remains and went back inside the building.

Back in the research room, the two began pulling books and leafing through old pages.

"Found it!" Delaney clapped her hands together.

"It reads Caleb Smith and wife, Carolinia, purchased the house from the heirs of Andrew Pettigrew." She showed Carly the entry.

"So, the first owner, Andrew Pettigrew, built the house in 1790. But to make sure, we need to check the lot owner," Delaney said.

Both Delaney and Carly searched until Brenda peeked into the room.

"Just checking. You two need anything before I take a break?"

Carly's head popped up from her volume. "Yes, how do we find when the owners received the original deed for a property?"

"If you have a name, we can search the mortgage books." Brenda looked at the book.

"We've found Andrew Pettigrew, and after he died, his heirs sold the house to Caleb Smith in 1802," Carly said.

"The South Carolina Historical Society holds the first mortgages, with original copies, some on microfilm or digitized on the computer. Don't forget about the College of Charleston and the city library. If you have names, you'll find a lot of information." Brenda shelved a book.

"Thanks, and we'll search Pettigrew's name in the mortgages." Carly pulled her purse strap over her shoulder. "We're on the right track—I'm sure of it."

Carly and Delaney headed next door to the South Carolina Historical Society. The sun replaced the rain, and the society's white building, standing between two ancient magnolia trees, contrasted against the blue sky.

Once inside, they approached a man at the information desk and asked where to begin looking for the original mortgage and property sale of Carly's house.

Tom Drummond, in his late fifties with brown eyes hidden behind wire-framed glasses, welcomed the women. "We hold an extensive collection of family papers and manuscripts of Charleston and South Carolina. If you know the address and name, we can find the mortgage and possibly the house plans. Also, we can search for any news clippings about your house," Tom explained.

Carly was encouraged because she knew if a murder had been committed in her home, the newspaper would likely have reported it.

Tom led them into a reading room first, explaining where to locate the information they needed.

"Some of the manuscripts are located in the map section." Tom showed them the reading room and pointed to a larger room down the hall. "Other items you must request, and we bring those to you. You can search through our vertical files and our online collection."

"I'm looking for Andrew Pettigrew and his wife, possibly the first owners of my house on King Street. I'm also looking for the original deed or mortgage." Carly pulled the notepad from her bag.

Tom leaned against the counter and polished his glasses. "Do you want to start with Andrew Pettigrew, or shall we start with finding out who bought the land and built the house?"

"Carly, let's start with Andrew. I think we'll find he's one of the people murdered in the house," Delaney said, and Carly nodded her head.

"Murder, hmm?" Tom looked at them over the top of his glasses. "Another place to search is the Charleston City Directory. If you know the year, we can find his name and occupation."

"We might be here for a while!" She smiled at Tom.

"Alright, let's go to the manuscript room and find Andrew Pettigrew in the plat books." Tom led the way.

They began searching the plat books and after thirty minutes located the original document showing the sale of a city lot to Andrew Pettigrew. Carly and Delaney couldn't believe their luck. Within fifteen minutes, Tom produced a page from the mortgages issued in Charleston for the years 1755 to 1799.

"Here's your proof." Tom read the line on page 393. "Pettigrew, Andrew. Mortgage for one town lot on King Street (Plat and Appraisement) 2nd May, 1789 from Hiram Pinkney, Esq."

"We did it." Carly squeezed Delaney's arm. "Now I know the names of everyone who've lived in my house. And we can figure out who won't leave it." She whispered the last part.

Before she could get the page copied, Tom found the name of Andrew Pettigrew's father, listed in the first census of 1790: John Halston Pettigrew, 53, Planter. He showed them the entry.

"Goodness, I'm so excited. Thank you!" She looked at the handwritten copy. "How do you read it?"

"The 1790 census was the first in the United States, so census takers took a variety of information. This page states that John Halston Pettigrew had one son, Andrew, aged 24, living at the plantation. It also lists the number of slaves as 68 and even tells their names and ages." He checked his watch.

"We're open until five o'clock, which gives me time to show you where we keep the newspaper records. There were at least five newspapers in the city, so there's several sources to search." He waited for their decision.

"I think we'll stay as long as we can today. Thanks for your help." Carly shook Tom Drummond's hand. It felt like a well-worn leather glove.

"Thanks for locatin' the census and city directory." Delaney also shook Tom's hand. Carly noticed that Tom's smile became warmer when he smiled at Delaney.

"My pleasure, now if you ladies need anything else, let me know." He left to help another patron.

The two hit the ground running with the new information on Andrew Pettigrew.

"You search the marriage records to see if Andrew had a wife, and check the 1800 census and city directory." Carly took the hair tie from her wrist, pulling her brown hair into a ponytail. "I'll check the newspaper files for any mention of Andrew or John Pettigrew." They walked toward the stairs.

"I think we're on the right track with Andrew Pettigrew. I've a hunch the person we're seeing isn't Caleb Smith." Delaney gave a 'thumbs-up' gesture as she went into the records room."

At four-thirty, Delaney texted Carly. "I hit the jackpot."

Carly texted back, "I hit the wall, but happy you didn't." The Historical Society didn't carry the years that Carly needed, with a date gap between 1789 and 1795. She finished the text, "Meet you downstairs in the reading room."

Carly arrived to sit beside Delaney at the table.

"Look what I found on our Andrew Pettigrew." Delaney smiled like a Cheshire cat.

She showed her the marriage license, city directories of 1795 and 1799, and death notices for both Andrew Pettigrew and his wife, Celeste.

"You found them!" Carly hugged her.

"Here's the scoop. Andrew married Celeste Faysoux at St. Michael's Church on September 21, 1791. It says her father, Peter Faysoux, is a physician," Delaney said.

"So he was married—good information." Carly shook her head.

"I checked the records for death notices and found them published in the newspaper on the same day." Delaney cleared her throat. "I'm certain the apparitions are those of Andrew and Celeste Pettigrew."

Carly read the copy of the death notices. A cold chill ran up her arms.

"Where did you find this? I couldn't find anything in the papers out in the main library." Carly asked.

"I found it online when I did a search for the Charleston Gazette. 'Died: 19 January, 1799. Andrew Pettigrew, Thursday, at his King Street home, the Customs Inspector, by a gunshot to his head, and equal in tragedy, a gunshot taking the life of his wife, Celeste nee Faysoux, beloved citizen and daughter. Committal at St. Michael's Churchyard.'"

"You're right! Here's the proof." She squeezed Delaney's hand.

"Now we know their names and what happened." Delaney leaned back into her seat. "I need them to tell me why they're still here."

"What's a customs inspector?"

"Well, it's an important position, because he collected duties from ships. They also kept records of merchant vessels coming into the harbor with imported and exported goods, and collected monies in taxes." Delaney blotted her forehead with a tissue.

"Tom mentioned the Charleston Gazette, housed at the College of Charleston. We could stop in to see their collection, or better yet, search online," Carly said.

"We've got several hours of daylight left, it's only four-thirty. How about grabbing a bite to eat at The Noisy Oyster and visiting St. Michael's graveyard? Maybe we can find Andrew and Celeste's graves." Delaney stacked up her books for shelving. "I've given a few tours in the graveyard, and it's open until dusk."

"Okay, I'm starving." She texted Austin to let him know of their plans.

Over dinner, Carly and Delaney discussed Andrew and Celeste Pettigrew's tragic end. They still didn't know the identities of the dark spirit and little boy. After dinner, the two walked from the restaurant up to Meeting Street and over to Broad Street to search the graveyard at St. Michael's Episcopal Church for the graves of Andrew and Celeste Pettigrew.

"Sure hope I have my digital camera." Carly rifled through her Coach purse. "I want to get some pictures of the graveyard, and my phone battery's almost dead."

"You can use my phone sweetie—it takes good pictures." Delaney searched her purse for her phone. "I hope we can find the graves, because some are hard to read, while others have fallen over and are broken in pieces."

"I've always loved this church. How about giving your spiel, tour guide?" Arriving at St. Michael's Episcopal Church, Carly craned her neck upwards, admiring the structure.

"Well, James Gibbs built the church. The most prominent features of this stucco and brick church are the giant classical portico and the 186-foot high proportioned steeple." She adjusted her sunglasses. "The history of the congregation of St. Michael's is rooted in that of St. Philip's Episcopal. The first St. Philip's church stood at this site from approximately 1681 to 1727. In 1751, the congregation divided, and the residents of the lower half of the city formed St. Michael's." Delaney motioned for Carly to enter the gates.

"Wow. How'd you remember all that?" Carly admired the ornate wrought iron gate, flanked by a brick wall on either side.

"I've rattled it off a few times, since it's part of my ghost tour!" Delaney took a picture as they entered the graveyard.

"Why did they bury people so close to the building?" Carly studied the headstones, noticing some of the graves were placed next to the church.

Delaney walked over to one headstone. "She was only twenty-one. I've heard the more pious the person, the closer to the church the grave was placed."

"It's a peaceful place." Carly read some of the gravestone inscriptions.

"I've been in here to point out the graves of prominent citizens, but I don't remember seeing the name Pettigrew on the headstones." Delaney examined each grave stone as she walked along the gravel path.

"Do you suppose they keep records for the burials?" Carly bent to read an inscription, covered with moss.

"I think the church has its own records, but I'll bet we can find the records at the Historical Society," Delaney said.

They spent the next hour walking through the cemetery, reading headstones, and then they split up, taking different sides of the graveyard. Delaney found a collection of older stones lining the brick wall that surrounded the cemetery. She poured water from her water bottle down the front of one headstone and rubbed it with a napkin, trying to read the stone's inscription.

"Carly!" Delaney then remembered her manners and respectful cemetery etiquette, and motioned to her. Another couple strolled through the cemetery; with the noise from the street, they didn't hear Delaney's shout.

"Did you find them?" Carly rushed over and bent down on one knee to inspect the writing.

"Found one—Celeste Faysoux Pettigrew's grave." She pointed to the writing. "The dates are hard to read, but looks like she was born on the 7th day of July, 1773. She died on— well, it's hard to read. I think it reads "1 7 9?""

"The death notice stated the deaths of she and Andrew occurred on the 19th of January, 1799." She read the printed sheet from the Historical Society.

"How about taking a couple of pictures with your camera, and I'll get a few with my phone." Delaney took several pictures.

They noticed the headstones on either side of Celeste weren't her husband. Both found it odd that the pair weren't buried next to one another. They spent another thirty minutes searching the cemetery. The shade hampered their search, along with nightfall approaching.

"Tomorrow I'll call the Rector at the church. I'll see what I can find out about the burials." Delaney put her camera back in her bag and tucked her strawberry blonde hair behind her ears. "It's odd—Andrew and Celeste weren't buried together."

"I don't know about you, but I'm bushed. It's been a long day," Carly brushed loose strands of her long brown hair from her face. The two friends left the cemetery and walked back through dusk to the parking garage.

"Do you want to come back to the house? Maybe Celeste will talk to you, now that you know her name." Carly leaned against the car door.

"Sure. I don't have anyone waiting for me at home." Delaney walked over to her car.

Carly pulled through the gate into the driveway, followed by Delaney. When they entered the dark house, Carly felt the presence of the spirits. Thank goodness that Delaney had returned home with her, because she felt weirded out—especially by the dark spirit. Carly flipped the lights on, illuminating the hallway.

Delaney stood at the threshold of the receiving room as if listening to the silence. Closing her eyes, she asked. "Celeste? Are you here?"

Carly stood in the kitchen doorway. The house held its breath.

"Celeste, we know you're here. We know Andrew's with you. We want to help you but tell us what's keeping you here, please." Delaney checked out the shadows in the room and into the hallway.

Carly felt dread begin as the temperature dropped. Once again, this cold, as if from the grave, sank into her bone marrow. Delaney stood there waiting, and her quickening breaths became visible clouds.

"There's someone's in here!" Carly felt shivers slide down her arms and felt the hair on her nape begin to rise.

Delaney rushed across the hallway, pushing Carly. Surprised, Carly shrieked. A large glass bowl sitting on a shelf flew down like it had been shoved, right where she'd been standing. The bowl exploded on the stone floor, sending glass shards everywhere.

"Lordy, are you okay?" Delaney hugged her and patted her back to calm her down.

Carly surveyed the damage. She felt nauseous. She'd never been physically threatened by these spirits and it terrified her. Backing away from the counter, she stared at the shattered bowl, glittering on the floor like shiny knives.

"Delaney, what am I going to do? I can't live like this! This place was supposed to be our dream house and now we're in danger of being seriously hurt! Only the guys remodeling the house had seen things moved around." She wiped the tears running down her face, and Delaney hugged her again.

"I promise, sweetie, I will help you figure this out and protect you as best as I can. We're going to figure out why they're still here and not at peace." Delaney helped her sweep up the glass and clean the floor. "Let's have some iced tea to calm down."

"Okay, doing something normal might help my nerves. Iced tea cures everything, don't you guys say that here?" She brought tea out of the chrome refrigerator and poured it into two glasses.

"Wait, do you hear that?" Delaney brought her finger to her lips. "I hear someone screaming 'No!' It's a woman's voice!"

Carly choked on her long sip of tea and stared into the hallway.

"I can't go through this again. Please don't make them mad, Delaney!" Carly's eyes were dull as she looked in the hall.

"It's okay, I don't get bad vibes from this voice." Delaney closed her eyes, holding her hands up. "Celeste, please, who shot you? Will you show me what happened?"

Carly could almost hear a faint voice moan—'Help him, I beg of you.' Delaney nodded to her as if verifying what she heard.

"It's Celeste Pettigrew's voice, I believe, can you hear it, too?" Delaney frowned and cocked her ear towards the hall.

"Good lord, I can't believe I'm almost hearing her too. This is unbelievable and creepy! Did she answer you?" Carly inched into the hallway, her senses heightened like a bloodhound. The two women held hands, united to solve this mystery.

As the women stood silent in the hallway, the temperature began to drop down again. Delaney turned. "I can see Celeste here…she's begging us for help and standing in the threshold, as if unable to enter the room." Carly squinted into the shadows of the hallway but could only see a lighter area at the threshold. But then she felt another presence, and resisted the urge to look behind her. The familiar chill curled up her back like a poison ivy vine.

"Delaney, ask her who she wants us to help- -Andrew?" Her eyes darted towards the hallway. She saw Delaney dart past her, as if chasing the apparition only visible to her.

"Wait, come back, Celeste! We will help, but you must tell me!" Delaney looked to the stairway at nothing and held one hand out.

"What's happening? Did she talk to you?" Carly ran up to her and grabbed her arm.

"I heard Celeste say 'No' to someone. Then, I heard her scream." Delaney pressed her hand against her forehead. "I think she said 'help him.' Someone or something wouldn't let her enter the room."

"Oh, Delaney, we're making progress, because you actually heard her and tried to communicate." She looked into Delaney's glazed eyes and gripped her shoulders. "But, I felt the dark spirit near me and the coldness, and I got so scared. I'll bet he's the one who tried to throw my antique bowl at me!" Carly's brow furrowed, and her voice raised in anger.

"I feel Celeste is controlled by the dark spirit. He controls the others in the house." Delaney swayed as if dizzy, and Carly helped support her.

"Are you alright? Here, let's drink our tea in the kitchen." She helped Delaney into the kitchen to sit down in a chair. She handed her an ice-filled glass of the southerner's magic potion. "I agree with you. Do you think there are more than the four spirits we know about here?

How can we get rid of them so Austin and I can claim our dream house back?" Carly's eyes grew large as saucers.

Before Delaney could answer, they heard a slamming door and both nearly jumped to the ceiling. Carly heard, "Hon, I'm home." Austin walked into the kitchen to find them sitting there staring at the entry.

"Hello, Delaney, good to see you." He poured himself a glass of tea from the pitcher.

"Umm...nice to see ya again." Delaney set her glass down and tried to smile.

"You two look tired. What happened?" He bent down, planting a kiss on Carly's cheek.

"Well, it's complicated, and I'm going to be late to lead my ghost tour." Delaney stood up with effort and gathered her purse. "I'll let Carly give you the low-down. You two have a good evening. Austin, please watch over Carly."

Carly and Austin walked her to the door. "I'll call you tomorrow." Carly hugged the older woman who felt fragile in her arms. She whispered to her. "I have a feeling we're in for an active night. Thanks so much for helping me today."

"You're welcome. Doing this exhausts me—guess I'm getting too old for communicating because it takes my energy as well. Just be careful and keep Austin close to you. I'll call the Rector at St. Michael's tomorrow, though." Delaney looked back over her shoulder at the house as she walked to her car.

Chapter 11

Austin returned to the kitchen and instructed Carly to take her tea and go relax in the den while he finished cleaning up the broken glass. Afterwards, he sank down onto the couch, pulled her into his chest and stroked her long brown hair.

"Thanks for cleaning up the broken bowl, hon." She burrowed her head into his chest and relished feeling safe for once.

"You two looked white as sheets. What in the world has been happening?" He began massaging her small feet.

"It's so hard to tell you about what's happened—it's been a day." She kept her face on his chest. "I had an odd encounter this morning after you left. And tonight, I think someone wanted to hurt me by dropping the glass bowl on me."

"What! We've never had something like that happen. It's not safe for you here, Carly."

"It sailed from the shelf and barely missed my head! I would have been hurt if Delaney hadn't pushed me out of the way!" She sat up, turning to face him with fear in her blue eyes. "This morning the cellar door was standing open, and I saw the toy horse on the floor."

"Damn, Carly! We can't continue living here if you're in danger. I'm not able to stay here and protect you, and I'd never forgive myself if you were hurt in our house." Austin kissed the top of her head and his voice cracked.

"Delaney and I are figuring out the mystery of why the spirits are still here." She measured his large hand against hers and kissed his knuckles.

"My rational mind is having a hard time accepting all this. I locked that door last night. You saw me!" He raked his other hand through his dark hair.

"I know, sweetie, I wouldn't have believed it if didn't happen to me. I know I put the toy horse in the nursery and closed the door." She massaged the back of his neck. He'd worked two straight shifts and then came home to chaos he couldn't control. "Something good happened today, though. We found the owners of our house all the way back to when the lot was purchased!"

"Seriously? You two amaze me with what you accomplish in a day. Wanna come help me with patients?" He tousled her brown silky hair and tried to laugh.

"We found out the first owners, Andrew and Celeste Pettigrew were murdered in our house!" Carly fetched her camera, notes and copies of the information. She handed them to Austin, who read over the census and murder announcement from the newspaper.

"I'm still struggling with all this, but let's say our star spooks are Andrew and Celeste Pettigrew. Who are the supporting cast?" He raised his eyebrows, trying to get a smile from his wife.

"Funny. We're closer to filling in the cast list, if nothing else. Delaney found the information for the burial notice at St. Michael's graveyard. Here are some pictures of Celeste's headstone." She advanced the digital images for him and told him how they couldn't find Andrew's headstone anywhere nearby. Explaining Delaney would contact the Rector to locate his grave, Carly began to tell him about the occurrences when they returned home.

Austin stretched his long legs out on the coffee table. "You mean she spoke to the Celeste woman?"

"Well, not exactly. I mean she heard Celeste speak before the bowl flew off the shelf."

"Good thing she saved you, sweetie. I don't want you to be in danger here" Austin said.

"Delaney started communicating with Celeste. She told Delaney to 'help him', but before she explained, she disappeared, and then the bowl was pushed off right where I was standing." She twirled a loose lock of hair. "I realize it sounds far-fetched."

"Well, what did the woman say next?" Austin said, and Carly could see him try to wrap his head around their conversation.

"Celeste's spirit couldn't say anything else, maybe because this dark spirit kept her from speaking. He seems to have some kind of control over the other spirits!" Carly wasn't sure what he was thinking. "Let's say I buy into this spirit thing. Then who the heck is 'him'? Her husband?" Austin took a long sip of tea. Carly could tell he wanted a wine or a scotch to listen to this.

"I don't know, hon. Think she meant Andrew was in danger."

"I hope Delaney can get them to leave before Thanksgiving. Remember, Dad and Mom are flying here for a few days. It'll be good to have something normal going on in our house for a change." He massaged the tension in her neck again.

She tried to think about and get excited about the holidays, but the spirits occupied her thoughts that evening. Carly needed Delaney to help figure this out and get these spirits out of her house. Without having the same sensitivity that her friend had, she depended on her for help. Shaking her head to clear it, she decided to embrace normalcy and ignore what was happening until Delaney could come over again and help with research and communicating with Celeste. She'd put together her menu for the Thanksgiving meal, the first social gathering in their new home. Snuggling up to the safety of her husband and his rational thinking, Carly tried to relax and not dwell on the extra guests in their house. For the rest of the evening, the couple enjoyed watching "Forrest Gump," a favorite of both of theirs. They had a silent pact not to talk about their uninvited guests.

Chapter 12

Carly and Austin sat on rocking chairs drinking coffee on the second floor piazza, watching neighbors leave for work. She was thankful he didn't have rounds and could stay here with her. The house's spirits were making her more nervous lately, and she loved their stately historic home so much. In fact, this humid low country coastal town had started to feel like home to her, even with the disturbing home event. As she rocked and gazed down King Street, her mind wandered back to that January evening in 1799. *Who murdered Andrew and Celeste Pettigrew?*

"Did you hear what I said, hon?" He nudged her bare foot with his.

"Sorry, I was thinking about Andrew and Celeste Pettigrew." She shook her head to move back to the present.

"I asked you about Thanksgiving. Mom just sent me a text about the meal. Have you thought anymore more about what we're having?" He rubbed his jaw, rough with morning stubble.

Even after nine years of marriage, Carly didn't look forward to spending time with her in-laws—or the "out-laws" as she secretly termed them. She didn't feel close to either his father or his mother, Myra, and it bothered her that she and Austin's first wife were still close friends. She imagined his marriage to her, with her blue-collar roots, was seen as a let-down to his prominent family. Now, her in-laws would be visiting, likely expecting to see a grand home worthy of their son and the money they'd given towards the purchase.

"Well, no, I haven't thought about it. Probably just a traditional turkey dinner." Carly tugged at her ponytail.

"I'm sure the folks will appreciate whatever you make, hon. You know Mom isn't much of a cook." Austin stretched his long frame as he rose up from his rocker. "It's only a couple of days—don't be stressed. Dad's patients get worried when he travels out of town near their due dates."

She dreaded the usual questions from Myra about when they could expect a grandchild announcement. Carly no longer kept track of her cycles and hardly thought about trying to get pregnant, since they'd discovered unexpected house guests who wouldn't leave.

"I've a busy day ahead. Going to the College of Charleston's library to search newspaper accounts of the murders. There should be a record of the trial, don't you think?" Carly stood beside him leaning on the rail and enjoyed the bucolic atmosphere early in the morning.

"I would think there would be a trial report, even back then. I know you can track it down." Austin kissed the top of her head. "Darn it, they need me earlier than I thought. Are you okay here alone?" Austin read the message displayed on his pager.

"I'm fine, and I'll be heading out soon." She'd grown accustomed to his leaving for the hospital at a moment's notice.

As she pulled up the antique coverlet on the bed and put away her long lace nightgown, a sound coming from the third floor caused her to stop and listen. What was making the sound…squirrels? Carly frowned, hearing what sounded like footsteps on the unfinished wood floor above the second floor. Added by an owner before the War Between the States, the third floor remained unfinished, so they used it as an attic for storage. Feeling her breathing speed up but also angry and fed up with all these house noises, she pulled her hair back into a ponytail, grabbed her iPhone and a flashlight and slipped on flip flops. Dang it, this house was theirs now and they wouldn't be chased out by rodents or ghosts.

Putting her fears aside, she tiptoed from the bedroom to the hallway. Nothing there. But, the sound continued from above, perhaps rodents were making homes. She crept up the narrow wooden staircase, her heart beating like that of a scared rabbit. Reaching the top step, she waited and listened—quiet now. She took a deep breath.

When she opened the door, the smell of rotten wood and neglect assaulted her nostrils. She surveyed the open space, her eyes adjusting to the bright sunlight streaming through the windows. The room contained studs as if someone began to convert it to living space, but for whatever reason, construction stopped. Walking around the room, she pushed a few storage boxes out of the way looking for rodents making the noises. Only a few spiders nested in the area, and she stomped a few of them, taking pleasure in winning one battle. Finally after looking around and listening for ten minutes, she found nothing and decided the noise was her overactive imagination. She told herself to stop jumping at every noise. She shook her head and started for the door to the downstairs without looking back.

On the first step, a hand pushed her from behind. Reaching for the banister to catch herself, she screamed and teetered, almost falling down the stairs head-first. She wrapped her right arm around a spindle, holding in a steady but awkward contortion. She grimaced in pain, afraid her shoulder had pulled out of joint. She regained her balance and holding her arm close, edged down to the second floor. All she could think was to get down to safety away from whatever or whomever had pushed her.

A man's laughter boomed from overhead. What in the world was going on? Was that the ghost of the dark spirit who pushed her and was laughing? She darted for the bedroom, slamming and locking the door behind her. Carly sat on the bed, trying to stop shaking. She pulled her sweatshirt off her throbbing shoulder and saw a bruise beginning to color blue on her wrist and forearm.

Carly knew somebody had tried to push her down the stairs. She felt the pressure on her back, she felt sure. If that was true, she didn't want to stay in the house any longer, and she'd need to tell Austin about this latest event. Surely he would understand how she didn't feel safe. Just then, the temperature started to drop, causing condensation to appear on the bedroom window.

To her, the chilly temperature was the last straw, a signal to get out of the house.

She'd nearly been pushed down the stairs, and the message got through loud and clear. She hurried down the main stairs and grabbed her purse. Carly refused to look over her shoulder as she slammed the door.

She received a text from Austin as she entered the car. She read her phone, "Hey hon. Hope you're having a good morning." She started laughing, but stopped on the edge of hysteria. She called him while he was on break.

Austin immediately told her he'd run into Dr. Hutchinson at the hospital and asked him about strange happenings in the house when he'd lived there. "He said they didn't notice anything until they started renovating and then all hell broke loose."

"Are you serious? It happened to them too? Did you tell him we think the couple was murdered there?" Carly gripped the steering wheel tightly with one hand.

"He admitted to hearing some of the same things we've heard and reassured me that we aren't crazy." Austin's voice comforted her with its normalcy. "Did you have a good morning after I left?"

"Well, no, I sure didn't. After hearing footsteps overhead, I went up to the third floor, but found nothing and didn't hear anything else. I know it sounds freaky, but I felt a hand try to push me down the stairs! After I climbed down, I also heard a man laughing when I closed the attic door."

"Are you kidding me? You felt a hand push you or did you just trip? I don't like to think this spirit is getting more violent towards you. I would never forgive myself if something happened to you." Austin's voice grew louder on the phone. "I'm guessing that's why Dr. Hutchinson moved out after his wife passed."

"We have to figure out why the spirits are stuck in our house in order to get rid of them." Carly pulled into the parking deck for the library. "I just arrived at the library. I need to learn more about the Pettigrews." She pushed her sunglasses onto her head and rubbed her eyes. "Love you."

"I love you, babe. We'll get through this. I'll call you later." Austin hung up the phone.

Walking into the library, she texted a message to Delaney. "Took a tumble this morning. The dark spirit again. Talk later!"

Library staff directed her to special collections on the second floor. She found the special collections room, and another staff person helped her search the microfilm records for the titles and dates she needed. However, as she began scrolling down the screen, Carly noticed the issues of the newspapers she needed were missing. At the bottom of the page, she spied *The Columbian Herald* and *The Evening Gazette*, both including issues from the years the Pettigrews were living in Charleston.

When she typed in "Andrew Pettigrew, Customs Inspector" into the search function, she received a hit and a link to *The Evening Gazette* appeared. She found a small article listing the name of Andrew Pettigrew, newly appointed Customs Inspector, July 9, 1797, which stated that the previous custom inspector, Isaac Holmes, who had been appointed by President Washington, had resigned after his inability to collect delinquent debts. Another article mentioned Celeste Pettigrew's father, Dr. Peter Faysoux, as the personal physician of Thomas Hayward, with whom the President resided during his Charleston stay. Carly could read between the lines that Andrew Pettigrew was likely given the prestigious appointment of Customs Inspector due to his connections with the Hayward and Faysoux families.

After more searching, Carly located two entries regarding exports on various cargo vessels, from November 1795 through December 1799, and all were signed by the Collector of Customs, Andrew Pettigrew. Reading the items, she was amazed to see the goods coming and going from the port of Charleston from so many different countries.

She sat back from the screen, rubbing her eyes as she felt a headache coming on. Before she called it a morning and went for lunch, she tried a search on the murder of Andrew Pettigrew, Custom Inspector. The source, The City Gazette, popped up on the computer screen, but a subscription to a genealogy site was necessary to read this resource and she didn't have access. With the possibility of finding out more information, she decided to subscribe to the genealogy site on her home computer. As she left the library, she noticed a text message from Delaney. "Got your message. I'll call you after work."

At home, she cautiously entered their house and found nothing out of the ordinary. Relieved, she made and ate a tuna salad for lunch and found the genealogical web site on the computer. She saw an offer for a free month's trial membership and signed up, hoping to solve the mystery in a short period of time.

Within minutes, she gained access as a member and found several entries for *The City Gazette,* Charleston, South Carolina. Scanning through the articles, her heart leaped when she read the words *'An account of the late murder, which appeared in the City Gazette of Saturday last'.* Slowly, she began to feel a tickle on the back of her neck and felt she wasn't alone in the room. Determined to continue with the task, she ignored the temptation to look behind her.

She sent the pages about the murder to the HP printer, then continued searching. The next newspaper article supplied the court's version of the arrest of the alleged murderer of Andrew Pettigrew, listing him as the Inspector of Customs, along with his wife, Celeste Faysoux Pettigrew. Again, she sent the page from the newspaper to the printer.

Walking over to the printer to get the articles, she felt a chill raise goosebumps on her arms. Her breath appeared visible in front of her. "Oh, Lord, please not again!" Her teeth chattered, and her heart raced with fear of what would happen next. The banging noise began again, and she knew the dark spirit wanted to get her attention.

She walked back to the kitchen desk to get her notebook, but the cellar door flew open with such force that it left the imprint of the knob on the wall. Carly screamed, backing away, with fear closing her throat. The banging echoed and grew louder throughout their dream house. Disregarding Austin's warning, she reached for the light switch to cellar. An energy as strong as a Kansas whirlwind raced through her, knocking her to the kitchen floor. The cellar door slammed shut. As suddenly as it started, the banging ceased.

Pulling herself up with her hand on a cupboard, she rubbed her sore shoulder. She was certain she'd have a bruise on her tailbone from this tumble. But as the pain subsided, her innate feistiness came back with anger. She winced from the shoulder pain when she yanked open the cellar door. "You think you can bully me into not finding out what happened to Andrew and Celeste? Think again!"

She slammed the door, relishing her new-found defiance. She and Austin wouldn't give up on their dream house and leave it to these spirits. With Delaney's help, she'd figure out what happened and make the ghosts leave. Carly grabbed her cell phone, texting Delaney about what happened and asked her to come by the house. Within seconds, Delaney's reply appeared. "I'll stop by after I get off work. Be careful!"

Carly returned to the computer, her hands trembling as she searched the columns of the paper, trying to locate the name *Pettigrew*. After a few minutes, she found a newspaper article with a detailed account of the murder trial. Scanning through the opening statement, her breath caught in her throat when the name Benjamin Hastings appeared as the accused. Is Benjamin Hastings the dark spirit who haunts her house? She printed the pages of the account. As she ate her lunch, her mind raced with thoughts of the encounters she'd experienced with the dark spirit. Lost in thought, her cell phone ringing caused her to jump. "Hello?" She cleared her throat and tried to sound like herself.

"Hey, sweetie. We haven't heard hide or hair from you in a month! Is everything all right?"

Hearing her mother's voice felt ordinary and comforting. "Mom, I'm fine. I meant to call, I'm sorry. I've been, um, busy." Carly felt her face flush with the lie, thankful her mother couldn't see her.

Her mother made some small talk and then questioned her daughter. "Honey, I can't get the boy's image in our photograph out of my mind. I didn't tell your father because I didn't want to worry him." Carly paced across the kitchen as they talked.

"I started doing research on the history of our house. Two people were murdered here in 1799." She tapped her finger on the table, waiting for her mother's reply.

"Oh my goodness! How awful. How'd you find that information?" Paula questioned.

"Suffice it to say, it's not been easy. I also found a friend who has a way with ghosts." Carly bit her lower lip.

For a moment, Paula Evans didn't say a word. "I don't believe in ghosts. But that doesn't mean I don't believe something strange is going on there. Why don't you come back to Kansas for the holidays?"

"Mom, you know I miss you all. Money's tight right now, with paying for all the renovations. But I promise, I'll come home this summer." Carly felt the tears pooling in her eyes.

"Well, maybe things will get better financially before the holidays. We understand, hon, but don't rule out a trip yet!" Paula's cheerful tone was comforting.

This would be the first holiday season Carly would be without her family. Even when she and Austin moved to Denver, she always made the trip back home for Christmas. This year, they would spend the holidays in Charleston.

"Tell Daddy hello. I miss you both, and love you!" She sniffed, wiping a tear from her cheek.

"I love you more, sweetie, all the way to the moon and back." Paula's voice grew husky as she said goodbye.

Carly returned to reading the newspaper account of the Pettigrew murder trial. She saved it to her hard drive, returning to the list of links. Another account told of the court proceedings from the murder trial of Benjamin Hastings. Jacob Hinman, a name unknown to her, was listed as another person involved in the murders of Andrew and Celeste Pettigrew. She leaned back. Another person involved? Maybe she's wrong about the dark spirit's identity.

The last entry puzzled her but she sent it to her printer. She thought, "It's no wonder we couldn't find you at the cemetery the other night. Someone moved you from the church yard at St. Michael's." She rubbed her eyes and sent a text to Delaney. "Do I have a tale to tell you!"

Chapter 13

As Carly finished cleaning the kitchen, the door bell rang. She peered through the peep hole in the front door, and saw Delaney with her jacket pulled up around her chin.

"Hey, Nanook of the North! I guess the winter chill followed me from Denver." Carly gave Delaney a hug. "How about some sweet tea? Just made a fresh batch."

"Hey, girl! Not supposed to be this cold yet, and I still want to wear my flip flops!" Delaney stepped inside the threshold and studied the house interior. "I'd love some, thanks!"

"Well, I've had an active day." She set two glasses in front of them and pulled out her research. "I think we're getting somewhere, my friend."

"Although I can't wait to read what you found, first catch me up on your tumble." Delaney put the papers aside.

"Oh my! It scared me to death. I think the dark spirit pushed me down the steps, and I heard him laugh afterwards." She glanced over her shoulder and whispered.

"He's getting bolder. We've provoked him by finding his connection to the Pettigrews, no doubt." She noticed the bruise on Carly's wrist. "My goodness, you did get hurt!"

"Yeah, my hand got tangled in the railing trying to keep myself from plunging down the stairs. Then, I had another encounter with him later." Carly rubbed her wrist and shoulder. "Later, the cellar door flew open. I swear, a wind blew up the steps and knocked me on my...um, rear." She took a long drink of tea.

"Lordy, I'm so sorry he's targeting you, but we're going to figure this out. There's a limit to how much physical force a spirit has." Delaney patter her hand. "Show me what you've found."

"I found four entries from *The City Gazette* newspaper about Andrew and Celeste and their murders." Carly leaned on the counter, waiting for her reaction.

Delaney read the newspaper account of the murder notice of Andrew and Celeste Pettigrew, January 19, 1799. When she got to the name of the accused, she looked up from the paper.

"Get out of town… Benjamin Hastings! So that's who I saw last night in my dream." She smacked her hand on the counter.

"You saw Benjamin Hastings?" Carly's eyes looked like twin saucers.

"After I fell asleep, I dreamed I was walking into the murder scene. The dark spirit, I think it was Benjamin Hastings, ran through me as if I were a wisp of smoke."

"I can't believe it! We've both had experiences now with Hastings going through us. He scares me, but I'm a Kansas girl." She put up her fists. "I'm ready to kick butt."

"Don't push him. He murdered two people in life; he's dangerous." Delaney's frown helped to calm her down.

"And, Austin ran into Dr. Hutchinson, the owner who sold us the house. He said they'd experienced noises and thought he saw a female apparition, too." Her brave expression was beginning to fade. "It seemed to start when they renovated the kitchen. The Hutchinsons also opened up the cellar when they updated the heating/cooling system."

"Hmm…interesting. Construction does stir up the spirits sometimes." Delaney said.

"They found the original house plans, and he told Austin they moved the air conditioning system into the cellar. When the wall was demolished, the cellar door and stairs were exposed again." Carly rinsed out their glasses, noting her hands were shaking.

"So how did the previous owners get to the cellar? Was there another entrance?" Delaney surveyed the kitchen for clues.

"According to Elise, our realtor, the cellar opened on the opposite side of the porch. Sometime in the 1800s, the house underwent another renovation, and the inside door was hidden behind the new wall." Carly said.

"Interesting…so that explains why the paranormal activity started. But, we don't know the whole story. Like, who's the boy spirit?" Delaney turned her chair to face the hallway.

"I'm thinking the boy dates from a different time period all together. Maybe he's the one crying, but the news articles about the Pettigrews don't mention a child." Tugging her hair into a ponytail, Carly browsed the articles.

Delaney continued reading the newspaper account. "It says that Andrew Pettigrew was shot in the head. I saw it... Benjamin took Andrew's gun and shot him in the head." She closed her eyes, remembering the scene. "They struggled, and Benjamin took Andrew's gun."

"I can't believe you dreamed about this. That's so cool, but also creepy," Carly said.

"The articles says that Celeste Pettigrew caught the murderer in the act, and she was then shot through the heart." This is why Celeste said, *'Help him'*! She knew Andrew was mortally wounded." Delaney pushed her reading glasses up on her head.

"This article states Jacob Hinman and Dr. Peter Faysoux came to the Pettigrew home to investigate why Andrew didn't arrive for his job the next morning." Carly leaned closer to the paper, then raised her head. "Peter Faysoux is the father of Celeste. Can you imagine how he must have felt, seeing his daughter and son-in-law murdered?"

"I feel Jacob Hinman and Andrew Pettigrew were old friends, or possibly business partners of some kind. I can't explain it." Delaney rubbed her temples. "I see them walking together, it's dark. That's where I lose them."

Continuing to examine the copies of articles, they read that Benjamin Hastings was arrested the following day, then was held at the Provost Dungeon. The article outlined the court minutes.

"I remember now…the dream I had awhile back, where I saw two men carrying a lifeless body to the wharf." Delaney talked in a low voice, intent on remembering. "I'm sensing the two men were Jacob Hinman and Andrew Pettigrew. I'd like to walk by the wharf, to see if I could remember something."

"The news account stated Jacob Hinman found the bodies of the Andrew and Celeste Pettigrew, but you saw Jacob and Andrew?" Carly watched in amazement as her friend tried to piece her dreams and the news articles together.

"I get the feeling he's involved in the murder plot. According to the accused, Benjamin Hastings, he followed the orders of his employer, Jacob Hinman. But why would anyone want to murder a powerful Customs Inspector and his wife?" She knit her brows and rubbed her hands together.

"I still have one article to print out." Carly walked to the printer and picked up the paper. "I went to the Historical Society where I found the will of Andrew Halston Pettigrew."

Carly held the paper like it was fragile as a robin's egg and read, "Andrew Pettigrew left his estate to his wife, Celeste, and her father, Dr. Peter Faysoux." Carly looked up from the will. "Is that common?"

"At that time, several women owned plantations in this area, but estates weren't always left to the wives." Delaney shifted in her seat. "I believe the reason he named her father as well was because Celeste was quite a bit younger than him and may have needed her father's help to manage his affairs."

"It looks like he was a philanthropist in addition to taking money and goods from his job." Carly's eyebrows lifted. "It reads that he bequeathed a portion of his estate to the Orphan Asylum and Poor House in Charleston, as well as the College of Charleston."

"There doesn't seem to be a smoking gun, no pun intended, in the will. Andrew appeared to be a good citizen, minus the fact he may have embezzled from the United States Customs. Many customs agents also double-dipped, and I recall some of the articles hinted towards Andrew doing that."

Carly looked at the clock on the kitchen wall, surprised it was already 6 o'clock. "Yeah, I've picked up on that too. I suppose all that money coming through the port was hard to resist." Carly's stomach rumbled. "Austin is working late, so how about I'll treat you to a meal at Tommy Condon's to celebrate what we've found."

"Well, all right then, sweetie. At my age, I can't turn down a dinner date. Be ready after I visit your bathroom." Delaney walked out of the kitchen to the bathroom and a chill washed over Carly.

Not wanting to be alone, Carly waited in the hallway until she came out of the bathroom. Delaney looked into the receiving room for a few minutes, squinting into the dimness and then looked away.

"Are you okay, Delaney? What is it?" Carly stayed back and watched her friend linger at the threshold.

"Oh, hon, it was so sad. I saw Andrew Pettigrew bleeding from a gunshot wound in his head. He reached out to me a leather pouch or envelope, as if wanting me to see it. I'm not sure what it was, though. I looked away, and then he vanished."

"Wow, I can't believe how you can do this. Wonder what he held in his hand? Maybe it's why Hastings murdered them?" Carly rubbed the chill from her arms. "Let's go eat, as these spirits make me hungry."

As the two walked out of the receiving room, Delaney's foot nudged the metal rocking horse. Carly bent and picked up the horse. "What?

I just put that horse upstairs in the bedroom earlier." She sat it on the hallway table and looked around. "I know you're here, little boy. I wish you'd tell us why."

The women gathered their purses and headed out the front door, talking about how good their meal would be. The door shut. Neither heard the pitiful cry echoing throughout the empty house.

<h1 style="text-align:center">Chapter 14</h1>

Carly heard her phone vibrating when she pulled into the parking garage on Cumberland Street. She read Austin's text telling her he had just pulled into the driveway to an empty house. "I don't want him to be there with no dinner. Do you mind if I ask him to join us?"

"Of course I don't mind. It'll be nice to see him again!" Delaney put on her tangerine lipstick, blotting her lips with a tissue.

They walked across the street to Tommy Condon's Irish Pub and Seafood Restaurant. Since they'd come before the dinner rush they got seated right away. When the waitress arrived a few minutes later, the ladies ordered tea for themselves and a beer for Austin.

Soon their drinks arrived and they got down to business.

"So, wonder what Andrew did to get him moved from the cemetery? It's odd for a member of the Stele church to get removed." Delaney took a long sip of tea.

"Here's what I've gleaned after reading articles." Carly leaned in closer to Delaney. "Jacob Hinman testified under oath, that he sent Benjamin Hastings to collect bribe money from Andrew, and Hastings admitted to that. But, Hinman said he didn't tell Hastings to harm Andrew." Carly tucked her hair behind her ears. "But, Andrew found Hastings pulling a loaded flintlock pistol from his safe."

"What a tangled web of deceit. So, Andrew was definitely skimming?" Delaney asked.

"Yep, like you said, seems Andrew kept some of the stolen goods for himself. But, he also paid Hinman 'hush money,' I think, to cover up a murder from almost ten years before." Carly's eyes widened with anticipation. Andrew murdered a dock worker ten years before, and Jacob helped him hide the body." She sat back, waiting for Delaney's response.

Before she could reply, the waiter led Austin to their table and he greeted Carly with a kiss and shook Delaney's hand.

Austin took a gulp of his favorite, Sam Adams. "Thanks for ordering. I need something a little stronger, but this one will do." Carly could hear stress in his voice.

"Bad night at the hospital?" Delaney cocked her head.

"No, not at work, but I think the natives in our house were restless tonight. One of our spooks wanted to intimidate me." He raked his hands through his hair, then rubbed them as if chilled.

"Oh no, hon! What happened?" Carly patted his knee.

"When I walked in the house, it didn't feel right. I know that sounds weird for me to say that." He lowered his voice. "I hurried upstairs to change clothes, and when I got to the top step, I swear it was the oddest thing. It felt as though the temperature had plummeted twenty degrees. I tried to move forward, but I felt like I ran into a brick wall."

Carly's eyes grew wide, her heart skipped a beat. Delaney squinted at him through her glasses and raised her eyebrows.

"I almost fell backwards. Then, I grabbed the stairs and pushed forward." He took Carly's hand.

"Oh my gosh, that's exactly how I felt when I got pushed down the attic stairs." She looked at Delaney.

"That's not all. When I came downstairs, I smelled gunpowder. I swear someone else was in the house. You two have experience with these spirits, but I don't. This freaked me out." He gulped the rest of his beer.

"Did you see anything?" Delaney put her hand to her temple.

"No, nothing except a dark shadow on the edge of my vision when I went upstairs." Austin almost whispered. "I didn't know what to do, Delaney."

The waitress took their order, and they resumed their conversation.

"We've found information about the murders and the trial from 1799." Carly said.

"You found the actual news accounts?" He sat back in his seat. "Enlighten me as to what you two sleuths uncovered."

"Well, we know that the dark spirit is Benjamin Hastings, who worked for Andrew's friend, Jacob Hinman. Turns out Hinman sent him to the Pettigrew's house the night of the murders to collect money owed to him as part of his blackmailing of Andrew." Carly drank more tea and widened her eyes.

"And I dreamed about the murder that caused the blackmail situation and saw two men carrying a body to the wharf." Delaney strummed her fingers on the wooden table.

"Wait, someone needs to explain Jacob Hinman. You found out about another murder?" Austin scratched his head.

"Okay, I found newspaper accounts of the murders of Andrew and Celeste Pettigrew." Carly handed the copy of the articles to Austin. "It says the bodies were discovered by Jacob Hinman, and by Dr. Peter Faysoux, the father of Celeste Faysoux Pettigrew."

He studied the copies as if putting it to memory.

"It's all there, the account of the murders, and the arrest of the murderer, Benjamin Hastings." Carly pointed to his name.

"Then, Carly found another article telling of a witness who saw Benjamin Hastings run from the Pettigrew home the night the murders took place. He remained in the Provost Dungeon until his trial." Delaney's voice rose in pitch.

Their food arrived and all three began to eat their blue crabs and salads.

"I do have a question for you, Delaney." Austin took a large bite of crab.

Delaney munched on an onion ring, her eyebrows lifting.

"I don't know if Carly told you, but my parents are visiting next week. I'd rather my parents weren't bothered hearing or seeing our troubled spirits." He wiped his mouth with the corner of his napkin. "Is there anything we can do soon to get them out of our house for good?"

"I have a friend who's a paranormal investigator. He's successful in communicating with spirits." She leaned in to speak softer. "We know the identity of the spirits, or at least three of them. I promise, it'll be low key, just Carly, Boyd, and myself. Of course, Austin, you're more than welcome to attend."

"Well, we've run out of other choices to resolve this situation, so let's try this investigation. It's hard to say no to two headstrong women." Austin waved his hands in mock surrender. Carly exhaled, feeling as if a weight lifted from her chest, and leaned into his shoulder.

Later that evening, Carly and Austin sat in the den, drinking coffee and eating leftover Danish rolls. He listened as she read aloud the newspaper report about the arrest and trial of Ben Hastings and Jacob Hinman.

"Charleston, January 23rd, 1799: On Thursday last at the court of general sessions, the trial of Mr. Benjamin Hastings, for the murders of Mr. Andrew Pettigrew, Customs Inspector, and his beloved wife, Celeste Pettigrew. Witnesses gave testimony to seeing Mr. Pettigrew at McCrady's Tavern shortly before 8 o'clock in the evening, having a drink of spirits with merchant, Jacob Hinman. On his walk to his home on King Street, Mr. Elias Hunt testified to seeing the accused, Benjamin Hastings, of this town, leaving from the cellar window of the Customs Inspector. Benjamin Hastings, a dock hand who found employment with Mr. Jacob Hinman, merchant of this town, denied any hand in the shooting of Andrew and Celeste Pettigrew. After a time in the Provost Dungeon, he implicated another in the murder.

Upon interrogation by the Provost Marshal, Mr. Hastings accused Mr. Jacob Hinman, his employer, as an accomplice in the murders. The jury heard the account of Mr. Hinman, who denied having connection to the said murder, however, upon further search of the home of the deceased, a ledger was found within the wall safe of Andrew Pettigrew. Within its pages, details of goods being stolen from various ships coming into the Port were written in the ledger. Jacob Hinman was the receiver of rum, whiskey, and a sundry of goods, all taken in a dishonest bargain. The accused, Benjamin Hastings, made claims in regards to blackmail being the reason for the corrupt bargain."

"So Andrew Pettigrew, the good Customs Inspector, was skimming goods, mainly spirits, from the duty on ships' exports and imports?" Austin asked.

"It seems so, according to Ben Hastings." She nodded. "But further into the account, it says Jacob Hinman forced Andrew Pettigrew to pay the bribe in exchange for his silence."

"Some friend." He examined the article. "Why didn't Andrew refuse?"

"Remember, Ben Hastings reported, under oath, Andrew Pettigrew murdered a dock hand, although sounds like self-defense, who tried to rob him after a night at McCrady's tavern near Adler's Wharf. Hinman and Pettigrew dumped his body into the Cooper River. And what's stranger, is that, well, Delaney is sensitive to these past spirits. She saw it in her dream."

"Good sleuthing, sweetie. Why did Hinman want to murder his *friend?*" His thick eyebrows were raised like twin arches.

"I found another account in *The City Gazette* which answered the question. Hastings went to get the cash bribe Hinman was expecting. Andrew kept a stash hidden in his wall safe." Carly jumped up from the couch to illustrate the story with gestures. "Hastings followed Andrew from McCrady's Tavern that evening, waiting until he and Celeste retired, then sneaked in through an open cellar window."

"Hastings murdered the couple for the cash in the safe?"

"The court account stated he shot the Pettigrews with Andrew's flintlock pistol." Carly looked over her shoulder toward the hallway and sat down.

"Wait, do you actually think we're smelling gunpowder from two centuries ago?" He poked her arm, getting her attention.

"Yes, Hastings's lawyer argued it was a murder-suicide." She turned around to face him. "He claims Hastings arrived to collect the money, as instructed by Hinman, but found Pettigrew and his wife dead. Panicked, he stole the cash in the safe and fled the home."

"I'm not a detective, but who's to say it didn't happen that way?" He walked to the hallway, looking in the receiving room. "I mean, if Celeste confronted him, maybe he killed her, then turned the pistol on himself to escape going to jail for stealing on the job?"

"Maybe, but it wasn't possible for him to shoot himself by the location the ball entered his skull." Carly shuddered at the memory of his wound. "The prosecution did their work in proving Hastings as the murderer. He implicated Hinman, telling of his blackmail over the years of Andrew Pettigrew."

"Wow. You found this out from the newspaper?" He stood up and stretched.

"Delaney researched the burial of Celeste Pettigrew at St. Michaels, but found something interesting about the burial of Andrew Pettigrew." She perched on the arm of the sofa. "Remember when I told you we found Celeste's grave in the churchyard but not Andrew's, even though the death account in *The City Gazette* stated the churchyard was their final resting place?"

Austin nodded. "Yeah, I remember you telling me."

"Well, the church records detailed the burial of Andrew in the churchyard, followed by a small note saying his body was removed."

"I don't understand, why did he get two burials?" Austin frowned and ate another roll.

"Delaney found out Andrew's body was exhumed from the church-yard after the trial and the revelation he murdered the dock worker. His act of murder caused his removal and reburial at the nearby Quaker Church cemetery. It's where Dr. Faysoux arranged his reburial." Carly put her hand on his neck, massaging the taut muscles.

"How'd she discover the reburial?" He let his neck relax under her touch.

"She met with the rector of St. Michaels, and he allowed her to search church records. She found Andrew Pettigrew's name on the roll of the graveyard." She kneaded his shoulders. "The Charleston Historical Society houses the church records on microfilm, and she found a small note written about the exhumation and reburial."

"Delaney and you are an amazing research team. So, he suffered the ultimate disgrace, getting the boot from the church graveyard." His eyes were closing with relaxation.

"With none of Andrew's family living, the move went unnoticed and forgotten. The estate went to Dr. Peter Faysoux, Celeste's father. The sale of the home happened within the year," Carly said.

"I guess I'm at a loss to understand why the ghosts still haunt our house." He sat up, adjusting his collar. "How'd the trial end?"

"The court only charged Jacob Hinman for receiving stolen property and blackmail. His punishment was a brand on his hand, but he did spend a short time in jail." She felt a chill, prompting her to look over her shoulder. "He must have left Charleston afterwards, as his name didn't appear in the city directory after that date."

"What happened to Hastings?" He yawned, sleepy from the massage.

"Benjamin Hastings received a guilty verdict for the murders of both Andrew and Celeste Pettigrew. He was hanged on February 2nd, 1800." She felt her chest tighten, the anxious feeling coming back.

"Not to change the subject, but my parents will be coming in a week for Thanksgiving. I hope this ghost whisperer can help move the spirits out of here." He carried their cups into the kitchen. She followed behind him, wrapping her arms around his waist.

"Thank you for agreeing and being supportive. I know this situation isn't one you're used to dealing with."

Austin turned, wrapping his arms around Carly. "I don't want to have you and our child living with any kind of danger."

"Child? Do you know something I don't?" She looked up with a slanted gaze.

"Well, we can start tonight." He breathed kisses down her throat.

They retired to their bedchamber for the night, hoping for peace. However, Carly awoke to the sound of weeping. She rolled over to face Austin, who was already awake.

Carly whispered to Austin, "How long has this been going on?"

"Just a few minutes, I didn't want to wake you."

Carly scooted closer to Austin, who wrapped his arm around her. "It's the boy. The sound makes me anxious, almost panicked. It makes my heart race, Austin."

Austin took his wife's wrist in his hand, checking her pulse. "You have an elevated pulse. Do you want a drink of water? Try to take slow, deep breaths."

Carly did as Austin directed, but she felt as if she couldn't breathe. "I felt this way before, it seems to come on suddenly when he is crying."

The effect the house was having on his wife agitated Austin. He got up from the bed and opened the door, walking out into the moon-lit hallway. "Stop it! Do you hear me?" Austin yelled.

"I feel like I'm having a panic attack! It's like I'm in a tight space; I can't explain it." She stumbled into the hallway to join him.

Austin pulled her close to him, wrapping his arms around her in a protective manner. "You've been dealing with this for months. We have to get Delaney's friend in here as soon as possible."

The temperature in the hallway dropped, and both of them were aware of a nearby presence. She tensed, feeling an impending encounter with Benjamin Hastings. But, the crying ceased all at once, and the house became quiet as a graveyard. All at once, an object shot up the stairway from below, narrowly missing her face. Both of them ducked as the object struck the wall behind her, leaving a small hollow where it hit.

"It's the toy horse? That's it! We're getting a hotel room tonight," Austin declared.

Carly bent to pick up the horse. She didn't feel the sense of panic as before; instead, now it was a feeling of determination. "Benjamin Hastings is trying to get us to leave. We are staying. He has chased others away, but we are staying. We have to."

He followed her back into their bedroom, where she placed the toy horse on an antique bureau. She climbed into bed. "I'm over letting Benjamin Hastings roam this house. I'll call Delaney as soon as it's a respectable hour. It's time to get some help with ridding the house of these spirits."

"Agreed, my love, as we can't have my family being unsettled by spirits in our house. Let's try and get some sleep. I start a long rotation tomorrow," he said, rolling on to his side. Carly poked her finger into his well-toned back. "Excuse me, but I didn't get my kiss." She trailed her finger across his back and to his stomach.

Austin smiled, rolling onto his other side, forgetting about the time. Neither were interested in sleeping nor spirits at that time, and the house remained quiet.

Chapter 15

The constant drops of rain pelting the window outside her bedroom stirred Carly from the peaceful slumber that had eluded her for many weeks. She smiled, remembering their passionate lovemaking, and stretched over to touch Austin, but noticed the empty space in their four-poster bed. She remembered him mentioning an early wake up and long hours at the hospital for the next few days.

She flung the duvet from her warm body and started a hot shower. As she let the water caress her muscles, the previous evening's events crept into her mind. The crying, flying metal horse, and Austin's fear all came flooding back. For the first time, Carly saw him give in to the fear she experienced. After her shower, she dressed and went downstairs to begin her once a week routine of cleaning the large house.

An hour into cleaning, she made coffee and sat at the table. As she drank her coffee, she glanced through the papers piled on the desk from the night before. Several copies provided information on Andrew Pettigrew's life, work, and his death. She rubbed her eyes, trying to focus on the information. "What am I missing, Celeste?" She twirled a loose strand of hair in her fingers, flipping the page.

Carly reread *The City Gazette* account of the trial and wrote down names and connections. She knew Benjamin Hastings received a death sentence, but where was he buried? She assumed in the pauper's section of the cemetery, but *which* cemetery? She wrote in large scribble: *Where were convicts interred in the city?*

Next, she reread the original story about Dr. Peter Faysoux and Jacob Hinman finding the Pettigrews' bodies. Lost in thought, she didn't hear her cell ringing at first.

"Hello." She answered.

"Mrs. Tabor, this is Tom Drummond from the Historical Society. We met a few weeks ago."

"Oh yes, Mr. Drummond. How are you?" She slid her foot underneath her, getting comfortable.

"I'm doing well, thank you." He cleared his throat. "Mrs. Tabor, the reason I'm calling is in regards to the murder trial you were researching."

A surge of excitement raced through Carly's veins. "Yes, what did you find out?"

"Well, after you and your friend left for the day, I couldn't get the case off my mind. I took it upon myself to delve deeper into the matter." She heard him rattling papers. "I cross-referenced the names of Andrew Pettigrew and Jacob Hinman into the database for other historic newspapers. I found the account of Jacob Hinman's trial in an article tucked in the back of the newspaper, which I've copied for you to pick up."

"Thanks very much. Maybe his trial will share information we're lacking. I know that Benjamin Hastings was convicted of murder and hanged. Do you know how I could find his grave?" Carly felt fortunate to receive his assistance.

"I would think most convicts went to one of the city cemeteries." Tom tapped his pencil on the desk. "The jail wasn't built yet, so I'm not sure what happened to convicts held in the Provost Dungeon. Let me do some research on that, and I'll get back to you in a few days."

"Great. I'm going to do research on the Faysoux family. I'll be in early next week to research more and will pick up the copies. Thank you again for your help." Her face lit up with an excited smile because they were gathering more clues.

Across town, Delaney searched through her address box for Boyd Hawley's business card. The off-white card had the logo LCI in the upper right corner. Low Country Investigations~ Boyd Hawley, Paranormal Investigator. She put the number for Boyd into her phone.

"This is Boyd, how can I help you?"

"Hi Boyd, this is Delaney Warrick. We met at an investigation awhile back at the City Jail." Boyd was sitting in his den, downing a bloody Mary, the ritual after a night of drinking. "Of course, yes, I remember you. You work for the Ghost Tours downtown, correct?" he recalled.

"Yes, that's right. Boyd, I have a friend who has a real problem on her hands. I'd like to sit down and talk to you about it, if we could. She and her husband need help and I thought of you," Delaney shared, hoping he would take the case. The thought of doing anything besides munching on the stalk of celery protruding from his tall glass of tomato concoction wasn't the least bit appealing. "Okay, sure. I can meet in, say, about two hours. What's convenient for you?"

"I'm heading into town to do some research, so I could meet you at the library. Would that work?" she asked.

"Sure, I'll get myself together and drive into Charleston. It won't take me long. See you then."

Relieved, Delaney replied, "Yes, I'll be looking forward to it. Later!"

After finishing tidying the downstairs, she started upstairs to change the bed linens, but before she reached the top, something drew her attention to the room down the hallway. The door to the small bedroom was ajar. She placed the sheets on the hallway table, continuing on to the nursery, as she liked to think of it. She knew she'd shut the door last night She felt a chill slide over her as pushed open the door. A scream caught in her throat—the apparition of Celeste Pettigrew stood in front of the antique crib. She advanced, but stopped two feet away from Celeste. She feared the sad ghost would vanish as before. Two centuries separated them in life, but only two feet came between them at this moment.

"I see you. I want to help you, but I don't know how!" Her voice squeaked, and her legs felt like spaghetti.

Celeste Pettigrew, frozen in place with such a sad face, simply reached out. Carly willed her legs to move closer, to grasp the outstretched hand, but the familiar coldness settled in the room. The apparition began to fade, and she sensed she wasn't alone. The door slammed shut, resonating throughout the empty house. She ran to open it, but the knob wouldn't turn. She shivered, crouching beside the door. Once again, Celeste vanished before she could connect. She rubbed her arms; now, the room as cold as a freezer.

"Benjamin Hastings, your day is coming. You're going to leave my house for good. You hear me? You murdering, low-life scum!" Tired of the ghosts playing with them, Carly became angrier about the dark spirit and how it prevented the others from communicating why they remained. She recalled each room had its own skeleton key placed above the doorways in each room by the builder, who had also been locked inside this bedroom. Rick had told her one of the crew heard him yelling and brought the keys to open the lock.

Pulling a small table over to the doorway, she climbed up and stretched on tip-toe to get the small metal key. The door opened with the key, freeing her from her unseen captor. She peeked around the door, afraid she'd encounter the ghost of Benjamin Hastings.

Trying to put the experience out of her mind, she began changing the linens and erase the fear. She stifled the urge to look over her shoulder as she made the beds. Feeling foolish, she began speaking to the ghosts out loud. "We're not leaving. This is our house now!" Her false bravado did little to settle the dread wrapping its tentacles around her insides. In less than a week, Austin's family would descend on their home. She feared they wouldn't have enough time to rid the house of its ghostly assemblage. Her nerves shot from the morning experience, she jumped when her cell chimed in her pocket. The display read Mom and Dad as the caller.

"Hey, Mom! What's up?" She walked to the den, sinking to the love-seat.

"How's everything going with you?" Paula's gentle tone reflected her concern.

Carly hadn't talked to her mother in a few weeks. "Well, I've been busy getting ready for the holidays. The Tabors are coming this week. Sorry I haven't called in a while."

"We're gonna miss having you kids up for Thanksgiving. Daddy is disappointed you're not going to be with us, honey." She could hear Paula moving a chair. "Honey, is anything wrong? I mean, with you or your house?"

Taken by surprise, she knew it was no good trying to lie once her mother asked her point-blank.

"Okay, I've been doing some research on the house. If I told you everything, you'd think I was crazy. Let's just say the ghosts are here, and I just have to learn to live with them."

"Carly, you know how I feel. You don't want to invite the devil into your home!" Paula's voice rose an octave.

"Mom, I didn't ask for this. I didn't invite them here." Her throat flushed, her dander rising.

"I knew something was wrong. I couldn't shake the feeling this morning. Maybe you should talk to your minister about it. Maybe he could come in and say a prayer for your house." Paula believed prayer was the answer to everything.

"We haven't found a church yet, Mom. I'm thinking about having a paranormal investigator come in and try to communicate with them." Carly waited for the sermon her mother was about to give.

"I think you're asking for trouble. Please, be careful. There are demons, just as there are angels on this earth." Paula's tone brooked no argument.

"I know, but we don't know what else to do. I want our house back." Carly turned to look down the hallway.

"I just want you to be safe, honey. I know you'd never willingly invite anything like that into your home. I'm sorry." She could hear the care in her mother's voice.

"It's okay. I'll keep you posted on what happens, but in the meantime, don't worry. Austin's my protector. He has my back!" She laughed, trying to ease her mother's mind. Carly changed the topic to the holidays. Her parents had purchased a plane ticket as an early birthday present for her to return home.

"I'll be home for Christmas. It will be here before you know it, Mom."

"A trip home will do you good, honey. Four more weeks, that's all!" The lilt in her mother's voice caused a smile to wash over her face.

After their conversation ended, she felt homesick. She'd muster all the positive energy left in her to prepare and get through the next week. Before she could put her phone on the coffee table, she saw an incoming call from Delaney displayed on the phone.

"Hey Delaney. What's going on?" She walked into the kitchen to fix lunch as she talked.

"Hi, sweetie. I'm sitting at the library with Boyd Hawley, the paranormal investigator I told you about. He'd like to get some information on the house, but I thought it best he hear it from the source." Delaney sounded upbeat and cheerful.

"Sure. I can meet you guys before I stop by the Historical Society." Carly said.

"Great. I've filled him in on the noises, but he'd like to talk to you." Delaney glanced at her watch. "I haven't said anything about the murders or the boy."

"Okay, I'll meet you in ten minutes." Carly finished her sandwich, gathered her tote bag with the research, locked the door and headed for her car.

Carly parked in the garage and walked the two blocks to the library. After the introductions, the threesome sat down at a small table toward the back of the reading area. Boyd Hawley was in his 30s, a dapperly-dressed man with small glasses and blonde, slicked back hair in a ponytail.

"Since Carly contacted me back in the summer, we've seen and heard three apparitions in the home. There's a fourth, a child, in the home. We've yet to make contact," Delaney explained.

"How do you know it's a child? I mean, what evidence makes you assume that?" Boyd raised his dark eyebrows.

"An apparition of a child appeared in a photograph Carly's father took. We've heard a child's crying and a banging noise coming from the walls, and a toy rocking horse shows up in different rooms throughout the house." She leaned in, lowering her voice. "The child's holding the toy horse in an earlier photo. A couple seems to have been murdered in the home."

"Murder, you say? It's no surprise her house is active. I'm listening." Boyd folded his arms, leaning onto the table.

"Well, we found out that in 1799, Andrew Pettigrew, who was the Customs Inspector, and his wife, Celeste, were victims of a double homicide. A dock worker named Benjamin Hastings committed the act. We located the information from several weeks of research," Carly recounted the information.

"That does lend itself to having spirit activity, my dear. So you feel the people who died are two of the spirits?" Boyd polished his glasses with a monogrammed handkerchief.

"Yes, I've seen them both, and my husband and I've smelled gun powder. Besides those two, there's a dark spirit. We're certain this is the murderer, Benjamin Hastings. He seems to be in control of the others," Carly paused, pushing a stray hair behind her ear.

"Does the spirit activity include objects moving or does it seem that someone threw them?" Boyd wrote a few notes into a small leather appointment book.

"Oh yes, this is common. But some of the objects have narrowly missed Carly and her husband, Austin. There've also been physical attacks, I believe." Delaney patted her arm. "She felt a push down the stairs, and we've all felt the spirit of Ben Hastings move through us. It's quite unsettling."

"It sounds like you want to move the spirits out of the house. Do you feel the presence in the home is demonic?" Boyd looked at Carly, then back to Delaney.

"No, I don't. I think the dark spirit, Ben Hastings, is trying to keep the others from leaving." She waited, looking at Delaney for input.

"I think the others are trying to tell us something. What it is, I don't know. Will you help us?" Delaney waited for Boyd's reply.

"I'd be willing to try. I'd like to bring along my associate, Tucker McGee, who's been investigating with me for about a year now."

Carly knew Austin didn't want many people involved. However, considering how desperate he sounded the night before, she decided he would understand the need for help.

"Whatever you think is best. We're under the gun time-wise. We've family arriving next week for Thanksgiving." Carly shifted in her seat.

"Dang, that might be a problem. Tucker is out of the country on business. He won't be back until after Thanksgiving." He ran his hand through his blonde hair, pulled into a tight ponytail.

"Oh. I see." Carly's shoulders sagged.

"I don't think they want to wait. Would you be comfortable investigating just with the Tabors and myself as helpers?" Delaney looked at Carly, then turned to Boyd.

"Surely, let's try. If you're free, I can meet you Monday afternoon— about 5." Boyd's handsome face shone with enthusiasm.

The three walked from the library, parting for the afternoon. Carly walked to the Historical society, barely making it before closing. Tom Drummond sat at the information desk, logging off his computer. "Hello, Mrs. Tabor," Tom Drummond recognized her, extending his hand. "I have the papers and would review with you, but we're about to close."

Carly smiled, taking the clipped stack of papers. "Thanks, Mr. Drummond. I appreciate you taking the time to search for me."

Before she could continue, Delaney walked into the building. "Hello, Tom. Good to see you as always." Delaney said, her infectious smile warming the room.

"Good afternoon, Delaney, always nice to see your familiar face." He shook Delaney's hand.

"I thought I'd walk Carly back to the parking garage." Delaney said.

"I think we're finished. Thanks for the research again, Mr. Drummond," Carly said.

The two walked down Meeting Street discussing the papers she'd received. Carly told her how happy she was that Boyd would help investigate the spirits and how Austin became a believer last night in the things she and Delaney had experienced.

"You mentioned getting locked in the nursery. Did that happen this morning?" Delaney walked fast to keep up with her taller and younger friend.

"This morning. Lucky for me, I remembered where the contractor put the skeleton key above the door."

"When did the toy horse fly past you?" Delaney stopped, turning to face her.

"This morning. The crying woke Austin, then me." Carly felt panic in her stomach remembering the episode. "We were in the hallway and felt the temperature drop. I think it was Ben Hastings."

Well, I think Ben Hastings's the cause for the mischief and trying to harm you. I'm hoping we'll figure out whatever it is that Celeste and Andrew want us to know when Boyd comes on Monday." Delaney patted her shoulder. "Don't worry, we're going to solve this situation, hon."

Carly drove back to the house, eager to read the court's account of Jacob Hinman's trial. Curling up on the sofa, she read the account from the Charleston paper, *The City Gazette.*

Charleston, February 10, 1799

Saturday came on the court of general sessions, the trial of Mr. Jacob Hinman, for the murders of Mr. Andrew Pettigrew and his wife, Celeste Pettigrew.

The accused, Mr. Hinman, was named as murderer by Mr. Hastings, dock worker.

On the afternoon of January 19th, Mr. Hinman and Mr. Pettigrew had met at McCrady's Tavern for spirits. Shortly after six o'clock in the evening, Jacob Hinman left Mr. Pettigrew on the corner East Bay Street, where the two parted company for the evening. Mr. Benjamin Hastings reported to the court that Mr. Hinman had been blackmailing the Customs Inspector, Mr. Pettigrew, for more than ten years. Upon the court pressing for details, Mr. Hastings revealed Jacob Hinman wanted to collect monies that were hidden in the residence of Mr. Pettigrew. He alleged the accused, Mr. Hinman, and Mr. Pettigrew had a long- standing agreement, to which the accused collected goods and monies were exchanged on a monthly agenda.

He came to Mr. Pettigrew's house to collect said monies, at which time Andrew Pettigrew pulled a pistol from his safe in the wall. At that point, the accused named Hinman as the person who killed the Pettigrews, and denies the murder. The accused was seen by a sundry of witnesses going into his establishment near six o'clock, while his person was seen leaving by various witnesses sometime after seven thirty, to which his wife gave an oath he was settled into his bed chamber near eight o'clock.

The jury heard testimony of the accused admitting to accepting a barrel of fine rum, but nothing more. He did further give testimony to the murder of a dock worker on the evening of 14 May, 1788. He admitted further to the fact that Andrew Pettigrew, deceased, had shot a sailor who meant to do him bodily harm during the attempt to rob him of his purse. When both men, somewhat under an inebriated state, tried to fight off the attack, Andrew Pettigrew shot the thief.

He also gave testimony that together, he and Mr. Pettigrew carried the body of the dead sailor to the river near the sloop, Leander, disposing of the corpse in the waters.

Upon hearing this revelation, the jury proclaimed the accused, Mr. Hinman, could not have committed the murders, as his alibi was sound. He was forthwith found guilty of blackmailing the deceased, as well as conniving to extort from the deceased various material goods from the Customs House. He was sentenced to be branded with a B upon his left hand, after which he would be sentenced to a period of two years in the Provost Dungeon of this city until the jail is completed.

Carly couldn't believe how accurately Delaney had dreamed the murder of the dock worker, with seeing the man shot, as well as the two young men carrying the body to the river's edge. She believed she'd found the proof the killer was Benjamin Hastings, not Jacob Hinman. His knowledge of Benjamin Hastings going to the home of Andrew Pettigrew that evening, on his direction, had cast a shadow on his innocence.

Missing in the account was the identity of the murdered dock worker, and presumably, Andrew couldn't be tried after his death. It seemed that for all intents and purposes, Jacob Hinman only paid for bribery and accepting stolen goods, and nothing more. What became of the Hinmans after his release from jail remained a mystery. She was unable to find his name in any later Charleston city directories, so hadn't pursued it.

Mr. Drummond had found and included another copy of a newspaper account, from *The City Gazette*, dated March 15, 1799.

Today in the city, the accused, Benjamin Hastings, of this city, was taken to the public gallows, where he was hanged by the neck until dead, for the murders of Mr. Andrew Pettigrew and his good wife, Celeste Pettigrew, nee Faysoux.

Disappointed, Carly found no mention of what happened to his body afterwards. Noticing it was six o'clock, Carly realized she'd missed lunch, so she fixed a salad for herself. Just as she turned from the sink, the doorbell rang.

She walked into the entry hall, and saw Elise Ravanel standing outside.

Carly opened the door. "What a nice surprise! Come on in. I've been meaning to call you."

Elise stepped through the doorway, giving Carly a hug. "Hey girlfriend. I thought you might be stressin' out over the big Thanksgiving meal. I got your text the other day—I'm as slow as a snail in getting back to ya." She slipped off her suede boots, placing them under the entry table.

"Oh yes, the dreaded major meal for the in-laws. So glad you're here." She led Elise into the kitchen. "I don't know the first thing about Low Country cuisine."

"Well, here's a little somethin' I picked up for you from the Mt. Pleasant shop that you love." Elise held out the bright bag.

"How sweet, you shouldn't have." Carly peered inside the bag.

She lifted a heavy, long item out, taking away the tissue paper that surrounded it like a mummy's wrap.

"Now what kind of spoon is this? It's pretty, and looks old!" She turned the antique silver spoon over in her hand.

"Honey, this is a rice spoon. Every home in Charleston and on the plantations around the area had several. You *are* planning on serving Carolina Rice?" Elise questioned.

"Well, I hadn't thought of it. Do you have a recipe for it?" Carly blushed, not knowing the tradition from her new home.

"Of course I do, I use one from my Grandmama, and it was passed down from her Grandmama. I know it comes well-recommended." Elise took out a recipe card from her Coach purse. "Why not make some shrimp to go with the rice? You could make the turkey, too. I bet they'll love having both, hon."

"Thanks so much and that sounds like a great plan. Where are my manners? Would you like a drink?" Carly put the spoon on the counter.

"Oh, I'd love some tea. Sweet, please!" She walked over to the window, admiring the reproduction plantation shutters.

Carly placed a glass and a small saucer with lemons on the table.

Elise took her glass, taking a long sip. "So, how've things been going around here? Are you still looking for a job?"

"Not exactly. I did mail a resume to the local television stations after we arrived." She joined Elise at the table. "I received a couple of notes saying they'd be in touch. You know, the typical brush-off."

"Well, don't get discouraged, sweetie. Just be patient, it'll happen." She took a sip of tea. "I hate to pry, but, did you ever find out more about the house to explain the weird happenings?"

"Yes, I've found out quite a bit. We definitely have a house full of spirits." She dabbed a spot of condensation from the table. "It's taken a lot of work between myself and a friend, Delaney Warrick. Maybe the three of us could do lunch sometime—you'd really like her."

"I'd love to meet her. Plan a date soon." Elise's smile wilted from her face. "I want you to know how sorry I am about the spirits—I didn't realize what had happened."

"It's okay. We're here now, and we're making the best of it. We love our house, but things get a bit tense at times." Carly took her empty glass to the sink. "Thank you for the spoon, I love it!"

"You're welcome. Do let me know how the dinner turns out." She hugged Carly. I'd loan you Jenny if I wasn't going to use her myself."

"You're lucky to have a housekeeper and cook all rolled into one."

"With our schedules, it made sense to hire someone to stay with the kids before and after school. Lord knows I'm not much of a cook or housekeeper; June Cleaver, I'm not!" Her laugh turned into a snort. "It gives us more time to do the things we want to do, and Jenny has become like family."

Elise stifled a yawn and looked at her gold watch. "It's after nine. I should be going home. Jameson took the kids to the movies while I showed a couple of properties. They'll think I dropped off the Ravenel Bridge!" She grabbed her Coach bag and suede boots from the hallway.

"Happy Thanksgiving! Let's plan on getting together with our husbands over the holidays." Carly walked Elise to the door, giving her a hug.

"We'd love to, as my job begins to quieten down with the colder weather." Elise hurried to her car, because a steady rain caught her without an umbrella.

As she drove away, Carly locked the door. Austin would be home soon, but at times she wished he worked normal hours; instead, she'd grown accustomed to this schedule. She retired to the den, and began reading through the newspaper accounts Tom Drummond had provided. Jotting down the facts she'd discovered, she created a timeline of the house before and after the murder, and the strange events that had happened in the house to them, hoping it would be helpful for Boyd on Monday.

Examining the photo her mother had taken, she found her digital camera in the desk and walked upstairs to take some photos. With dread, she felt a presence nearby. The hair on her arms stood up as she entered the nursery. Letting out her breath, she flipped the lights on. The room felt cold, having been closed off for the day.

She began taking pictures of the area where she and her parents had posed that July afternoon. She moved the toy horse and placed it on the hearth and photographed it.

Feeling somewhat silly, she said in a low, gentle voice, "I know you're still in this house, sweetie. We can't help you move on if we can't see you." Sitting in the middle of the room, Carly listened for sounds within the house. After a few moments finishing the last shots, she flipped off the light, closing the door behind her.

She heard the door close downstairs, and assumed Austin had returned. Deciding to check the camera later, she placed it on the dresser in their bedroom. Walking into the kitchen, she accidentally scared Austin when she came up behind him.

"So, how'd your day go, love of my life?" He set his glass of water down and nibbled on her neck. She arched her back, moving into his toned body.

"Very good, because I found out more on the trial of Jacob Hinman. I also met with Delaney and her friend, Boyd Hawley, who agreed to come on Monday." She waited for a reaction from him.

"I didn't expect you to have any lucky getting someone to come that fast. I don't know if I'll be able to join you, it depends on my schedule." He put his arm around her as they walked into the den.

"It's okay. We'll start after we have dinner here, probably after six o'clock. His partner is unavailable, so Delaney and I, and you if you're free, are going to help him."

The rest of the evening, Carly and Austin discussed their day and holiday plans. She showed him the rice spoon that Elise brought over.

"Oh, that reminds me. Mom called earlier today and gave me their flight time. I can't wait for them to see our lovely house that we've worked so hard on. I just hope we don't have uninvited guests, too." He sat his glass on a coaster.

Carly forgot about the pictures on the camera, as they went up to bed. Austin soon was snoring away, but she curled up just listening to the soft rain dripping down the window of their dream home. Within minutes, she fell into a deep sleep.

Chapter 16

Carly awoke on Monday morning feeling apprehensive. She looked at the clock, then back at the empty space in the bed. Austin didn't have to be at the hospital until later that morning. She slipped on a pair of yoga pants and a University of Kansas hoodie. When she reached the bottom of the stairs, she saw Austin using a dust mop on the wood floor.

"Well, look at you! How long have you been at it, Mr. Clean?" She put her hands on her hips, admiring the view of her husband cleaning in his scrubs.

"Some people sleep till all hours of the morning." He turned, winking at her. "Nervous energy, I guess. I wanted to help."

She wrapped her arms around his waist, stretching to kiss him. "Thank you for helping- especially since your folks will be here in a couple of days!"

"I don't mind, hon. Since it's just the two of us, it doesn't get too messy." Austin flipped her ponytail. "Are you ready for the ghost whisperer to come tonight?"

"No snide comments about Boyd, understand?" She pointed her finger at him. "Besides Delaney, he's our only hope at this point."

"I know, I'm teasing you. I hope he rounds them up and sends them to the big corral in the sky. I can't say as I'll miss them."

Both of them worked on cleaning insides of the windows and the elaborate wooden trim and polishing silver for the remainder of the morning and into the afternoon. Everything in the house remained quiet, and it seemed so normal that Carly could imagine none of the spirits had ever appeared.

Carly prepared a family recipe for a pork chops marinade for tonight. She already prepared the salad and put it in the fridge to chill until supper. It wasn't until mid-afternoon that she remembered the pictures she had taken upstairs in the nursery. She went back upstairs to get the camera from her bedroom, and then studied the display. However, she noticed nothing unusual in any of them; maybe the child came with the photo album into the house, not the Pettigrews. In just a few hours, she might get an answer.

Carly set Austin to work grilling the pork chops and veggies to prepare for Boyd and Delaney to dine with them. She decided to use the formal dining room for a change as it could be a trial run for the upcoming meal on Thursday with Austin's parents and sister.

She surveyed her formal dining room and wished she'd had more time to decorate. The sideboard and table were reproduction Queen Anne style. She found the six chairs at a primitive shop when she and Austin took a vacation to New England. Ivory heavy damask draperies graced the two large windows that opened to the street. The average-sized room, painted a robin's egg blue, was bright and cheery, even on this gray day. A Thomas Sheraton round, convex mirror, typical of the period, hung above the sideboard.

Strangely, the house had remained quiet the last couple of days, almost as if holding its breath in anticipation. Carly wasn't sure if that was a good sign. She had butterflies in her stomach, not sure what they would encounter later in the evening.

At five o'clock sharp, Delaney pulled her car inside the gated entry, while Boyd Hawley parked his black Ford Explorer on the street and walked into the yard. Before the pair reached the door, Austin walked onto the lower porch.

"Welcome! Good to meet you, I'm Austin." He extended his hand to Boyd. "Hi Delaney, good to see you."

Austin opened the door into the hall, where Carly waited.

"Boyd, this is Carly Tabor." Carly and Boyd shook hands.

"Thank you for coming. I see you've met Austin." She welcomed them into the receiving room.

"You've a lovely home, ma'am. I'm looking forward to investigating it." Boyd stepped farther into the room giving it a second look around.

"Is there anything I can help you bring in, or did you want to wait until after dinner?" Austin noticed he had parked on the street.

"How about you and Carly show me where you have the most interaction with the apparitions. I'll put cameras in those areas. It takes about thirty-five or forty minutes to carry everything in and set up all the equipment." Boyd gave them a broad smile.

Carly and Austin led Boyd and Delaney on a tour of the house, marking the areas where they had experienced either physical contact or heard sounds. Carly showed Boyd the upstairs level.

They stopped outside the nursery. She opened the nursery door, not going inside.

"This room is home to the toy horse that keeps appearing in different areas of the house. The photograph showing the ghost of the boy was taken over by the fireplace."

"Well, it sounds like you've several areas of the house with spirit activity. From what I gather, you hear the crying and banging sounds from inside the walls throughout the house. You also have seen the most activity in the front room downstairs. It seems like the kitchen area is also hot." Boyd turned toward the door leading to the third floor.

"That's an unfinished story that we're using as an attic. I've heard footsteps up there, and I felt a hand try to push me down the stairs." Carly shivered as she looked up to the third floor.

"Sorry to hear that. Perhaps we should check out the kitchen next." Boyd waited and allowed the group to proceed downstairs.

"We felt a spirit down here in the cellar." Carly unlocked the cellar door and flipped on the light.

"Okay, sounds like you have a lot of places showing activity. How about we carry the equipment inside, and we'll set things up after dinner?" Boyd rubbed his hands together, his blue eyes dancing in the kitchen lighting.

While Austin and Boyd carried the cameras and cords into the house, Delaney helped Carly with dinner preparations.

"This afternoon I stopped in the Historical Society to find the Quaker Cemetery where Dr. Faysoux moved Andrew." Delaney sighed, rubbing her eyes.

"Did you have any luck?"

"Yes, and no. I found the original site of the cemetery—and it's now right under the parking garage on King Street." Delaney raised her eyebrows. "After a search, we found they were moved to the Court House yard for urban expansion. I saw the plaque listing the names of the people who were reburied, but Andrew wasn't listed."

"I don't understand. If he was part of the move, why wasn't his name listed?" Carly took the pork chops from the warming oven.

"Sad to say, but I found that several cemeteries were relocated or built over. In my dream, I'm positive I saw Peter Faysoux leading the procession to the Quaker Cemetery. If his grave wasn't moved, it's a moot point... seven stories of concrete are over him now." Delaney filled the glasses with ice.

"I can't believe it. Strange he was buried a few blocks from our house." She poured iced tea in the glasses.

"Well, at least now we know that he was buried at the Quaker graveyard. Maybe that's all we need to know." Delaney pulled up a bar stool.

Austin and Boyd made three trips to the car carrying in cameras, computer equipment, and sound equipment, as well as miles of extension cords that would snake throughout their home. Carly had no idea that paranormal investigations required so much high tech equipment.

During dinner, the conversation began with polite pleasantries, and then focused on why they were here and what was going on in the house. Due to writing down experiences in her notebook, Carly was able to fill in Boyd on occurrences, while Austin described his fewer ghostly episodes, as well as the conversation he had with the previous owner. After Delaney added her sightings of the Pettigrews and Benjamin Hastings, Carly handed the picture of the boy to Boyd to inspect.

"Wow, definitely not a photo bomb. When was this taken?" Boyd studied the photograph.

"My dad took that picture just a few months ago." Carly put the pitcher on the sideboard. "I took a few pictures up there last night as well."

"Really? I'd like to upload them to my computer, and see what shows up on there. Sometimes I get an orb or a mist, not so much a full body apparition like this." Boyd adjusted his glasses.

"I didn't see anything, but you're welcome to upload the pictures." She walked into the hall. "I'll get the card out of my camera for you." Carly released the memory card from her camera and joined the others in the dining room.

"Thanks, I'll upload it before we start, then you can put it back in the camera for tonight." Boyd took the memory card and put it in his shirt pocket.

After the group had finished pecan pie, Austin and Boyd began setting up the cameras. Delaney and Carly helped run the miles of cable and extension cords throughout the house.

"We'll put the computers in your den. It will be the command center." Boyd carried the two laptops into the den.

Boyd planned the receiving room, kitchen, and upstairs landing as locations for the cameras which would automatically record happenings in those rooms. As their investigation began, as if on cue, a storm was brewing off to the west and brought hammering rain on the roof.

Delaney brought her digital voice recorder, hoping to capture the sounds inaudible during the investigation. Boyd opened his laptop, with sound bars scrolling across the screen. Carly and Austin took their place on the loveseat while Boyd gathered his paranormal gadgets, spreading them on the table.

Cary felt inept in the field of paranormal investigating, and she knew Austin had no experience with this type of thing. Neither had watched any of the ghost investigation shows on television. However, the amount and technical sophistication of the equipment impressed the couple.

"We aren't up on our paranormal gear. What exactly is all this?" Austin touched a small device.

Boyd held up the small tape recorder. "This is a digital voice recorder with a K-II meter attached. These will capture my voice and anything that is audible or inaudible. I use it to try and capture an EVP."

"Does EVP mean electronic voice phenomenon?" She examined the meter on the coffee table.

"Yes, that's right. You know more than you think." Boyd smiled at her.

"This full spectrum camera will take video and still shots in ultraviolet and through visible light. It can see things that our eyes might not see." He showed the group the camera. "Let's begin if all of you are ready."

"First thing is to turn the lights off. I know you've been able to see the spirit activity during broad daylight, but I like to make it dark inside so it takes out the daytime shadows and lighting issues. I've had just as much activity during the day, when the house is empty." Boyd stood up and pointed to the bag on the floor behind Delaney. "Delaney, will you grab the flashlights in my backpack? I forgot to tell y'all that we'll need flashlights."

Austin and Carly turned off all the interior house lights. Delaney handed out the flashlights from Boyd's large backpack.

"Any questions?" Boyd surveyed the group.

Austin settled into his chair, listening to the soft hiss coming through the various cameras throughout the house. Without any objections, the investigation of the Tabor's King Street home began.

Chapter 17

Boyd stationed Austin in the den to observe the computer screens recording the numerous cameras throughout the house. He gave Austin a walkie-talkie and brought the other one with him. Boyd led the way into the darkened receiving room, followed by Carly and Delaney. Their flashlights shot lasers of illumination all around the room. Creaking as if in protest, the old floor boards made noises as the group gathered in front of the fireplace. Delaney held the spirit box close. Only their flashlight points identified where each person stood.

"We're here at the Tabor home on King Street. Is there anyone who would like to speak? Celeste? Andrew? You have our attention, and we're here to listen." Boyd held the digital recorder.

"The lightning… it is bright…lighting up the sky." Delaney's low voice shared with them as she started her Electronic Voice Phenomenon (EVP) session. She reported what she could see that nobody else could. "Andrew puts another log onto the fire, peering out the window at the rain. It's a cold rain; he's still wet from being out in the downpour." Delaney's flashlight turned around to the doorway as she held the spirit box.

Carly saw the K-II meter showing activity. She pointed her flashlight at the device so that Boyd could see it.

"There's a rise in activity on the meter—that's a good sign. What else is Andrew showing you?" Boyd moved to another part of the room.

"He hears a noise, to his left, and moves to the safe inside the wallboard. He takes out his flintlock pistol, loading two round balls inside." Delaney paused, turning toward the wall safe. "He takes something from the safe… it looks like a paper wrapped with a leather binding of some kind. He shoves it into his jacket pocket." Delaney's flashlight bobbed over to the wall safe, touching the panel which hid it from view.

"Andrew, why did you get your pistol? Did you see someone when the room was lit from the lightening outside?" Boyd moved to the hallway.

A bolt of lightning flashed outside the window, causing everyone to jump. The static on the spirit box was silent, followed by an electronic voice saying in a garbled tone, '*fight*'. Carly looked down as the K-II meter flashed.

"I'm hearing something in my headphones in the receiving room." Austin's voice crackled through Boyd's walkie-talkie.

"What about a fight? Did you and someone get into a fight that evening, January 19th?" Boyd asked, and they saw the K-II flash green.

"Oh no, I'm getting an odd feeling that someone's standing near me." Carly turned to be sure it wasn't Boyd or Delaney, but in the darkened room she couldn't see. Carly saw the flash of Boyd's full spectrum camera.

"Andrew, who fought with you in this room?" Delaney moved away from the fireplace.

"Wow, did anyone else feel the temperature change in here?" Boyd whispered, rubbing his arms.

"It's him—Hastings." Carly watched the meter continue to flash green.

The rain began to ping on the windows with icy pellets. "Is that hail?" Boyd moved to the window.

"Sounds like it, although the forecast hadn't called for anything like that tonight." Delaney joined him, and shone her flashlight outside.

"Benjamin Hastings, are you in this room?" Delaney asked. The spirit box continued to give off a static sound.

"Do you see anything else, Delaney?" Boyd moved his camera to the fireplace and took another photograph.

"I can see Andrew, the room isn't well-lit, just lit from a few candles in the holders on the fireplace, along with the fire. The door to the safe in the wallboard is ajar." Delaney's voice sounded like a monotone. "Andrew is holding his pistol, loading another ball. There's someone in the room that's larger than him. Oh no, the bigger man knocks him back then they struggle for the gun."

Delaney crossed the room to the doorway. "Who's the intruder, Andrew?" The K-II displayed another green flash, a beacon in the velvet dark. Carly and Boyd moved closer to Delaney and listened.

"Andrew and the intruder both have hold of the pistol. I can see his face." Delaney's voice caught in her throat. "Yes, it's Benjamin Hastings!"

"Delaney, where's Celeste? Is she in the room?" Boyd's gentle voice moved as his flashlight moved into the hallway. "Let's go out into the hallway, it's cold in here." Boyd led the trio from the receiving room.

Austin's voice crackled from the walkie talkie telling them he's seeing a light float from one side of the room to the hall.

Delaney began her EVP session again in the hallway. "Celeste, we know you're tryin' to show us something, and we want to help you. What's in your hand, sweetie? Do you want to show us something?"

The sound on the spirit box caught them by surprise, as a soft voice bleated *"help."*

"She's here. I can see her." Delaney whispers.

Boyd and Carly begin to move slowly into the kitchen, where a camera was recording.

"Celeste, did you see Andrew and Hastings fighting? Did you come downstairs and find Benjamin Hastings shooting your husband?" Delaney moved a chair over to the center of the room and sat down.

"The sound, the banging, do you hear it?" Carly asked Boyd, and turned toward the cellar. The storm had picked up outside, thunder boomed nearby, but the banging was competing with nature's noise.

"Yes, I hear it," Boyd moved further into the kitchen. As he talked, the crying began. "That's an affirmative on the crying."

"Celeste, are you cryin'?" Delaney opened her eyes, turning toward the hallway.

"Celeste, who is crying?" Boyd called out, and held the K-II in front of him.

"Oh no, I'm feeling a panic attack or something coming on, you guys. I need to get some air." Carly's arms and legs began to shake, followed by a feeling of the air sucked out of the room.

The spirit box and K-II meter responded at the same time. *"Dark"*. *"Help him."*

The room began to feel more like a meat locker than a kitchen, as the temperature dropped. Carly sat on the cool tile floor, trying to get her breath and calm herself.

"Are you okay, hon? Do we need to stop?" Boyd bent to check on her.

"Help who? Who do you want us to help? Hastings shot your Andrew, Celeste?" Delaney paced back and forth.

The crying and banging grew louder, reverberating through the dark house. The meter continued flashing, the voice recorder capturing the sound that came onto the spirit box, *"Run."* As the words displayed on the small device, the cellar door slammed shut with a force that rattled the frame.

"Weird, the horse just fell off the mantel upstairs, Boyd." Austin's voice rang from the walkie talkie in Boyd's belt. Outside, a loud clap of thunder followed by a lightning bolt lit up the street. A large tree outside their house took a direct hit, sending a large branch onto the power line. Carly and Boyd heard the refrigerator stop humming.

Austin radioed in an urgent voice. "All the equipment just went dark, so looks like the electricity is out with the storm. Is everybody okay?"

"Are you okay, hon?" Delaney turned her flashlight toward her friend.

"I'm feeling better, but I think we should go back into the den." Carly stood, grabbing the counter for support.

Boyd glanced out the window, the sparks still visible as the hot wires flapped like ripped clothing in the wind. "I hope we didn't lose all the evidence. I've a surge protector on the cords, so let's hope our work isn't lost."

As the three made it back into the den, Austin was lighting the candle on the coffee table. It illuminated the room enough for Carly to bring a few more candles from the receiving room to light the den.

"Well, we've had an eventful evening, even if we didn't get to investigate the whole house. I'm going back to my house tonight and listen to the recordings and review the camera recordings." Boyd unplugged the computer cords and wrapped them up.

"I jotted down a couple of things I saw, two instances in particular. I saw a light…a kind of blob, traveling from the receiving room to the hall and marked it on the log. Just before the power went out, I saw the toy horse in the nursery fall off the mantel." Austin leaned back in his chair, raking his hand through his hair.

"I'll review it all tonight, and tomorrow, I'll call you to set up a time to meet. Like you, I think the crying is from a child. You had three spirits in the house tonight." Boyd carried a candle with him as he walked into the receiving room to take down the cameras.

"Okay, I appreciate you coming. Maybe Delaney and I can do some more work here and in the research department. We still have a couple of days before our company arrives." Carly held another candle for Boyd to pack up.

"I don't want to dash your hopes—this might take more than a couple of days. There's more going on here than just the murder of two people." Boyd stacked the equipment near the door, while Austin stacked the equipment from upstairs.

Delaney and Carly helped gather cords and equipment in the semi-darkness. An hour later, Austin and Carly collapsed onto the sofa, exhausted from an evening of paranormal investigation. Finally, they saw lights from a power company truck outside the window and workers putting up safety cones around the downed line.

"It's slightly odd for the power to go out right at the time the creepy things happened in the house." Austin joined Carly at the window.

"Nothing surprises me in this house. I'd hoped we'd get all the answers tonight, but we aren't any closer than before Boyd came." She turned into Austin's embrace.

"You know I didn't believe in the paranormal stuff before, but I've resigned myself to believe some things defy explanation. We'll get to the bottom of this, hon." He massaged her back, working up to her shoulders.

Carly thought about the words the spirit box emitted. Why did she always have the sensation of a panic attack combined with a feeling of suffocating when the spirits were nearby?

"I hope Boyd captured the EVPs and images from the cameras. In the meantime, I'm putting my bet on Celeste. She's going to be the key, I feel it." She walked over to blow out the candles and led Austin upstairs.

Carly and Austin awoke to the sound of the crew working a wood chipper to dispose of the branches from the previous night's storm.

"Power's back on—it's eight-forty-five. What's on the agenda for you today?" Austin rolled to face Carly. She rubbed her hand across her forehead, the thought of having to do anything seemed to be more than she could face.

"I hope Boyd calls to tell us he's solved the mystery of the Pettigrews and Ben Hastings haunting our house." She yawned and stretched her arms. "What's on your plate?"

"Got some patients going home in a day or two. So I'll need to finish my notes." He rolled onto his back. "It looks like a short workday, so we can head downtown to eat at Mike's Bar-b-que. It's been awhile since we've eaten there."

The two rolled out of bed, and by nine o'clock, they were both downstairs in the kitchen eating breakfast. Carly's phone began ringing the second she sat to eat her toast and drink her coffee.

"Hey Delaney, what's up?" Carly answered.

"I wanted to call and see if y'all had anything else happen after we left last night. I expect you'll hear something today from Boyd."

"Yep, you know Austin saw a couple of things. I'm hoping we captured several EVPs. I wish we could've walked to the cellar," Carly said. "I wanted Boyd to investigate down there—especially since we've both had experiences with Hastings there." She chewed up a bite of toast.

"Maybe we should have Boyd and his partner, Tucker, come back after your in-laws go back home. I'd like to see what they find down there, too." Delaney's voice sounded perky this morning.

"Well, I'll let you know if he calls. In the meantime, I'm going to follow up on a couple of leads. I feel like Celeste is the key to finding the answers. Something tells me she's trying to give us the answer to what's going on here." Carly sipped her hot coffee.

"You might be right. I'd love to know why both she and Andrew had a paper or something in their hand when I saw them," Delaney said.

"I think whatever it is, it involves Ben Hastings." Carly recalled the instance in the nursery when Celeste reached out to her with something, and then the door locked by itself.

"All righty, have a good rest of the day. In case I don't get to talk to you before, do have a happy Thanksgiving!" Delaney's voice sounded positive.

"You too. If you don't have plans, you're welcome to join us. We'll be eating around noon," Carly said.

Carly ended the call and began to worry—in less than twenty-four hours, Austin's parents and sister would be arriving. She checked each of the bedrooms to be sure all was ready. She hoped the other guests, the unseen ones, wouldn't interfere with their family gathering.

The menu for Thanksgiving lunch consisted of Carolina Rice, shrimp, turkey breast, cornbread stuffing, sweet potatoes, green bean casserole, and cranberry salad. She also planned on serving the traditional fare of her grandmother's pumpkin pie and yeast rolls. This holiday would be her first time to make a holiday meal, which always fell on her mother. At least she didn't worry about her mother-in-law judging her cooking, since Myra Tabor wasn't much of a cook. But, she continued to worry about the spirits in their house and how they might behave with visitors.

Carly wanted answers to the reason why Celeste and Andrew Pettigrew and Benjamin Hastings remained in her house after two hundred years. She also wanted to know how the spirit of the young child figured into the mystery. She logged into her account on the ancestry web site for more information on Peter Faysoux and found two entries for his name. In *The City Gazette*, Peter Faysoux was mentioned in a story about his treating the inhabitants of the Poor House, as well as the inmates of the Charleston Orphan Asylum. She found another link with him serving on the board of the Orphan Asylum. She searched through the account once again of Benjamin Hastings' trial. It listed Dr. Peter Faysoux and Jacob Hinman as the first to find the bodies of his daughter and son-in-law after the murders. Finding his daughter's body must've been a father's worst nightmare.

Dr. Faysoux must have found a burial site for Andrew, once the church demanded his coffin exhumed from the churchyard at St. Michael's. She remembered the will of Andrew Pettigrew leaving Faysoux the personal effects and home of his daughter and son-in-law.

She clicked on a link for the 1799 City Directory of Charleston. She scrolled down the page, finding his name and his family: Peter Faysoux, physician, 57; his wife, Susan Faysoux, 48, and two unmarried children, Elias, 22, and Louisa, 20.

With a jerk back to the present, her cell phone rang and she answered this unfamiliar number.

"This is Boyd Hawley. I hope I didn't wake you." Carly heard his cheerful voice.

"Hey Boyd—good to hear from you." She pushed her chair away from the computer.

"Well, I reviewed the video clips and listened to the recordings from last night. Is there a good time to meet this week?" Boyd asked.

"Today is good, but the rest of the week Austin's family from Kansas City are visiting. What about this afternoon?" Carly bit her lower lip.

"I work from home, so I can stop by around two? I tried calling Delaney, but didn't get her," Boyd said.

"Let me try. I spoke to her earlier today. Two o'clock works for me."

"Okay, see you later." Boyd ended the call.

Carly attempted a call to Delaney, but didn't reach her, so she left her a voice mail to join them at two o'clock today if possible.

Delaney and Boyd arrived just before two o'clock. Carly hurried downstairs, seeing their vehicles parking in front of the house.

"Hey there. You two are right on time." Carly closed the door, feeling a rush of cold air settling in the entry hall. "Let's talk in the den; I made us hot tea and a snack."

Carly poured tea and served the apple turnovers. She carried her plate and cup over to the loveseat.

"Let me tell you what I found. I discovered Dr. Faysoux had two other children living at home as listed in the 1799 City Directory." Delaney took a sip of Earl Grey tea.

"You aren't going to believe it, but I found the same thing today on my genealogy site." Carly almost choked on her tea.

Boyd plugged in his laptop and cued the video to the time on his paper. "Okay, I have some interesting things from last night's investigation you might want to look at. When the investigation began, you were seeing Andrew and Ben Hastings in the receiving room. When the temperature dropped, we all felt it. As the EVP session continued, we walked into the hallway. If you look right here, you can see a large orb." He pointed with a small probe at the screen. "Austin saw this on the screen right as we commented about the coldness and Ben Hastings being in the house. If you notice, the orb follows you, Carly, right out into the entry hall."

Carly shivered as she watched the orb float behind her.

"Wow, that's quite a large orb, comparatively speaking. Did you pick up anything on the spirit box?" Delaney moved in closer to see the screen.

"I thought I heard the word '*run*'. Listen, and see what y'all think." Boyd turned up the volume. The three listened as he replayed the recording. A low, but audible, voice said, '*Run*'.

"That's odd. If she came into the room after Hastings shot Andrew, why would she tell him to run?" Carly took another bite of turnover.

"Remember, I saw Andrew and Hastings through someone's eyes, and it wasn't Celeste." Delaney closed her eyes, remembering the scene.

Boyd continued to search the video for more footage for either movement or EVP activity.

"I heard something on the digital recorder, Delaney, that I thought you'd find interesting. When you were trying to get Andrew to communicate in the receiving room, I noticed a mist in the corner of the room, it seemed to hover over by the large chair." Boyd continued to run through the recorder.

Delaney peered over his shoulder as he paused the part of the video to share. As Delaney was talking to Andrew Pettigrew, a mist formed behind Carly.

"It looks like whatever it was had a direct effect on Carly." Delaney watched as Carly appeared to have difficulty breathing and began coughing.

"It isn't the first time. It's happened in the cellar and in the receiving room." Carly pulled the sleeves of her sweatshirt down to cover her now cold arms.

"Well, we know Benjamin Hastings came into the house alone on that evening. We also have the account in the newspaper saying he came to collect money Jacob Hinman thought he owed to him. What happened in that room is pretty clear; Andrew Pettigrew pulled his pistol from the safe and intended to use it." Delaney pointed her finger at the computer screen.

"But, Hastings overpowered him and turned the gun on Pettigrew." Boyd advanced the video to the next segment.

"And let's not forget Andrew shared drinks earlier at McCrady's Tavern with Jacob Hinman. Maybe he was getting Andrew smashed so that Hastings could sneak in after he went to bed and take all the money from his safe." Carly's eyebrows rose as she made her point.

"That's true, but who else was in the house? Celeste retired for the night, as she was in her night clothes. The attack on her husband surprised her," Delaney added.

"Do you think the other person might have been Jacob Hinman?" Boyd squinted at the computer screen as if it would reveal the secrets.

"I don't think so, because as long as Andrew was livin', the money would keep flowing in each month." Delaney looked inside her bag for her notes. "Don't you have something in the papers from the Historical Society saying Jacob Hinman went into his shop after six?"

"But, his wife stated under oath that he was at home with her that evening and in bed by eight-thirty. No one questioned it during the trial. I get the feeling the person in the room isn't Jacob Hinman." Carly picked up her cup, drinking the last of her tea.

"Okay, so that brings us back to the same question. Who was the third person in the room?" Boyd scratched his head and rubbed his temples.

"Celeste tried to make contact with Carly earlier in the nursery with something in her hand. Earlier, Andrew held out something for me, too, so it seems they both want us to find something, a ledger or papers of some sort." Delaney cracked her knuckles.

"We already know Andrew Pettigrew's ledger more or less convicted Jacob Hinman, revealing the 'payments' he'd given him over ten years. It had to be something the public didn't know, or something personal only the killer and the Pettigrews knew." Carly poured Delaney and Boyd more tea.

"Wish I had more for you, Carly. I'd like to come back with Tucker. I think we should move one of the cameras to the cellar, and keep the others in the receiving room and kitchen," Boyd said.

"Sure, we're up for that. Maybe I'm wrong about Jacob Hinman. His wife could've lied to keep him from the gallows." Carly pulled her long hair back into a ponytail. "Did you find anything on the memory card from the pictures I took upstairs in the nursery?" Carly asked.

Boyd reached into his backpack and took out the small media card, handing it to her. "No, I enlarged it and took out some of the noise. Sorry, I didn't see anything."

"I wish we knew the child's name and what happened to him. He doesn't fit with the Pettigrews, but he's here making his presence known." Delaney helped Carly clean up the dishes from the den and carry them into the kitchen. Carly and Boyd agreed that his presence was an additional mystery.

After Boyd and Delaney left, Carly logged into her computer genealogy account to search for information on Dr. Peter Faysoux. Disappointed, she found no descendants within the data. She assumed after Celeste's brother passed away, the line ended. She typed in Celeste Faysoux Pettigrew and crossed her fingers. Solving the mystery remained their only hope to create peace in their house.

Chapter 18

Leaving Austin sleeping in for a change, Carly started her day before dawn, preparing the two pies for Thanksgiving dinner. She decided on the regional Southern pecan pie and the traditional pumpkin pie. In addition, she used her Grandmother Evans's recipe for cranberry salad, a Thanksgiving staple for as long as she could remember. However, she couldn't shake the feeling someone was standing behind her. She blamed it on nerves, anticipating the proverbial other shoe to drop.

After stuffing and basting the turkey, she placed it back in the refrigerator. She'd prepare the rest of the meal with the help of Austin's mother and sister.

"Now where did I put the recipe for the rice?" She searched the counter for the hand-written recipe card, remembering having placed it beside the mixing bowl. In a panic, she retraced her steps in search of the missing card.

Austin walked in to witness her turning the kitchen upside down for the recipe card. "Hey, sweetheart, I'm heading over to the airport. Mom texted me and said they're on the runway."

"Oh, okay. I'll hold the fort down." She didn't look up, preoccupied with finding the recipe card.

"Let's not do anything to stir up the natives, okay?" He kissed her and picked up his keys from the hall table and left the house.

Frustrated, she groaned out loud, and then as if by magic, the recipe card floated to the floor.

"Thank you. Now everyone behave! Capeesh?" She downed another cup of coffee before continuing her meal preparation. An hour later, Carly heard the door close as she finished tidying the guest bathroom.

"Hon, we're here!" Austin's voice echoing throughout the downstairs.

Carly met the Tabor clan in the entry way, getting hugs from each of them. "How was your flight?"

"It wasn't bad. Lovely drive from the airport through Charleston. What a lovely historic town." Myra Tabor examined the interior as Carly led them into the den.

"You've gotten into the Primitive and Early American style, haven't you?" Ainsley Tabor touched the small wooden bowls and boxes and admired the antiques.

"We decided to try to add pieces which were typical during the eighteenth century. It's fun trying to find the right pieces." Carly hugged her sister-in-law, Ainsley again.

"How about giving us the ten cent tour, son? We've been trying to imagine what kind of house you found for under a million down here." Austin and his father, Kent Tabor, talked in the doorway. He laughed, patting his son on the back.

"Sure, let's all take the tour. Carly, you wanna start at the receiving room?" Austin extended his arm, waving the group into the hall.

Dr. Kent Tabor stood over six feet, five inches tall, keeping a slender frame in good shape from an active lifestyle of racket ball and golf. Myra, a petite porcelain-skinned beauty, remained lovely and graceful. A former Miss Kansas in her younger days, Myra had a flair for fashion and kept up with the latest beauty regimens. Together, they shared a love that remained strong over forty years. Carly watched as they oohed and aahed over their beautiful home, and was satisfied they seemed impressed with the décor for the "diamond-in-the-rough."

Ainsley Tabor, eight years younger than her brother, had just turned 30 years old. Taking a job as a photo journalist in Kansas City after a recent break-up, she'd moved back into her parents' large home to save money. While Austin favored his father, inheriting his handsome features and height, Ainsley resembled her mother, beautiful with dark hair and a petite frame. Carly stood in the receiving room, feeling like an outsider, as well as a female giant, with his upper-income family, while the rest of the family climbed the stairs.

"You'll love the third floor, sis. It'd be a good size for an apartment and studio." Austin looked back at Carly. "Hon, are you coming?"

She hurried up the stairs, catching up with the tour outside the nursery. Hesitating before opening the door to the nursery, she dreaded their questions and comments about a baby.

"This is the nursery, when we need one." She opened the door, allowing the family to walk through. Myra and Ainsley Tabor admired the baby bed and wardrobe, along with the christening gowns.

Ainsley picked up the metal rocking horse that was sitting on the mantel. "Well isn't this cute. It looks old, where'd you find it?"

"It came from an estate auction, and I found it in an antique store in Mt. Pleasant along with an old photo album." Carly took the photo album out of the wardrobe, turning the page to a photograph of a small child sitting in a chair with the toy.

"The toy is worth even more because you have photographs showing it with a child." Myra placed the antique toy back on the mantle.

"It wasn't cheap, that's true. I just felt drawn to it." Carly ran her fingers over the cool metal.

The elephant in the room could hide no longer. Myra cleared her throat. "We hope there'll be a little someone in that bed before long."

"So do I Myra." Carly turned away, trying not to sound curt. A chill settled in the room, and it wasn't from an unseen spirit this time.

"Let's go upstairs, I want to show Ainsley her future digs." Austin ushered everyone out of the nursery, waiting to put his arm around Carly's waist and kissed her forehead.

"Hold on tight, the stairs are narrow." As the group climbed the narrow stairs, Carly remembered her recent tumble and she grabbed the railing.

For the remainder of the evening, Austin and Carly played tour guide. Before it got dark, they had taken the family to the Battery and to a few cemeteries and churches close to their house. They drove past the City Jail, Powder Magazine, and Provost Dungeon. "Wish you guys could stay a bit longer." Austin pulled his car into the driveway after they'd finished the tour.

Carly unlocked the door, hesitating before going inside. Taking a deep breath, she turned on the lights. Thank goodness, nothing was amiss, and no strange noises or temperature drops greeted them.

That evening, after the Tabors settled into their rooms, Austin and Carly breathed a sigh of relief. So far, so good, Carly thought, setting the alarm for early in the morning so they could begin preparing the meal before dawn.

When Carly awoke at five o'clock with the alarm, she felt rested, sleeping through the night without the sounds of banging or crying waking her. She looked over at Austin, who yawned and stretched his arms over his head. "Well, that's one night down, two to go. I hate to jinx things, so I'll just say,"thank goodness!" Austin got out of bed and dressed. When Carly finished dressing, they walked arm in arm downstairs to begin preparing for the noon Thanksgiving meal.

The Tabors came downstairs a little after seven. Carly already had their lunch underway, and Austin checked on the turkey deep-frying inside the large "green egg" cooker. She poured coffee for the Tabors and placed a breakfast casserole on the table.

"Did you sleep well?" She looked at Myra and Ainsley and saw they looked tired. Perhaps things last night weren't as peaceful as she and Austin thought.

"Umm, well, I had trouble sleeping, you know, strange place." Ainsley dipped a helping of sausage and egg casserole, not making eye contact.

"I always have trouble sleeping the first night or two in a strange bed, so hopefully you'll sleep better tonight." Carly passed the casserole to Myra.

"Oh, I slept fine. I was asleep as soon as my head it the pillow. Kent didn't move a muscle all night." Myra took a small helping, passing the dish to her husband who agreed.

Carly breathed a sigh of relief. "Well, I'm glad you're all here for our first Thanksgiving in the new house. We've missed you." Carly remained on pins and needles worrying the spirits would cause problems. No one mentioned any night encounters or odd noises, so perhaps the spirits were behaving for company.

At noon, the family gathered in the dining room for lunch. Carly's dish of Carolina rice and shrimp went over well, as did the turkey and traditional fixings. Kent and Austin retired to the den after the meal to watch football, while Carly and the ladies cleaned up the dining room. As they carried the dirty dishes into the kitchen, the women planned to hit the early *Black Friday* sales. Meanwhile, Austin and his father discussed a visit to the hospital and a round of golf, weather permitting. She enjoyed her time shopping with Ainsley and Myra, picking up some good bargains for gifts for her parents, as well as Austin. Myra and Ainsley enjoyed the shops that Carly ushered them to, and they found the city of Charleston charming and festive.

Everyone arrived back at the house about the same time, and they relaxed in the den, worn out from the day's events.

"Did you enjoy your tour of the hospital, Kent?" Carly raised her head from the back of the leather chair.

"I did, thank you, and we talked to Dr. Hutchinson…he certainly sang our Austin's praises." Kent nodded at his son.

However, that evening, as the family sat watching the classic movie channel, the peaceful evening came to a crashing halt. The sound cut through the stillness like a jackhammer. Everyone bolted upright at the start of the banging.

"What in the world?" Myra sat up from the loveseat.

Austin and Carly looked at one another, afraid to speak. Hoping to avoid an explanation, he stated, "We've experienced some weird sounds in the house."

His father and mother traded worried glances. "You mean this is normal?" Kent cupped his hands to his mouth to be heard above the clamor.

"Well, it happens often." Carly pushed her hair back from her shoulders, feeling her husband's anxiety. "But, don't worry, we're dealing with it."

"How do you stand it? Have you contacted someone to check out the heating and cooling?" Myra moved around the room, trying to locate where the sound was originating.

"That's coming from inside the walls, it doesn't seem to be in the duct work." Kent put his ear to the wall. "Let's go downstairs to take a look."

Austin and Carly jumped to their feet, knowing the past experiences that occurred in the cellar. Austin stammered, "It's not necessary, Dad. We've had that checked out. It doesn't seem to come from the heating or plumbing."

The banging continued, and Kent, Myra, and Ainsley looked at one another with nervous smiles.

"We haven't told you about this because we didn't want you to think we're crazy." Carly's eyes filled with tears, as her apprehension and anxiety increased.

"Well, I didn't want to say anything, but I heard Carly crying the other night. Is this why?" Ainsley asked.

"It wasn't Carly, sis. Umm…well…we are of the opinion that we aren't alone in the house." Austin raked his hand through his hair.

"What do you mean… you aren't alone?" Kent sat back down, trying to speak above the noise.

"We think we have ghosts or spirits in our dream house." Carly reached for a tissue. "We've had several encounters over the past five months, and I asked someone trained in the paranormal to investigate what's going on here." She blew her nose, avoiding looking at her mother-in-law's slack- jawed expression.

"Son, you don't believe in all that ghost absurdity. Surely you don't?" Myra walked over and sat next to her son.

"Mom, I was the last person to believe our house had ghosts. Believe me, Carly and Delaney have researched and experienced numerous encounters, as have I, with the spirits." He reached for Carly's hand to reassure her that they were a team.

"Well, there's got to be a rational explanation. This is real, not something a ghost catcher is telling you." Kent stood over his son, his shadow falling over him like a death shroud.

"Who's this Delaney person?" Ainsley returned to her chair, pulling a woven afghan over her legs.

"Delaney's a friend of mine who happens to be a sensitive, someone who can see and communicate with spirits. We've seen the people who died in this house." Carly wiped her eyes and couldn't meet the Tabors' gazes.

"Mom and Dad, we found out through court records that the original owners, a couple, were murdered. It happened in the receiving room, and the person who killed them was found guilty and hanged. We're certain that all three of these people's ghosts are still here in the house." Austin exhaled, squeezing Carly's hand like a drowning man holding on to a life preserver.

"So the crying I heard last night?" Ainsley pulled the afghan up to her chin.

"There's a child here. The antique toy horse appears throughout the house. And my parents took a photo in the room which shows the child's ghost." Carly showed them the enlarged photograph that her father had taken earlier in the summer. The image of the small apparition holding the toy horse caused a simultaneous gasp from Myra and Ainsley.

"Oh my! That gives me chills." Myra held the photograph to get a better view.

"Daddy took the picture when he and Mom were here last summer. Mom sent the picture to me after she got the prints developed," said Carly.

The family sat and listened as Carly and Austin recounted event after event, along with the investigation prior to their arrival. Afterwards, no one spoke. The banging had subsided to a faint pounding, then silence.

"I don't know what to say, kids. We've never experienced this sort of thing. But, we believe you, even though it's hard to accept something like this." Kent bent over to clasp both Austin and Carly's hand.

"I wasn't going to say anything, but the first night, I saw the bedroom door open. I felt like someone was standing in the room watching us sleep." Myra rubbed her hands together, feeling a chill.

"I'm sorry you had to experience this. We hoped they wouldn't bother our guests." Austin's broad shoulders sagged.

"We've had a good visit, son, don't apologize. You can always sell the house and make a profit." Kent gestured towards the work they'd completed.

"We're not selling!" Carly and Austin chimed in unison. The Tabors stared at them, confused.

"We'll get to the bottom of this. We're figuring out the mystery of the murders, as we research more." Carly walked back to the desk, putting the photograph inside. "We're going to have the investigator return. The spirits are trying to tell us something, but we just aren't getting the message."

"Well, it's obvious the message is for you, and anyone else, to get out. Doesn't take a mental heavy weight to figure that out!" Ainsley shook her head, making a 'pff' sound.

"No sense getting snarky, Ainsley. It isn't like we can just walk away. We've invested a lot of time and money in our house." Austin stood, walking over to stand with Carly.

"I didn't mean to ruffle any feathers. Just stating the obvious. Sorry, Carly." Ainsley threw up her hands in mock defense.

"It's okay. We knew everyone would think we're crazy. That's why we haven't said anything, and wouldn't have, if you hadn't heard the sounds for yourselves." Carly leaned into Austin, feeling his arm circle her waist.

The group tried to resume a normal evening. Austin and Carly served pecan and pumpkin pie, along with coffee. No one mentioned the strange goings on in the house, but when the time came to retire for the night, everyone remained on edge. That night, everyone slept well and nobody woke up with crying or banging.

The next morning, Carly made French toast for the Tabors and everyone had a normal and cheerful breakfast. The Tabors kept their original plan to depart on Saturday and they enjoyed a relaxing day of seeing more Charleston sights and dining out. When they were leaving, Austin helped his parents carry their luggage out to the car. Myra forgot her purse and returned inside to find it on the hall table.

She rejoined the family outside, giving Carly a hug. "I can't understand it, but I believe you, honey. You have a lovely home, and you were such a good little hostess for us." Myra kissed her daughter-in-law on the cheek.

"Thank you, Myra. I'm glad you know the truth. We'll be okay." Carly opened the car door for her.

"I hope you and Austin will get busy on a niece or nephew for me. It doesn't look like I'm going to be giving the folks a grandchild anytime soon." Ainsley embraced Carly.

"I think we can give it a good try!" Carly winked at Austin, while the Tabors laughed and said goodbyes.

Chapter 19

Carly stood on the porch as Austin and the Tabors pulled out of the driveway headed for the airport. Feeling a sense of relief that Austin's family had experienced the spirit activity and didn't think they were crazy, she sighed and decided the incident strengthened her resolve to end the haunting of their dream home. So, she closed the door, made a cup of hot tea, and decided to find Celeste Pettigrew in the newspapers on-line. Searching for Peter Faysoux in the many databases on the genealogical web site, she received the same hits as previously but scrolled down the choices, in hopes that Celeste's name might appear in her father's links.

In fact, she remembered reading about Peter Faysoux serving as the physician to both the Charleston Poor House and the Charleston Orphan Asylum, so she searched and found several hits appeared. Although most of the accounts were minutes from board member meetings, Carly scanned them for ties. Next, when she searched in the *Charleston Orphan Asylum*, several hits for Faysoux appeared and revealed that he served as the physician to the Orphanage from its beginning, in 1794. She found it interesting that the city's Orphan Asylum was the first orphanage in the United States. As she read the meeting accounts, her heart leaped when she saw Celeste Pettigrew's name. The accounts listed several staff member names, as well as patrons who came to the institution to offer clothing or supplies for the inmates, as they were called.

Reaching for her cell, she phoned Delaney. "Hey, I found a lead on Celeste! There's a connection to the Orphan Asylum in town."

"Are you kiddin', sweetie? What else did you find?" Delaney's voice perked up.

"I found a list of microfilm files and locations, but I still have to read through them. Maybe I'll find even more details." She saved the page to her computer files.

"Let me know—I think you struck gold today! By the way, we need to try and get another investigation set up with Boyd and his assistant, Tucker," Delaney said.

"Definitely, after Austin's family were scared by our spirits. I'd like to get them over here next week, if you could call them." Carly picked at her cuticles and felt tired from the adrenalin burst. "I'll stop by the Historical Society first to look at the microfilm files. I'll be in touch, Delaney." The friends said goodbye, ending the call.

Later in the morning, Carly received a text from Austin, "The folks got on the plane. Hospital called. Emergency surgery. Don't wait up. Love you." Not feeling rested and her normal energetic self, she decided to wait until Monday to visit the Historical Society. Instead, she researched information about the Charleston Orphan Asylum and was appalled by the number of orphan and abandoned children in Charleston. She read entries from the minutes from the Orphan House, i.e. Asylum, but to access the information she'd need to see the actual records from the institution.

Following a hunch, she called the Historical Society and left a voicemail for Tom Drummond. "Hi Tom, this is Carly Tabor. I found some information on one of the owners of my home, Celeste Pettigrew. I need more information on her involvement with the Charleston Orphan Asylum. I'd like to know if you could help me locate the records. I'll be into your office on Monday, thanks." Carly noticed a book, *The Charleston Orphan House*, and noted the author's name, as it may be a good source as well. Armed with new information and feeling more energetic, she prepared to go to the library.

The library was busy, but she found the book *The Charleston Orphan House* in the research section, and she also happened upon the city directory of 1799. She wanted to see if Andrew and Celeste had children or servants living in the house, which might lead her to the person who witnessed the murders. Carly located the 1799 city directory online and found Andrew Pettigrew listed as Inspector of Customs. Noting only he and Celeste were listed for their residence, she surmised they had neither servants nor children. So, she scratched the notion of possible other witnesses in the house on the night of the murders. How did the ghost of a child who appeared in the photo fit in with the Pettigrews? She texted Delaney asking her to check for a possible Pettigrew child in the baptism records at St. Michael's Church. Since Celeste's wedding and burial took place there, it made sense any child would've been christened and buried there.

The research room at the library held the book on the Orphan Asylum, and after skimming through, she learned of the early days of the orphanage and names of early teachers and house workers. While reading the location of the original facility, she realized it was only a couple of streets away from her home on King Street and she decided to look for the site. Also, President Washington had toured the Asylum while visiting the city in 1790. Although interesting to read, she needed the actual records of the facility and had a hunch Celeste Pettigrew's involvement would be noted. As she left the building, Delaney sent a text, "No luck with the Pettigrew child theory." Carly sent a reply thanking her for trying, but felt like a deflated balloon.

The rest of the weekend proved uneventful in Carly and Austin's home. It was the last week in November, and Carly worked decorating their dream house for Christmas early since she would spend Christmas in Kansas. Much as she tried to put it out of her mind, however, she remained preoccupied with the spirit activity in the house. Even so, she loved the holidays, especially Christmas, so the holiday season this year would be a welcome diversion.

"Austin, do you mind bringing down the Christmas totes from the third floor?" Carly hollered upstairs to Austin, who'd finished his shower.

"Do you need them all down today?" He rubbed the towel over his wet hair.

"No, it's okay. I don't need to decorate today," she sighed. "I wanted to enjoy the decorations before I have to leave."

"How about next weekend? You don't really want to have decorations lying all around if you have Boyd and Delaney back with all their equipment, do you?" He walked to the landing, waiting for her to tell him what to do.

"Yeah, you're right. I'll wait until next weekend," she said. As usual, Austin made perfect sense, even when he was just trying to get out of going up in the attic himself.

He finished getting ready, and came downstairs to find her in the receiving room, on hands and knees in front of the wall.

"What are you doing?" He watched her hands pushing against the wainscot paneling below the wall safe.

"I thought maybe there might be another safe in the wall, one that Ben Hastings didn't know about." She moved her hands along the wall near the fireplace.

"Well, it wouldn't surprise me if Andrew had another hiding spot. However, I don't want to rip off the paneling to find out."

Carly stood, brushing off her jeans. "I know, but I can't get it out of my head that whatever Andrew and Celeste are trying to show us is somewhere in this house. Maybe it's money that Hastings and Jacob Hinman didn't know about."

"Didn't you say that Hinman and Celeste's father found the couple? Maybe he came back and took whatever they seem to want you to find?"

She didn't think Peter Faysoux would leave the house unattended. "It has to be something else, I just have a gut feeling." She tapped her hand on the mantle.

"Well, let me know if you find anything good. I'm heading down to the hospital. What are your plans for today?" Austin crossed the hall and grabbed a bagel from the bread box. He took a cup from the cabinet and poured coffee into it.

"I'm going to the Historical Society today to see if Tom Drummond can help me find the minutes from the Orphan House meetings." Carly wiped the crumbs off the counter in front of the bread box.

"Sounds to me like you've got your day planned. I'll call or text you later." He leaned over to peck her cheek. "Love you."

Carly poured the last of the coffee into her travel mug. She finished her breakfast of oatmeal, and within the hour was on her way to the Historical Society. Before pulling into the parking garage, she got a text from Delaney. "Heard from Boyd. Would Wednesday work for another investigation? Tucker McGee will be joining him. Bringing out the big guns! See ya later."

She found a spot on the second level and sent a reply. "Wed. is fine. Going to Historical Society. Keep me posted."

Carly put her phone in the back pocket of her jeans and went into the Historical Society. She glanced to her right, searching the reference desk for Tom Drummond. He leaned over the desk and was just hanging up the phone.

"Hi, Mr. Drummond. I was hoping you could point me in the direction of the Orphan House or Asylum records." She adjusted her Coach purse strap on her shoulder.

"It's nice to see you again, Mrs. Tabor. I got your message." Tom moved from behind the desk. He led her into the Carolina Room. "I believe we have the information you need, as a few years ago the records were brought here and put on microfilm. We also have the original records. What else did you want to check?"

Carly had her questions ready. "Do you know where executed prisoners from the Provost Dungeon would've been buried? I tried to find it in some of the research I've been doing, but I've struck out."

Tom thought for a moment. "I know the city opened several new burial grounds in the mid to late 1790's due to overcrowding. Once the graveyards filled, new ones needed to be secured. The early forefathers thought the burials were polluting the air."

"A lot of those early graveyards aren't where the early maps indicate. What happened to all the people buried in those graveyards?"

"The graves were moved to new cemeteries as the urban sprawl took over. Just outside here, where the King Street garage is—that's where the old Quaker cemetery used to be." He pointed out the window.

Carly knew of that cemetery, since Peter Faysoux chose it as Andrew Pettigrew's final resting place. "I know they moved coffins for reburial on the Court House yard. Sad, isn't it?" She shook her head. "People moved around like cords of wood."

"It seems it was a common practice. The town didn't know what to do with the dead who weren't church members or were colored. If you're interested in learning more about the city cemeteries, I can show you where we keep those records."

In a short time, Tom brought her the volume containing the years 1790 through 1800. Excited to get started, she sat down at the computer and began her search. She felt as though she was seeing an old friend when Peter Faysoux's name appeared as the first physician to both the Poor House and Orphan Asylum. She stifled a squeal when the name of his daughter, Celeste Pettigrew, was mentioned as one of the Orphan House patrons. The minutes mentioned her in various entries as attending to the children from the years 1794 up until her death in 1799. She was a frequent donor of clothing and food, as well as a teacher during the early years at the Orphan Asylum.

She stopped reading and looked up. Did Celeste volunteer her time to the Orphan House because she was unable to have children of her own? As she searched the text from each of the entries, she wondered if Celeste and Andrew had bonded out one of the orphans.

"Is there anything I can help you with?" Tom popped his head in to check on Carly's progress.

"Actually, there is." She pushed her chair away from the computer. "Where are the records for the names of the children brought in by date, and also who adopted or bonded them out for work?"

Tom walked into the room, searching on another computer. "Yes, we have a book that was transcribed from the original records and minutes. It includes a section on the employees of the Orphan House or Asylum, as it was known, including the names and information on all children who came to the institution."

"You're the bomb, Tom!" Carly patted him on the sleeve of his starched shirt.

"Well, err…thank you, I guess. I think this book also lists the names of the children, the parent or guardian who brought them to the Orphan House, and the whereabouts of the child in regards to bonding out." He handed her the call number. "It also lists the date of death or when the child no longer was a ward of the institution."

"Thank you for locating it. I'd love to see it." She felt like a kid at Christmas.

"I can do you one better, Mrs. Tabor. I'll make you a copy of the sections of the book that you need. I think it holds a wealth of information on the children." He went down the hall, leaving her to revel in this discovery.

During the next hour, she located six different entries listing Celeste Pettigrew's name as a contributor of goods for the nourishment and dress of young boys and girls at the Charleston Orphan Asylum for many years. After fifteen minutes, Tom appeared with several copied pages about the residents of the asylum for her to review.

"I made a quick call over to Harlan Greene, in special collections at the College of Charleston Library and asked him about your question regarding executed prisoners. He said the burial place would depend on whether the family claimed the body." Tom cleared his throat. "And if the event of no next of kin, the body was interred at one of the public burial grounds for poor people and those who didn't have membership in churches." Tom handed her another piece of paper with Harlan Greene's contact number.

"That makes sense, just as Andrew Pettigrew's father-in-law secured his reburial in the Quaker cemetery." She slipped the paper into her folder. "Thank you, for everything."

"Quite welcome. I took the liberty of looking in our collection, and found *The Silence of the Dead: Giving Charleston Cemeteries a Voice*, by Michael Trinkley, which lists all the public and potter's burial grounds in Charleston." He handed her the large volume. "In 1792, the city acquired a public burial ground, "The Strangers and Negro Burial Ground," now bordered by Calhoun Street to the South, Coming Street to the West, Vanderhorst to the North, and St. Philip Street to the East."

"Wonderful! I've wondered where those burial grounds were and that makes perfect sense."

"Charles Fraser, in *Reminiscences of Charleston,* published in the 1850s, wrote about seeing public hangings in that general area as well. Here's a copy of his book for you to review." He laid the book on the table.

"Again, I can't thank you enough, Mr. Drummond. I'll stop by the College of Charleston Library and talk to Mr. Greene," Carly said.

"Glad to help the younger generation develop an interest in our history. Now, is there anything else I can help you locate?"

"I don't believe so, you've been so helpful." She gathered all the copies and notes, and then paid the copying fee and checked out the books.

Down on the street, she squinted at the area around her, trying to put herself back in time and envision the area in 1799. The last time anyone saw Andrew Pettigrew alive, he was having a drink at McCrady's Tavern, not far away on East Bay Street. Farther down Calhoun Street, once called Boundary Street, stood the large building called the Charleston Orphan Asylum, with brick walls around the yard and the poor children within. Fortunately for Celeste, it wouldn't have been that far of a walk to visit the children or help her father to care for either the sick or dying children. According to the minutes, bringing with her fruit and vegetables for the children, as well as fabric for clothing. The Pettigrews had a well-documented benevolent tie to the Orphan House.

She wondered if Andrew Pettigrew had enlisted the help of the inmates at the Orphan House, perhaps using them to do odd jobs for him. There was something about Celeste's connection to the Orphan House and the child in the photograph. "Could this be a child that Celeste and Andrew had adopted, then the child passed away?" Carly pulled her jacket up to her chin, the brisk wind giving her chills. Consulting the map of the cemeteries in the town during the years 1762-1800 that she'd purchased, she could see the potter's burial ground where Hastings may have been buried would have only been a short walk from the Orphan House. She had marked the final resting places of the Pettigrews with a small red dot.

The nip in the air caused her to shiver as she walked along Meeting Street. The streets were brightly decorated for the Christmas season, and the businesses and homes adorned their doors and displays with greenery. She paused before crossing the street to the parking garage. She wished she could see what Celeste Pettigrew saw as she brought her contributions to the children housed within the Orphan House. Wrinkling her nose, she imagined the terrible privy smell would have reached her before she stepped inside the gate. She read in the Orphan House book the city received complaints about the privies and other issues from the large care establishment.

She drove back home, thinking of all the information Tom Drummond located. Reaching into the antique mail holder near their home's door, she retrieved a stack of bills and junk mail, and went inside. She walked into the kitchen, laying the stack of mail on the desk. Out of the corner of her eye, she thought she caught a glimpse of something across the hall in the receiving room. It had been so quiet, so maybe it was nothing. Shaking off the feeling, she made a sandwich and poured a glass of tea. But, an acrid smell wafted into the kitchen. Gun powder. She sensed she wasn't alone in the empty house. "Please don't start this again." But, she had no control over these guests.

Walking into the entry hall, she noticed the smell growing stronger. She waited, and within seconds the apparitions of Andrew and Celeste became clearer. Both stood near the fireplace, their death wounds visible. Still chewing a bite of turkey sandwich, she tried to swallow, but choked as she saw the ghastly sight. On the floor, a pool of crimson progressed towards her, so she stumbled backwards to avoid the mess moving closer to her feet. The scene had never appeared this strong and real. The Pettigrews' outstretched arms appeared to move closer towards her, a silent scream forming on their lips.

Carly screamed, and in her haste to move out of the way, tripped over an object, causing her to tumble to the floor. She lay there grabbing her ankle in pain. The toy horse lay underneath her, causing her to spit out curses as she picked it up and tossed it into the hallway. Surprised, she noticed the clean wooden floorboards showed no bloodstains and the sad couple were no longer in the room. It had all seemed so real this time. Feeling foolish, she tried to stand, putting all her weight on the other foot, but her other ankle throbbed in pain. She hopped into the kitchen, preparing a baggie of ice to place on her swollen ankle.

"Well, this is the last thing I need." She plopped down in the chair, trying to hold the ice on her ankle and calm down. She still wasn't used to seeing the appearance of apparitions, but felt she must accept that it could happen any moment in their home. Delaney told her that she had the sensitive gift, otherwise she wouldn't have seen the apparitions or smelled the gun powder. Carly knew the toy horse signaled the child's presence, who was connected somehow to the Pettigrews and the murder. The Pettigrews were trying to lead them to discover what really happened on the night of their murders.

As Carly set with her foot elevated at the kitchen table, the doorbell rang, causing her to jump. She sat the ice bag on the placemat, limping to the front door. "Come on in! What a nice surprise." She opened the door to Delaney.

"What happened to you?" Delaney looked at Carly leaning on the door frame.

She ushered Delaney into the hall, explaining her tumble and encounter with the Pettigrews.

"Bless your heart, honey. You want me to take that toy horse to my house for a while?" Delaney touched her swollen ankle.

"It isn't too bad. I didn't even see it lying in the floor when I walked into the receiving room. I guess I'm turning into a klutz." Carly shifted in her chair.

"Keep it elevated, and take some ibuprofen." Delaney went over to the freezer to add more ice to the bag.

Carly reached into her files on the table. "I hit the jackpot today! Celeste was an active contributor and visitor to the Orphan House." She handed the copies to Delaney. "I think the child in the photograph is from the Orphan House. That explains his appearance of looking under-nourished and sickly."

Delaney read over the pages. "I think you're on to something. We'll have to concentrate on the child when Boyd and Tucker come on Wednesday. Do you want me to take the toy horse home with me?"

"No, it's okay." Carly gave a sideways glance at the toy still lying in the hallway. "I'll put it inside the armoire upstairs in the nursery. And I'm locking the door this time."

Carly made a pot of hot tea, and they discussed the information that Tom Drummond had located about the indigent and criminal burials within the city.

"I checked out a couple of books on cemeteries, and Tom made copies of the list of all the children entering the Orphan House from 1790-1799. I'll read it tonight." Carly sipped a cup of peach tea.

"Keep me posted on what you find. I'm anxious to get on with the investigation." Delaney handed her the papers. "You've made great progress in finding the answers to questions about the Orphan House and Ben Hastings." The two women agreed that in a couple of days when Boyd and Tucker conducted another investigation, perhaps the house would share some of the secrets it had harbored for the last two hundred years.

Chapter 20

Winter's chill had taken hold in the low country. Carly turned on the gas logs in both the den and receiving room fireplaces to warm up their house in preparation for the paranormal investigators to come later in the day. Walking out the front door to get the newspaper, she noticed the neighbor lady watching her from behind a partially closed curtain. Even though it was awkward, she did what her Kansas upbringing had taught her and waved at the mortified elderly woman. The woman quickly pulled the drapes together. Smiling at the woman's behavior, Carly shook her head and closed the door. As soon as she entered the hallway, her cell phone rang from the kitchen, so she hurried to get her phone. Although the number was not one she recognized, she answered the call.

"May I speak to Carly Tabor, please?" A woman's voice asked.

"This is Carly." She pulled out a stool by the bar and sat down.

"Hello, this is Larae Forrester, and I own the Mount Pleasant Antique Emporium."

"Yes, I remember you. You're from the shop where I bought the toy horse."

"Well, I'm callin' because I've acquired a collection from of the Forsythe family here in Mount Pleasant which might have a connection with the album and toy horse that I sold you. I'm almost certain there were Forsythe names on the back of the photographs you purchased. Would you be interested in taking a look?" Larae asked her.

"That's thoughtful of you to remember me. I'd forgotten I left my name and telephone number with you." Carly thought for a moment, would this be helpful information?

"It surprised me when I saw the name on the items. I purchased the lot of goods I sold you from the same dealer whose husband was the auctioneer for the estate sale. Do you think you'd want to have a look… if you're interested, that is?"

"Oh yes, I'm very interested. I can stop by later in the week, if you wouldn't mind holding them." Carly wrote herself a note on her calendar to stop by the store.

"Surely, I'd be happy to put them back for you. The family tree is written on silk; it contains several generations. The birth and death records date back to the early 1700s. That'd be an early Charleston family connection." Larae's voice sounded excited about the discovery.

Carly thanked her, pleased to have another piece of local history to display, if the price wasn't too high. She wrote herself a note to drive out to Mount Pleasant on Thursday.

Carly spent the afternoon cleaning house. She wanted everything ready when the paranormal investigators and Delaney arrived. The pot of chili she'd prepared filled the kitchen with a delicious aroma. She put a few beers in the refrigerator in case the guests wanted something stronger than sweet tea. Hearing the doorbell, she opened the door to her friends. Delaney gave Carly a hug as she stepped into the house, and Boyd hugged her, too. He introduced his partner, Tucker McGee, to them. Tucker was a handsome man in his mid-thirties, with short dark hair, spiked up into a faux hawk, which gave him a more youthful appearance. She invited the trio into her kitchen, offering them some chili. She'd been brought up to feed her guests, whether it was a plate of cookies or a sit-down meal.

"If nothing else comes of our investigations, we always get a good meal out of it." Boyd patted his flat stomach and winked at Tucker.

The foursome sat around the table, with Carly and Delaney providing Tucker an update on the spirit activity in the house. Carly shared with the group the latest encounter with the Pettigrews and the possible connection of Celeste with the Orphan House children.

"I'm starting to believe the spirit of the child is an orphan Celeste knew. I don't know how they're connected, but she spent a lot of time there. A good portion of Andrew's money went there after he and Celeste passed." Carly finished setting the table and put the pot of chili on the table.

"Boyd showed me the investigation he did a couple of weeks ago, and it seems the house is an active location. Maybe the child will reveal himself tonight. We'll put cameras down in the cellar as well as placin' the thermal cameras throughout the downstairs." Tucker helped himself to chili and poured a beer.

After the meal, everyone pitched in to help clean up. The group carried in the equipment from Boyd's SUV. The set up took about forty-five minutes, with Boyd and Tucker placing the cameras on each of the three levels. Cameras were specifically placed in the "hot spots"—the receiving room, kitchen, nursery, and cellar. As Carly led Boyd and Tucker into the cellar, all of them immediately felt the drop in temperature. Tucker blew into his hands as he set the cameras in various areas of the cellar.

"I don't like it down here. Delaney and I have seen Benjamin Hastings down here and had a few scary encounters." Carly shuddered, remembering their fright.

Boyd surveyed the cellar noting its construction. "Wonder why the window was closed long ago with cinder blocks? These large stones on the cellar walls are also interesting."

"The contractor assumed a previous owner closed off the cellar in the 1800s. All we were told is the wall started showing structural issues and the Hutchinsons had it re-done when they moved the heating and cooling down here." Carly shivered and rubbed her arms.

"Okay, we'll keep the thermal camera on down here, as well as puttin' another video camera down in this area," Tucker adjusted the camera stand and put the camera back on the tripod.

"Carly, do you have the metal horse downstairs? I'd like to use it as a trigger object," Boyd asked as they climbed the stairs.

"No, after my last encounter, I stuck it back in the armoire upstairs." Carly left her spot at the make-shift command center and walked to the nursery. She hesitated, feeling the fear of a child walking into a dark room. She adjusted the flashlight to shine throughout the room. Reaching inside the armoire, she took the small toy rocking horse and made a hasty retreat to join the others.

"From the notes you've taken, I can see that it's a trigger object for the child. We're goin' to use it to communicate with him." Tucker placed the toy horse on the floor beside the barrel-back chair in the receiving room.

"This room is the most common location, but we've found it all over the house." Carly studied the spot where the crimson stain had inched towards her just hours before.

At six-thirty, the city had grown dark, and Carly and Delaney began turning out the lights. Everyone had flashlights, and Carly took the first shift of watching the split-screens on the computers in the den. Boyd,

Tucker, and Delaney each carried walkie-talkies, while Carly was given a small walkie-talkie to communicate with the others from her position in the den. The group hoped it wouldn't take too long for the host of spirits in the Tabor house to make their introductions.

The weather outside on this cold December evening was eerily similar to the reported weather on the night centuries ago that Benjamin Hastings entered the cellar of the Pettigrews' King Street home. A wintry mix of rain and sleet pelted the windows, as the street lamps outside sparkled with minuscule ice pellets clinging to the iron globes.

Carly let her mind wander to the image of the young boy holding the toy horse. Boyd and Tucker finished checking the cameras and batteries, while Carly walked over to the small desk to retrieve the photograph of the boy. "Tucker, I don't believe you've seen this before. It's amazing that he's holding the toy horse," Carly commented.

Tucker studied the image, then, handed it back to Carly. "That is one of the clearest images of an apparition that I've ever seen."

"I feel like the child wants to make contact with us, but the dark spirit, Ben Hastings, controls the house," Delaney said. The investigators agreed that might be possible.

Carly's job consisted of monitoring the split computer screens of the group from the den and she had a walkie-talkie to communicate with the others. Carly sat transfixed, watching the three on the split screen of the computer. Delaney walked into the hallway with a flashlight, her attention drawn to the front of the home. Boyd held the digital voice recorder and K-II meter, while Tucker held a mini digital video camera and spirit box. Both had head lamps affixed to a band around their heads.

"Celeste, are you able to speak with us tonight?" Carly heard Boyd ask, as he watched for any signs of an EVP on the device.

She saw Delaney close her eyes and Carly heard her speak slowly on the walkie-talkie: "It's a raw winter evening, there's someone coming down the street, the rain is starting to turn to sleet. I see a person on the street in front of me. It appears to be a man, but I can't tell who. He's going the same direction as I am."

Carly observed Tucker join Delaney in the hallway and heard them ask questions. "Andrew, were you coming home after drinking at Mc-Cradys Tavern with Jacob Hinman?" Delaney asked.

"Is there a little boy with us tonight?" Carly heard Boyd question on the two-way radio. Carly watched the screen, looking for any anomaly to appear.

Delaney walked back into the receiving room. "Did anyone else hear a woman's voice?"

"I think we got something on here, Tuck." Boyd watched the light flash in rapid succession on the K-II.

"Keep talking, Boyd, I think you're getting something." Carly watched and heard Tucker hurry into the receiving room.

"Celeste, can you see who is in the room with Andrew?" Delaney stood in the center of the room, her eyes closed.

Carly heard the K-II meter, as well as the spirit box, set off a series of sounds and lights, and "*shot*" came across the display, and the word was repeated by the spirit box. Carly leaned in toward the screen, straining her eyes to pick up anything that might appear.

"Who got shot?" Tucker turned to the doorway.

Carly made a note of the time and watched a small orb appear on the nursery camera, streaking across the room. She noticed a similar anomaly appearing in the receiving room, and noted it.

"Celeste, we know Ben Hastings shot you, and he shot Andrew. He paid for his crime." Delaney looked down. "I'm seeing the word *"run"* appear on the spirit box.

"Celeste, who do you want to run? We know someone else is here; who're you tryin' to protect?" Carly would hear Tucker asking and saw him looking into the hallway.

"We smell gun powder, and it's strong. Carly, can you see anything?" Boyd waited for Carly to respond.

Carly watched on the computer screen as Delaney reached for the fireplace mantel and heard her say, "She took a ball in the heart." Delaney reached to her chest, as if hit herself.

From the den, Carly watched Delaney close her eyes, and saw her friend choreograph the murder scene.

"Something moved over there, but it's dark in here. There's blood everywhere on the floor; Andrew is bleedin', the look of terror frozen on his face. The flame from the fire is casting a glow onto the pool of blood. I see Benjamin Hastings, holding the pistol, its barrel still smoldering from the two shots he fired." Delaney kneeled before the fireplace.

Carly watched Boyd and heard him ask. "What else do you see, Celeste? Someone else was in the house that night. Who was it?"

Carly watched a filmy mist appear on the camera in the cellar, while upstairs she heard the spirit box squawk, "*boy*." Tucker, Boyd, and Delaney heard the word too. Carly watched the mist move out of the camera's view.

"So there was a child here—I knew it!" Carly observed Delaney moving closer to Boyd.

"I'm seeing some activity in the cellar on the digital camera." Carly radioed everyone and documented the time of occurrence.

"Celeste, you don't have to be afraid of Ben Hastings. He's gone." She saw Delaney turn toward the doorway. "Tucker, Benjamin Hastings is here."

Carly watched the thermal camera positioned in the kitchen. Her heart skipped a beat when the outline of something glowed red in the doorway.

"He's not happy, and it looks like he still has a rope around his neck." Carly heard Delaney report.

"I'm seeing a form on the thermal camera, guys. It looks like the shape of a man." Carly noted the change in temperature in the doorway.

She saw Boyd move closer to the door, holding the spirit box. "Carly, do you see anything else?" Boyd spoke into his walkie-talkie.

Carly looked at all the cameras displayed on the screen. The image on the thermal camera had faded to a light purple, showing a very cold temperature. As she watched the image change on the screen before her eyes, the spirit box said "*dark.*"

Carly felt her chest begin to get heavier with the smothered feeling, and the room's temperature began falling.

"Carly, are you seein' anything on the thermal?" Boyd repeated on the walkie-talkie.

Feeling light-headed, Carly tried to remain calm, not wanting to stop the investigation. In a split second, the K-II meter with Boyd began flashing, Delaney suddenly reported she saw someone running through the house.

"I'm fine, just light-headed for a moment. I don't see anything, other than everyone's breath when they speak." Carly heard her heartbeat growing louder in her ears.

"Someone's running through the hallway. I can't tell who it is, though. It's too dark." She watched Delaney move into the kitchen.

Carly watched Boyd look down at the digital recorder and spirit box.

Soon, everyone heard the now familiar sound reverberating throughout the house, causing the three investigators to move into the entry hall.

"Let's split up. Delaney, you stay on this level. Boyd, you take the second floor, and I'm goin' down in the cellar." Carly heard Tucker say, and she saw him pick up the large lantern flashlight.

Carly watched the trio move in the darkness, their headlamps and flashlight moving slowly to their assigned locations. She was still feeling short of breath, and the beating of her heart was now followed by a wave of nausea. Trying to resist fear and not be overwhelmed by panic, she breathed deeply and slowly. It was then that she heard the crying, soft at first.

"Does anyone hear crying?" Carly asked into her walkie-talkie. The pitiful sound seemed to be coming from within the den.

"I'm just hearing the banging, nothing else." Delaney tilted her head to listen.

"The banging is quite loud up here. It is coming through the walls." Boyd speaks into his walkie-talkie.

Carly observed Tucker standing in the middle of the cellar, his head lamp lighting a small section of the room. He shook his head to show he couldn't hear what the others were saying over the two-way radio.

"I'm not hearing any crying, just the banging. And it is colder than a gravedigger's knee down here." Tucker commented on his radio. "I feel like someone else is here too."

At the same instant, Carly saw something appear on the screen in the receiving room, or more accurately, something disappear.

"The toy horse is gone, y'all. Did one of you move it?" She heard Delaney looked around the room.

Neither had moved the horse. Carly looked at the screen, shifting her weight in the chair. She tried to get a better look at the images displayed on the monitor while steadying herself. It was then that she felt something beside her.

"He's here!" Carly's voice cut through the static of the radios. She turned towards something only she could see. "Oh my goodness, the boy's here with me." Feeling the room begin to swirl around her, she lost consciousness.

Delaney darted into the den to find Carly slumped over in the chair, the small toy horse lying beside her.

"Boyd, Tucker, come back to the den! Carly's passed out!" Delaney yelled and then put her radio in her back pocket; she tried to help Carly sit upright. "Oh my goodness, I can see the child just sittin' on the floor beside Carly! His eyes are so dark—he's the boy in the photograph. Wait, he just disappeared!"

By the time Boyd and Tucker reached the den, Carly began regaining consciousness.

"What happened?" Carly said, unsure what had happened.

"You said he's here, the boy is here." Delaney helped her into the chair.

"I saw him holding the toy horse." Carly took a drink from her glass of tea.

"When I came in and found you slumped over in the chair, I saw the boy on the floor for a split second. It was the boy in the photograph," Delaney said.

Boyd walked over to the computer desk, making sure to hit 'save', just in case.

"Are you okay? Do you want us to stop the investigation?" Boyd asked.

"No! I'm fine. He's never appeared to me or anyone before. We're too close now." Carly straightened in her chair and adjusted the earphones.

"Carly, we can take a break." Tucker sat on the arm of the loveseat, clearly shaken by the experience.

"Before you passed out, I had the feeling I wasn't alone in the cellar. It was like someone moved behind me. It's been awhile since I felt that way." Tucker shifted his K-II meter back and forth in his hands.

"Every time Celeste tries to make contact, Benjamin Hastings appears, along with a drop in temperature. We've all felt it. This time, the boy made contact and moved the horse." Delaney summed up their experiences. "Were you here in the house when the Pettigrews died?" Delaney lowered her voice to a gentle cadence to engage the child and perhaps draw him back into the room.

As if cued by an unseen director, the crying began, followed by a banging louder than ever.

"Did you run out of the house before the bad man saw you?" Boyd changed his tenor as if talking to a child.

"Did Celeste tell you to run?" Tucker prodded gently, speaking above the clamor as he noticed a change on the thermal camera.

Carly looked to the screen, watching a mist move in the receiving room, disappearing into the wall.

"I saw a mist move from the receiving room. Delaney, it moved in your direction." As Carly described what she saw, Delaney walked into the hallway.

"Celeste, we know the boy's here." Carly heard Delaney speak louder. "Is that who you want us to help? Wow, I felt something move past me, as if a whirlwind crossed through the room."

The spirit box broke the long silence, divulging a name: "*Freddy*". The weeping stopped and the banging ceased. The house became as quiet as a tomb.

Chapter 21

The name "Freddy" still displayed on the spirit box echoing throughout the house. Finally, the group had another name to help figure out the mystery.

"Thank you, Celeste." Delaney walked into the hallway, feeling the spirit activity had ceased for the night.

In the den, the clock displayed 12:47 am. The investigation had lasted roughly six hours.

"Wow, this was a long spirit contact. Let's get the lights up and get back to my house. I need to go over all the time stamps and digital evidence while it's all fresh in my mind." Boyd walked over to the main light switch in the hallway. Turning to Tucker, he asked, "Do you wanna crash at my house tonight?"

"Yeah, that's fine. Let me send Jill a text so she won't freak out if she wakes up, and I'm still not home." Tucker took his phone from the holder on his belt. "The wife doesn't always understand my crazy hours."

"Thank you both, for everything," Carly said, hugging both men.

"Hey, it's our pleasure getting to investigate such a great place. There's a lot of evidence to go over tonight. Try and get some rest, okay?" Boyd squeezed Carly's shoulder.

For the next forty-five minutes, the group disassembled the cameras and computer monitors, along with the sound system and miles of extension cords. By 2 a.m., the equipment was inside Boyd's Explorer, and everyone was ready to leave.

"Thanks again, and give me a call when you can meet up to go over the investigation," Carly reminded them and the men left the house.

Carly walked into the kitchen where Delaney was sitting at the table. "Are you okay, kiddo? You really scared me there for a minute when you passed out."

"Yeah, I'm fine." Carly walked over to the sink to fill her kettle. "How about a cup of chamomile tea to settle our nerves?"

"Tomorrow, after you've gotten some rest, we'll start our search for Freddy. But for now, you need your rest—after a cup of chamomile tea." Delaney dug through her purse to find her keys.

"It's late, why don't you stay with us tonight?" Carly poured the hot tea.

"Now don't worry, I'll send you a text the minute I walk in the house. I'll be fine." Delaney walked to the door, followed by Carly.

"Thanks again for arranging the investigation tonight. We know the boy's name, thanks to you." She hugged Delaney goodbye before opening the door for her to leave.

Even after sipping some chamomile tea, Carly's nerves were still on edge after the evening's events, so she went upstairs to take a hot bath. She hated to admit it, but she felt afraid to be alone. In the months of seeing and hearing the unexplainable, seeing the boy affected her in a different way. The look of terror on his face kept haunting Carly's thoughts. As she let the warm bubbles soothe the tense muscles in her neck and back, she heard a text come in on her cell phone in the bedroom. She decided to ignore it in favor of relaxing in the much-deserved soak. After her soothing bath, she came into her bedroom and checked her phone to read a text from Delaney, "Sweet dreams. We'll chat tomorrow. D."

However, Carly couldn't get the image of the little boy out of her mind. It was one thing to see the boy in a photograph, but it was quite another to see him sitting beside her, his dark eyes staring into hers. What became of you, Freddy? Her eyes welled with tears thinking of the pitiful waif. She curled into her comforting nest of blankets and tried to sleep.

At eight o'clock, Carly rolled over, squinting to see the time on the clock. She saw the blurry image of Austin, sleeping soundly beside her. She assumed he crawled in bed sometime during the early morning hours, as she tossed and turned until after four. She started to rise, but felt a wave of nausea overtake her. Still feeling shaky from the previous night's fainting spell, she eased back onto the bed. The room continued to spin for a moment. Carly waited until the nausea passed before making another attempt to rise from bed.

Finally, at nine o'clock, she plodded into the kitchen. Nothing sounded good for breakfast, so she opted for a cup of tea and a blueberry muffin. Turning around, she noticed the small reminder, a post-it note affixed to the counter reading *Thursday~ Mount Pleasant Antique Emporium- Larae* . Carly sipped the hot tea, enjoying the sensation of the liquid easing down her throat and into her empty stomach. She'd forgotten about the appointment to see the items related to the picture album and toy horse.

Before she finished her muffin, Austin stumbled into the kitchen. He bent to kiss the back of Carly's neck.

"Well good morning to you, too." She leaned back to enjoy the stubble of his unshaven cheek against her neck. Austin made a pot of coffee, and the smell wafted across the room to her.

"How'd it go last night?" He peered into the refrigerator for something to eat.

"It went well, I think. We found out the name of the boy in the picture. Delaney and I both saw him." She nibbled her muffin.

"What? You saw him?" Austin shut the door abruptly, turning to face his wife.

"Yes, he sat beside me in the den. It scared the bejeebers out of me. I actually fainted!"

"Are you okay?" He placed his hand on her forehead. "You look a little pale this morning."

"I feel a little weak. I know it sounds strange, but I think Benjamin Hastings is the cause. Every time I hear crying or get close to finding out what Celeste is trying to show me, I feel like I can't breathe." She took a sip of tea.

"Why don't you let me make an appointment with one of the doctors at the hospital? Something else could be wrong, so let's get you checked out." He brought her another muffin and sat down beside her.

"If I'm not feeling better after the holidays, I'll get checked out, okay?"

"Okay, but after you get back from seeing your family, you're going in for a physical. Deal?" Austin patted her hand.

"Deal." Carly shrugged. "Now, stop acting like a doctor and be my hubby. I need a hug before you leave for the hospital."

Carly felt better by lunchtime. She took a granola bar and bottled water with her as she hurried out the door for Mount Pleasant. But, she couldn't get the image of the little boy out of her mind. It was one thing to see the boy in a photograph, but it was another to see him sitting beside her, his dark eyes staring into hers. What became of you, Freddy? Carly thought, her eyes welling with tears at the memory of this pitiful waif.

When she arrived at the antique shop, Larae was sitting behind the large counter. *Dressed to the nines,* as Carly's mother would say. Many of Charleston's upper income ladies did dress as if each day were a fashion show. Larae Forrester, with her auburn coiffure and artificial tan, looked much younger than her likely age of mid-fifties. Her manicured nails were painted a salsa shade of red, and her slender fingers showcased several antique gold rings.

She said hello when Carly entered, and she introduced herself. "Hi, I'm Carly Tabor. You called me yesterday about some items you thought I'd like to see."

Putting her book down, she hopped off the stool. "Of course, I remember! Please, come back into the office, hon. I have the items in there."

Carly followed Larae into the office where she lifted a large box from a shelf. "This came in last weekend, and I immediately thought of you. Although I couldn't place your name, it only took a minute to go back through my receipts and find you."

"You must keep excellent records, because that was way back in July."

"I loved the items you purchased, and the lady who brought them here was a long-time friend of my mother." Larae moved a box out of her way. "The Forsythes were intimate friends of Miss Jalene's, and she'd saved several items from their family and brought them in last week."

The first of the items was a large hand-written family tree. Carly watched as Larae unrolled the delicate treasure, careful not to rip the delicate item. In total, the finished piece measured three feet across by four feet tall. The tree itself was a work of art, traced onto the slik material colored in pastel water colors now beginning to fade from age.

The artist had inscribed each name with beautiful penmanship. The tree began with the year 1647. Carly noticed the name *Forsythe* listed on a branch of the tree. Listed closer to the top of the tree, near the year 1710, was the surname *Faysoux.*

Carly gasped, causing Larae to jump. "What's wrong?"

"I saw a name I recognized. I'll take it...all of it." Carly hadn't even seen the rest of the items in the box.

"You want it all? Wouldn't you like to see the rest? Some of it is quite old." Larae's well-groomed brows arched in disbelief.

"No, I want all of it. What do I owe you today?" She rifled through her wallet for her credit card.

In total, Carly had purchased without seeing several other items for over $500: an 1850 antique china doll—with chest, a gutta percha mourning cameo, and an original Civil War portrait of General Bernard Bee, a relative of the Faysoux family. Other items were likely pre-Civil War era, possibly Revolutionary War. Her purchases went into several large boxes, which Larae wheeled out to Carly's car on a dolly.

"I hope you enjoy the Forsythe collection, although I'm not sure why you're so interested in them. I put the paper that went with the photo album inside the box. Come back and see me sometime soon." Larae waved goodbye to her.

Carly closed the car door and sat in disbelief and begin to feel nauseous. The large purchase was the first she'd made without first seeing everything. What were the odds that Peter Faysoux would be the ancestor of the Forsythe family in the photo album? How ironic that the owner of the toy horse had transfixed the spirit of a long-dead boy into the present. She made it home in time to see Austin walking into the house. He met her at the door, "Looks like we timed that just right, sweetie!"

"Hey, handsome! Want to help me haul in my loot from the antique mall?" She hoped the cost of her loot wouldn't come up because she felt guilty.

Austin closed the door and walked out to the car, seeing the large box inside the trunk. "Did you get all of this at the antique shop in Mount Pleasant? I hate to ask what you spent."

"What would you say if I told you the toy horse that keeps moving around our house once belonged to an ancestor of Celeste Pettigrew?" Carly avoided the question.

"Are you kidding me? How did you find out about that?" Austin sat the box down in the receiving room.

She carefully removed the family tree from the box, laying it on the large wooden coffee table.

"Well, if that doesn't beat all! If I didn't see it, I wouldn't believe it. Peter Faysoux's name is right here, and his son, Elias," Austin mused, looking over the family tree.

"My Granny Evans would call it a 'God thing.' How else can you explain it? It goes to prove why Freddy wants the horse. It belonged to Celeste's great-great-nephew. It gives me chills." She placed the family tree inside a tissue paper-lined container.

Carly began removing the rest of the items and sharing with Austin. She admired the small china head doll dressed in original 1850's clothing, noticing the perfect condition of not only her clothing, but the original sawdust stuffed body. Next, she removed a small wooden butter mold. A yellowed piece of paper with faint, but legible handwriting: *This butter mold belonged to the Elias Faysoux family of Charleston, South Carolina, 1820,* was stuffed inside the mold. Turning the mold over in her hands, she felt thrilled to hold an item that once belonged to Celeste's brother.

The next treasure she unwrapped was a miniature of a young woman, with dark brown hair in curled locks held back with a thin gold band. The portrait once hung as necklace on a black velvet ribbon, now faded and threadbare. Was this a portrait of Celeste Faysoux Pettigrew? She stared at the image of their ghost…the likeness was convincing.

"Honey, I hope you didn't spend more than our house payment on this box?" Austin examined the portrait. "This isn't yard sale stuff here."

After she confessed the considerable amount paid for the items, she waited for the sermon sure to come, but what she heard was quite the contrary.

"You have a good eye for antiques, and I think it was meant for you to have it. Like it or not, we inherited the ghosts as baggage from this family. We might as well have something to show for it." He tugged on her ponytail and kissed her.

She stood, her arms reaching around him in an embrace that was as much in gratitude as in relief.

"Before we look at the rest of your treasures, I want to show you something." He led her to the den, and Carly eyes widened. While she was in Mount Pleasant, he'd carried down all the holiday boxes from the attic and put up their Christmas tree.

"You're the best. Thank you for doing this!" She kissed his cheek.

"Well, I had some time since I got called off rounds today." He pulled her closer. "My patient didn't make it."

"Oh, I'm sorry." She tightened her embrace.

"I worried she wouldn't make it, but she didn't pass until I got to the hospital. I wanted to speak with her family before coming home. Dr. Lowe checked on my other patients during early rounds this morning. I wish I could've saved her... Carly, she was only sixteen." His voice cracked.

She hugged him again, feeling the tension in his body. He kept his grief inside when he lost a patient, but his feelings over the loss of a child were hard to hide.

"I guess you needed to keep busy. Thank you for bringing all the totes down for me. Maybe we can decorate the house together later?" She touched the bows of the tree. "I want to finish exploring this treasure chest first."

The rest of the afternoon, she finished going through the items in the box and found several Civil War items belonging to the famed South Carolina general, Bernard Bee. His family tied in with the Faysoux family tree. The delicate *carte de visite* showed him in uniform, along with a small palmetto cockade on a black mourning ribbon. A note attached read: *General Bernard Bee, killed at the First Battle of Manassas, July 1861.* She found a small leather wallet containing a paper explaining General Bee died honorably after encouraging his South Carolina regiment to rally around the Virginians, as their general, Thomas Jackson, stood like a stone wall during the battle. He would forever be known as "Stonewall" after General Bee's admonition. "Well for goodness sakes. This is a piece of history for sure!" She packed the items into the box again.

The afternoon turned to evening, and at six o'clock, when they sat down to eat dinner, Carly's cell rang. She recognized the incoming number and answered.

"Hey Carly, it's Boyd Hawley. How are ya doing now?"

"Hi Boyd. I'm feeling much better, thank you." She raised her eyebrows to Austin; both were anxious to hear what Boyd had to say. She put her phone on speaker.

"Tuck and I finished reviewin' all the evidence. We captured quite a few EVPs on the digital recorder, and we picked up a couple of surprises to boot. If possible, I'd love to meet with you and Austin, when he's available," Boyd asked.

"Of course, just name the day and time." She winked at Austin.

"I was thinkin' about Friday evening. Would that work for y'all?"

"I think that's fine. Hold on a minute." She looked at Austin who shrugged his shoulders. "He'll have to check his schedule tomorrow morning, but I'll be able to come. Do you want me to call Delaney?"

"Thanks, that'd be great, hon. Just give me a buzz if y'all can't make it tomorrow. I was thinking around six for dinner and movie- my treat!" He laughed at his joke.

"It's a date. Thanks!" Carly put her hand up for Austin to give her a 'high five'.

"I'll text you directions to my house. It's in Goose Creek. Goodbye for now."

After their call ended, Carly sent a text to Delaney who confirmed she could attend then as well.

On Friday evening, Austin and Carly left their home and traveled out of the city to Boyd's house in Goose Creek, a pleasant thirty minute drive. His two-story home was typical of the stylish suburban homes in the area. The stone colored siding on the house with dark green shutters had a nice curb appeal, augmented with pink crepe myrtle trees and Confederate Jasmine curling up the side of the lower porch. Delaney's non-descript small car was already parked in the driveway, and just as they walked up to the green front door, Tucker McGee roared up in his glossy black Escalade. They waited for Tucker and all entered Boyd's house together.

Boyd Hawley had decorated his home in a contemporary style, with masculine accents of dark colors. Although Carly knew he'd been divorced she didn't notice any photographs of children, so she assumed they had no children together. Right away, Boyd asked for drink orders. Austin declined, as he was on call. Carly, Delaney, and Tucker each requested a glass of white wine and made small talk about the unusual cold snap while Boyd finished a gumbo they could smell simmering on the stove. Carly teased Boyd about his ability to cook making him a good catch.

During the meal, Carly shared the box of family memorabilia and the family tree she'd purchased. The group marveled over the connection of the toy horse to the Faysoux family. They agreed with Carly's hypothesis that it was a connection showing the crying child ghost in the house wanted to be close to Celeste's ghost in some way.

Following a tasty pecan pie dessert, the group gathered in the family room, which contained a large seventy-inch television mounted above a large gas log fireplace. The soft leather furniture made the room cozy, as the soft flames of the fireplace illuminated the room with its warm glow.

Boyd positioned his equipment on the sofa table and began the anticipated show. "Tucker and I spent most of Thursday morning going over the different camera shots from the investigation. It seems like the upstairs camera caught a few orbs, but nothing substantial." Boyd cued the recording to the time stamp he wanted to share.

"One thing we noticed was the K-II meter did a great job pickin' up on EVPs that happened in y'all's receiving room," Tucker added.

Carly shared that she'd noted several orbs and mists in that room throughout the evening.

"We listened to all the EVPs, and a couple of them were clear as a bell. I'll let you listen to the ones that we picked up when Boyd was trying to draw out Celeste. I think you were talking to her as well, Delaney." Tucker turned up the volume on the video recording.

As the static cleared, the group heard the word, *"run."* Boyd advanced the video recorder to the next EVP. The voice was a child, and it followed after Boyd asked if there was a child in the house. The sound of the small child's voice was sad and chilling, *"it's dark. I'm scared."*

Carly looked at Delaney, and tears welled up in both of their eyes, in response to the sound of Freddy's voice.

"We played it back to the time stamp on the notes you made, Carly. It came before the temperature dropped. That was when we got the next EVP. This one left us both a little freaked out." Tucker rubbed his hands together.

The sound of Carly's voice came on first, advising the group of a dark orange glow on the thermal camera. Carly grabbed onto Austin's hand when the next voice came over the recording. She'd heard him tell her to get out of the house before, and it was the same deep and gruff voice who said, *"dead"* and *"all die."*

"Did you get anything when Carly saw the apparition of Freddy?" Delaney shifted her position on the couch.

Tucker moved to the laptop, programming the video image of the investigation to stream to the large television. The group watched as each camera followed the group in night vision. The camera captured their breath as they questioned the spirits of Celeste and Hastings. They saw the large orb near the toy horse, visible on the floor. The camera stopped, no image visible, at the moment Carly tells the group the horse and the boy are in the room with her.

"That is amazing. We have proof of the boy Freddy communicating. We also have Celeste giving the name of the child. Now we have to figure out what happened to Freddy." Carly turned around to face Boyd and Tucker.

"We captured the banging sound on the digital recorder, but we tried to hear the cryin'. It wasn't until Delaney hears it that Carly time-stamps it. I went back this morning to amplify the digital recorder at that moment, and this is what I got." Boyd cued the video recording.

"The crying was very low, but as we cleared the clutter and noise, it was obvious the boy was speaking between sobs," Tucker whispered.

The sound of Freddy's small voice uttered, *"can't breathe"*, then *"afraid."*

For a long time, the group sat completely silent, affected by Freddy's small voice giving an account centuries later of what likely became of him. Boyd replayed the two EVPs so that the group could hear them back to back.

"Carly, wherever Freddy was, he didn't make it. From the sounds in the house, the banging and crying, it would make sense to assume the child died in the house." Tucker exchanged looks with Austin, who put his arm around his wife.

Carly felt shocked; it was one thing to have murders committed in the house, but harder to process that a small, innocent child died alone in the darkness. The rest of the findings on the digital recorder and cameras were harder to distinguish.

"So, what do you suggest we do? Damn it, they're causing Carly to be physically ill, and the ghosts have even appeared to my family." Austin moved his arm down to take Carly's hand.

"Several times, I've felt the sensation of choking, or shortness of breath, whenever I hear the crying. Do you think it's how Freddy died?" Carly leaned over the back of the couch, looking at the screen.

"Maybe, but I'd like to try to get Freddy to communicate with me. I saw images of the street and someone walking to the house. Maybe it was Freddy?" Delaney asked.

"Carly, how do ya feel about another go at it with just Delaney? Maybe he would connect with both of you women. He's drawn to you for sure," Boyd said.

"You might do some searching in the information about who Freddy was. Didn't you get names of the orphans from the time Celeste was volunteering there?" Tucker continued to advance the video on his laptop.

Boyd and Tucker provided the equipment and the ability to bring to light the name of the child, Carly thought. The picture of the child and the connection of the horse to the descendants of the Faysoux family members only strengthened her belief the child was from the Charleston Orphan Asylum.

"Okay, I'll start tomorrow. I have records from the Historical Society printed out listing the inmates at the Orphan Asylum. After this, we have a first name to search." Carly was encouraged by the new information.

"And I'm pretty sure Freddy is still in your house. He's never left." Boyd turned off his computer.

Austin stood, extending his hand to first Boyd, then Tucker. "Thank you both for all you've done, and Carly and I appreciate it. We're ready for these ghost people to move out of our dream home."

"You're welcome. We haven't investigated a house with so much activity in a long time. It has such a connection to early Charleston history." Boyd shook Austin's outstretched hand.

"If you want us to come back, just let us know. Been a pleasure to work with you both." Tucker shook hands with both of them.

On the ride back to their house, Austin and Carly recounted hearing the voices of Benjamin Hastings and Freddy. She felt that Freddy had crossed whatever barrier was keeping him from communicating. She told him that perhaps Benjamin Hastings was losing his hold and they could finally reclaim their house.

Chapter 22

After returning home from Boyd's house, Austin and Carly retired for the evening. While showering, she sensed someone watching her. Thinking Austin was goofing around, she wiped the condensation from the shower door, finding she was alone in the bathroom. As she finished her bedtime routine and climbed into bed, he put his book on his nightstand, holding the covers so she could slide in.

"Sweet dreams. Love you." He kissed her and rolled over to face the opposite side of the bed. She pulled the blanket up to her chin, trying to shake the feeling of someone being in the room.

At 3 A.M., she was awakened by a dull thump. She sat upright, trying to distinguish the origin of the sound. In a few moments, she heard it again. This time the sound grew louder, and she heard the faint crying, but Austin didn't stir. He really needed his sleep for his early morning, so she didn't wake him. Summoning her nerve, she threw off her covers and picked up a small flashlight from her nightstand. The light outside on the street illuminated the hallway through the piazza doorway. She moved like a prowler, down the stairway, stopping to peer into the lower hall. The flashlight shone against the front door, into the den, further up the hall, and the entrance into the receiving room.

Advancing into the receiving room, something caught Carly's eye. The panel which hid the wall safe was ajar. Her first thought was an intruder had left the safe open. She turned on the hall light, illuminating the rooms on either side, and then opened the safe to check that the deed and other important papers were all accounted for. However, what she didn't expect was the apparition of Celeste Pettigrew to appear standing in the hallway, her hand outstretched, beckoning her to follow. Carly nearly screamed with surprise, even though she felt this spirit meant her no harm.

Following her to the cellar door, she watched as Celeste disappeared into a vapor. The door had remained locked since Austin's encounter, but had been open during the investigation two nights before. She touched the knob wary of being shocked, as it had done to Austin. The sobbing continued, becoming softer. The banging stopped. Carly waited, frozen in indecision about whether to go into the cellar and dreading what she might see. Before she could decide, she heard what sounded like a hammer striking wood resonating from the cellar. Losing her nerve, she ran from the kitchen to her bedroom, not stopping to see if anyone gave chase. Terrified, she leaped into bed, causing Austin to wake.

"What's wrong?" He sat up, looking frantic.

"I heard crying again, so I went downstairs…the safe was open, everything of ours appears to be there. But, Celeste was standing there." She scooted closer to him. "I was so afraid, but she wanted me to follow her to the cellar, so I did."

"Hon, you followed her to the cellar? What if you'd run into robbers in the house?" He slid back under the covers, pulling her down onto his chest.

"I watched her walk through the cellar door! Then the crying stopped, and I heard a sound like a hammer striking wood. Maybe an intruder is hiding down there!" Carly buried her face in his chest.

"Okay, I'll go down there and make sure it's nothing. Just stay up here, all right?" He reached into his bedside table, pulling out his larger steel flashlight that could be used as a weapon. He pushed his glasses on before walking down in the cellar to whatever awaited him.

But, if intruders were inside Austin might be at risk and out-numbered! He needed a back-up just in case. Carly grabbed her flashlight and followed him. She watched as he tip-toed into the kitchen, not making a sound as he turned the knob on the cellar door. She stood in the hallway, watching as he placed his foot onto the first step. The crying started again. Hiding in the hallway, she felt the temperature drop. Under her breath, she whispered, "God, please keep him safe."

Austin's voice carried up from the cellar below. "Freddy? Where are you?" Austin called. The crying grew louder, followed with a loud banging noise.

Carly edged into the dark kitchen, listening to the sounds. She moved toward the cellar door, pausing to grab a long metal flashlight from a drawer in case she needed to protect them. But, Austin heard her.

"Sweetie, I thought I asked you to stay upstairs?" He turned and looked up the stairs. "Go back to bed, there's no one down here. But, I do see a cap or stone cover on the stone floor that runs along the section of the wall that previously led outside. Wonder what its purpose was? I'll call our builder to see if he knows."

"I want to come down there to see it." She called downstairs and shone the flashlight down the stairs from her vantage point to the opposite side of the room.

The crying grew louder. After seeing that no one was hiding in the cellar, Austin pulled the string to turn off the light bulb.

"No, please, it's okay. I'm coming up now." Austin started to walk back upstairs, she saw him jerk around to look back into the dark and heard him curse. "Damn, I just felt someone grab my shoulder. And now I'm seeing a man! It's Benjamin Hastings! It looks like he's been hanged and has a frayed rope still knotted at his throat. And he looks ready to kill someone!"

"Oh no, Austin! Are you okay?" Starting to run downstairs to help him, she saw her husband bounding to the top of the stairs. But when he reached the door, it slammed shut between them. Carly screamed. She'd missed it by inches. Austin pushed against the door, afraid of what was waiting below.

Pounding with both fists, he called, "Carly, open the door! Hastings' ghost actually touched me!"

She grabbed the knob, pulling and turning. As before, the door flew open, the force pushing her into the opposite wall. Austin jumped into the kitchen, slamming the door and locking it. They both heard a definite evil chuckle from the other side of the door. He moved away from the door, staggering and trying to keep his balance. He slide down on the floor next to Carly, his heart still racing.

"What happened? Are you okay, hon? Did you say Hastings pushed you?" Carly hugged him tightly.

"Definitely felt a cold hand on my shoulder. And his eyes were so black and full of hate!" Austin tried to take deep breaths to calm down.

"And we both heard Ben Hastings laughing! What did you say you heard and saw down there?" She turned the kitchen light switch on to try to add normalcy.

He recounted the sound of crying, followed by the discovery of a cistern or well cap within the floor. "I reached to turn on the light, to investigate the difference in the floor, when the noises grew louder. I decided to come upstairs to tell you what I found, when a hand, colder than ice, grab my shoulder. When I turned around, I saw him!" He shook his head, as if trying to erase the memory.

"I bet Hastings was trying to keep you from something—and to make a point that he's down there." Carly patted his back.

"I called out to Freddy. I know it sounds stupid, but after the EVP recording tonight, the crying got to me." He raked his hand through his disheveled hair.

"You don't have to explain feeling compassion for Freddy. It breaks my heart when I hear it, then I feel like I have a panic attack." She pulled his head onto her shoulder. "I understand."

He straightened up from the floor, helping Carly stand. They walked into the receiving room to check the safe before going back to bed. Seeing everything looked in place, Austin closed the safe door, turning the lock and closing the panel.

"I still can't believe this happened, and I actually saw a ghost! I'll call Rich Trevenour later today to find out if we once had a cistern or well down in the cellar." He turned off the light. "Maybe Freddy fell in and drowned. Maybe he wasn't killed, maybe it was an accident. It's worth a try."

"I didn't notice the floor being any different down there, just raised in a spot. The north wall is different too, so maybe the floor had some issues as well," Carly said.

Austin checked the front door's locks as Carly flipped off the kitchen lights. "Let's go to bed. I'm not feeling well," she said and stopped by the bathroom for some water. The encounter had left her feeling queasy again, not to mention terrified.

Carly couldn't remember sleeping in so late on a Saturday morning, but the early morning had been too eventful. She went downstairs to make coffee, finding Austin's note. "I didn't want to wake you. Heading to the hospital. I'll call Rich today. We'll get through this. I love you. A." Smiling, she checked her phone and saw three text messages. One was from her mother, who was worried about her, as usual. Fortunately, in only two and a half weeks she'd be flying to Kansas to spend Christmas with her family and would be able to reassure her parents that all was good.

The second message was from her mother-in-law who was inquiring about the ghostly encounters and wanting to be sure that Carly and Austin were safe. She read the third message: "This message is for Carly Tabor. I would like to contact you in regards to a position at WCSC, Live 5 News. Respectfully, Bonnie Hargrove, Personnel Director."

Carly stared at the message, "Well if that doesn't beat all. I didn't think they even read my resumé."

She sent a text to Austin's mother, reassuring her that all was well and they would call her soon. She felt guilty for lying to her, but no sense getting her upset over something she had no control over. Sending her mother a text, she promised to catch the family up on all the latest when she arrived in two weeks.

She wanted to go back into television reporting, so maybe she should check out the position WCSC may offer before deciding. She texted, "I'd like to discuss the position with you at your earliest convenience. Thank you. Regards, Carly Tabor."

After the excitement of the morning, Carly decided to indulge in a morning of leisure- drinking coffee and watching cooking programs on television. Later in the day, after straightening up the house a bit, she went to the den where she'd placed the papers for the Orphan House. Lying on the desk was the picture of Freddy. It was the same boy who appeared to her during the investigation.

Reviewing the Orphan Asylum or Orphan House data from Tom Drummond, she found much information, including the names of people directly involved in the daily care at the orphanage. The names and ages of the children and the circumstances involving their arrival to the asylum were also listed. The list included the names of the workers, when their employment began and also the date of resignation. To be admitted, the child was assigned by a church or city warden, parent or guardians. Children who were without a father, mother, without any parents, or even children who had two living parents could be admitted to the asylum. The children were also indentured to the Orphan Asylum, taking away all parental control, who had the right to bind them out at a later date. The boys went on a "binding out list" at fourteen years of age, while girls could go on the list at the age of twelve. The ending ages for the apprenticeship were twenty-one for boys and eighteen for girls. She couldn't help but feel sorry for these pitiful children, not only orphans but then they became indentured servants until adulthood.

Carly underlined the date of the minutes and the volume number of the indentures for future reference. Tom Drummond had copied the records from the first orphans indentured to Orphan Asylum, until the year 1800. Even though she had the name *Freddy*, she wasn't sure if that was a first or middle name, or even if Freddy was one of the orphans. She searched the list, reading each name, and feeling the hopelessness that any parents of the children must have felt to have to give up their children due to poverty. Also, the date listed the birth years of the children along with the date of their indenture, and to whom they were bound. For some of the children, the death dates were also noted. She remembered reading that at the first Orphan Asylum, the children who died received burial on site. Later, they would receive burial at nearby cemeteries. By 1850, the Orphan House children were laid to rest in a special area of Magnolia Cemetery on the outskirts of Charleston.

However, when she reached the letter R she found the first child with the name Frederick. Her heart skipped a beat as she read the entry: "Richards, Frederick. Admitted September 25, 1794, aged three years by his mother, Susannah Richards. Runaway January 19th, 1799. Born June 11, 1791. (Minutes, January, 30th, 1799)." Frederick Richards was later listed as a runaway at only 8 years old. She put a star beside the entry, with an intuitive feeling this might be the boy who was haunting her house. She wanted to be sure, even though the date of his running away matched the date the Pettigrews died. Only one other Frederick was listed, but the dates didn't match up with the Pettigrews. Carly felt she now had a name and the story of this young child. Freddy was Frederick Richards so perhaps this would help solve the mystery and get rid of the spirits.

Carly was upstairs putting laundry away, Christmas music played from one floor below. She noticed her cell had a text message from Austin. "Hey, I talked to Rich Trevenour this morning. I explained the raised part of the floor in the cellar. He's going to stop by this morning on his way to a jobsite to take a look. Make sure you're up and dressed!" She rolled her eyes; he knew she'd be slow to rise after their late night ghost adventure. Walking out onto the second floor piazza, she watched a carriage weighted down with nosy tourists pass by the house, so she smiled and waved, feeling like a mannequin stationed at their historic house. As she turned to walk back into the house, she saw Rich Trevenour's construction truck pull in front of her house, so she walked down to the street door to let Rich inside.

"Carly, your husband wanted me to take a look at your cellar. Is it a good time?" Rich asked, taking off his cap.

She led him into the kitchen. "Please, come in. Thank you for making time for us. I'll flip the light on for you." Unlocking the cellar door, she led him into the cellar, which didn't seem scary in the daylight.

"This is the spot we think maybe was a cistern or well," Carly said, tapping the area with her shoe. Being in the cellar in the sunlight made it difficult to remember the terror the last time she and Austin were down there.

Rich inspected the floor, shining his flashlight onto the area and the walls. "Yep, it looks like at one time there was an entrance here—see the patches? Maybe it was a cistern, since it was common for them to be indoors or under roof to keep the animals out. Sometimes they put them into the ground and covered 'em with a cap. Rainwater provided the house's drinking water." Rich pointed with his flashlight. "The area seems like the right size, and the stones are higher in elevation than the other section of floor."

"Okay, that makes sense. Now what about this wall?" She pointed to the north wall in the cellar.

"Yeah, seems this part of the cellar wall wasn't made from the same material as the rest of the foundation. I'd expect the area to be larger, but maybe the structure was unsound, causing the homeowner to repair the wall." He ran his light along the whole section. "The city's seen its share of earthquakes, so it wouldn't be a stretch to have foundation damage. I see there's a bit of crumbling down here near the floor." He pointed the flashlight to a section near the wall that faced the street.

Carly stooped down to run her finger along where the floor and cellar wall met. "Is it safe? I mean, is the wall an important load bearing wall?"

"Nah, don't think so. Timbers support the upper floor, so I feel like this wall doesn't have to be in this location." He studied the room. "I'd say there are supports on the opposite side of the wall. My guess is the room was larger, but for some reason long ago they wanted to make it smaller."

"I think Dr. Hutchinson, the previous owner, told Austin this was added not long after an early owner had issues with odors coming from the sewer gas or something to that affect," Carly explained.

"Interestin' but don't think it's a problem. If y'all ever want to expand the cellar for more storage, you ought to contact me and the city inspector, just to be safe."

"When you guys were remodeling the receiving room, did you find anything in the walls other than the safe?" Upstairs, she walked into the hallway with him.

"The crew knows that in old houses, anything that they find is provided to the owners. If my crew had found somethin', they woulda told me."

"I just wondered if maybe there was another wall safe we didn't know about." She showed him to the door. "Appreciate your coming and taking a look at the cellar. We've heard some noises down there and wanted to have it checked."

"Might be a critter found its way in. But, if you aren't seeing droppin's, it probably found its way back out." Rich reached in his pocket for his keys.

After he left, she texted Austin that his hunch was right, since Rich thought it was a cistern in the cellar, and she thought that maybe Freddy had fallen inside.

Deciding to call Delaney, she left her a message on her voice mail. Carly was anxious to share that she'd maybe found their Freddy, as well as the latest spirit encounter.

Chapter 23

Carly waited for Delaney to pick up her phone, after reaching her voice mail the first time she called.

"Hello?" Delaney's voice sounded sleepy.

"Hi! I hope this isn't a bad time?" Carly tucked her foot underneath as she settled into her chair.

"Hey there, I just dozed off in the chair. You know how dumb you feel when you wake up in a fog. And, I dreamed about Andrew Pettigrew," Delaney said.

"Really? Well, maybe we need to get you a man closer to your own age, lady." Carly said.

"Ha ha, no thanks! You're feeling better, I see."

"So what did you dream?" Carly smiled hearing her friend's spark come back.

"Well, I could tell the weather that January evening was raw, because ice pellets had formed on Andrew Pettigrew's cloak as he walked from McCrady's Tavern. He ran into Robert Grant, who seemed to be a neighbor, who was also having a drink at McCrady's."

"You saw the witness who testified seeing him at the tavern that evening. How'd you know his name?" Carly walked over to the stereo to turn the holiday music down quieter.

"Yes, Andrew called him by name when the two spoke. Robert left early, so they walked along and separated when Andrew turned south and walked on King Street."

"Wow, I'm speechless. What else did you see?" She closed her eyes, trying to visualize what Delaney saw.

"I saw Andrew walkin' down the street, pulling his coat around his neck. Benjamin Hastings trailed him by keeping several paces behind to remain unnoticed. Hastings watched Andrew go inside his house." Delaney's voice assumed a monotone as she recounted her dream. "The fire's glow lit the room, but Celeste must have already gone to bed. At the safe, Andrew put a large number of coins into a leather pouch, along with a wallet containing a long piece of parchment. The parchment looked like it was closed with a red wax seal."

"Did Andrew see Ben?" Carly sat on the edge of her seat.

"I woke up when Andrew heard a sound, and I can't remember anything else." Delaney's voice sounded disappointed.

"It's amazing how you can dream like that. I do have some great news though—I did find Freddy!" Carly picked up her papers from the desk.

"Found our Freddy? Where?"

"I was reading the minutes from the Orphan House, and I saw his name. I've emailed it to you if you check on-line. I couldn't believe my eyes!" Carly emphasized the point it was the boy in the photo and her house.

"Sure, let me check now—my laptop is right here." After a few minutes, Delaney almost shouted into the phone. "I can't believe it, sweetie! This has to be him. It even states he was a runaway."

"Definitely, but now we need to find out why he ran away, or why he ended up in Andrew's house. We're missing something." Carly tapped her pencil on the desk.

"When I was dreamin', I saw Andrew putting a sealed parchment into the safe. Hastings was following him, and surprised him at his safe."

"I'd like to do another investigation, maybe just the two of us if you're up for it, because I feel Freddy and Celeste are reaching out to us. But, I leave for Kansas to see my family on the 23rd. Delaney, I'm just so tired of all of this." Carly's voice cracked. "We don't feel safe in our house. Hastings pushed Austin while he was checking a noise in the cellar, so he's getting more aggressive. I want to have our house free of spirits, for good."

"Oh, honey, I'll help you anyway I can. I can come over and work around my two jobs, so let me know what works. Maybe we can go out for what you younger ones call a girl's day, no paranormal talk, just us having lunch or shopping," Delaney said.

"Awesome! Oh, one more thing. Well, actually two things, then I'll let you go." Carly said. "First, Austin had a hunch about where Freddy is. We recently found a patch on the cellar floor which could've been a cistern. Austin thought he might've fallen inside and drowned."

"Well, it sounds like a possible explanation," Delaney agreed.

"And second, I was contacted for a job interview with Channel 5 news." Carly looked at her calendar, the name written in red.

"Congratulation, dear. You might have a job come the New Year!" Delaney said. "Maybe you could report on your resident ghosts."

"Ha, I'm hoping they'll be old news by then. Get it?" Carly laughed at her joke. "Well, we'll see. I haven't even talked to anyone yet. I'll keep you posted though."

The two finished their conversation, planning to meet the first of the week. Carly planned to research some possibilities for why little Freddy Richards would have been in the Pettigrew house instead of the Orphan House on that winter's evening.

The December days sped by, as Carly and Austin finished decorating their King Street home. The real seven-foot pine Christmas tree was illuminated each evening, giving off a glow in the room. She used her antique Christmas decorations and toys to decorate the den. Placing an artificial tree in the receiving room, she decorated it in an 18th century style, with wooden peg dolls on a garland and strands of wooden buttons. Bringing the old toys in the nursery down to the receiving room, she worked to make the room appear as it might have during the time the Pettigrews living there.

Using Photoshop to edit the photograph of her and her mother in front of the fireplace, she cropped the picture to only show Freddy and printed out a 5x7 version and a smaller size. Hoping it might comfort his sad spirit, she placed the smaller print inside an antique metal frame and made it into an ornament to hang on the tree. She stood the larger picture of Freddy's ghost on the mantle, next to a Nativity scene and beeswax candle. Adding the small portrait of the lady she'd purchased from the Mount Pleasant collection to the mantel, Carly was satisfied with her make-shift shrine to their house spirits.

Nevertheless, each evening, the couple awoke to sounds coming from the walls, and banging and weeping. Exhausted from lack of sleep, Carly was to the point she couldn't will herself to move out of bed to investigate. Austin decided to ignore them after his last investigation and run-in with the ghosts and decided to stay with her. However, the hauntings were beginning to negatively affect both of them; not only did she feel fatigued, but also suffered with stomach issues, probably brought on by stress. He experienced difficulty staying awake at the hospital due to the lack of sleep and anxiety.

The weekend finally came, with hopes of rest and relaxation for the Tabors. They decided to dine out Friday evening at The Noisy Oyster.

"I spoke to Rich again today about the cistern in the cellar." He watched the crowd milling through the city market.

"What did he say this time?" she asked.

"He said it'd be possible to take out the small section of stone, get a better look at what was down there, if we wanted. It wasn't uncommon to have an old well or cistern closed up after a couple of hundred years." He sipped his sweet tea.

"Do you think Freddy could have fallen in the cistern without anyone even realizing he was in the house?" She fidgeted with her napkin.

"I don't know, might be a wild goose chase. I mean, if he did fall in, little evidence would remain. Besides, someone would've figured it out. If that was your drinking water, a corpse would have contaminated it." Austin moved his glass as their appetizer of calamari arrived.

"I agree. The house was vacant for a time, but the estate was settled, and Peter Faysoux sold the house. They would have continued to use the cistern." Carly dipped her calamari into the sauce, taking a bite.

"Well, we might be barking up the wrong tree. It's just a hunch," he said.

They enjoyed a dinner of the fresh catch of the day and talked about holiday shopping remaining to be done.

When they arrived home, the neighborhood glowed with Christmas decorations and white lights. Even among the adjacent houses, their larger house appeared warmer and more welcoming, particularly with candles in the windows. So lovely, Carly mused, and who would think it was haunted. Walking inside, Carly felt something wasn't quite right.

"What's wrong?" Austin saw her hesitate and look down the hallway.

"Umm...don't know. Something feels wrong." She stood in the hallway, looking right to left.

He flipped on the lights in both the receiving room and the kitchen, while she walked to the den and turned them on. Nothing appeared out of the ordinary in the den, so she joined her husband in the hallway.

"Hon, maybe you're getting too stressed out with these spirits. I don't see anything out of the ordinary in the kitchen or receiving room, but I'll check the dining room." He walked through the kitchen and into the adjoining room.

"Nothing here either," he said.

"Maybe you're right and my nerves are shot." She hugged her husband. "Let's watch some TV in the den and chill out."

After watching reruns of "Friends" for a few minutes, Carly heard a text arrive on her iPhone and checking she saw it was Delaney.

"Just checking in with you. Thought if you weren't busy I'd stop by tomorrow. This week got away from me, sorry." Delaney had typed.

"Don't worry, we're under the weather too. Just worn out. Tomorrow is fine. Austin working Sunday, but will be here tomorrow all day." Carly typed back.

In a few minutes, Delaney replied, "Sounds good. Don't worry about fixing me anything. I will have eaten an early dinner. I'll be over around seven, if that is okay and not too late."

After another text, they agreed upon seven o'clock the following evening. She was glad her friend wanted to try once again with Freddy.

The next day was quiet with Carly trying to sleep in later and nap, after doing some holiday shopping with Austin. In the evening, Delaney was right on time, coming into the house with the chill of winter on her heels.

She shed her coat and after giving both Austin and Carly hugs, followed them into the den. The logs in the gas fireplace painted the room in yellow tones.

"Your decorations are lovely, Carly, and especially love the antiques! And your tree…I love the fresh smell of a pine tree." Delaney looked at the ornaments on the tree.

"Thanks, Christmas is my favorite time of the year. Austin did a lot of the decorations though. He likes Christmas as much as I do, even if he hates to admit it!" Carly said.

"Yeah, I enjoy seeing the house all lit up. It should be lit up for a while, as much time as it took." Austin winked at Carly. "She has another tree in the receiving room and one upstairs in the landing."

"Oh, I'd love to see them, if you wouldn't mind." Delaney waited for a reply.

"Sure, I'd be glad to show you." Austin led her up the stairs.

When they returned, Carly had brought in a tray and three stoneware mugs.

"Smells heavenly of cinnamon, I do believe?" Delaney peered into her mug.

"This is my Grandma Evans's cider recipe. I have cinnamon sticks here as well, if you'd like." Carly put a stick into her cup.

"It smells delicious, thank you." Delaney breathed in the scent, then took a sip.

"Would you like something sweet to go with it? I have homemade sugar cookies too." Carly's lifted the tray.

"You know me all too well, my friend. No way can I turn down a cookie!"

The three sat and chatted, enjoying the cider and cookies. Carly explained the history of the Orphan House and showed Delaney the pages of the orphan names copied from the original minutes.

"Breaks my heart to read about these poor children. I guess for some, it was a chance to get a good start in life, once they finished with their indenture, but still… so pitiful." Delaney flipped the pages, reading through the names.

"I felt that way too as I was reading down the list. Conditions weren't good, even though the city and churches kept tabs on the children. Celeste accompanied her father in his medical visits to care for the sick children. She would've had intimate access to the children, and no doubt came in contact with Freddy Richards." Carly flipped the page to where Freddy Richards' name was included, showing it to Delaney.

"Yes, I see what you mean about the timing and also the situation. Did anyone look for him? Did you find any mention in the minutes about them goin' out to search for the runaway?" Delaney asked.

"It seems odd a child would go missing and become a 'runaway', if he turned up later. It looks like they concluded he was gone, and that was that." Austin said and took the page Delaney offered.

"We'll have to look, just to be sure. But I believe it's our Freddy. I think he knew Celeste from her dealings with the Orphan House. That's how I'll approach the investigation tonight." Delaney finished drinking the last of her cider.

"Do you want me to start turning down the lights for you?" Austin set his cup on the tray.

Delaney looked over her shoulder, feeling eyes watching their every move. "No, I don't need the dark to communicate. Most of the time the spirits speak to me or show me things in their own way. I think we should just leave things as you have them."

Carly and Austin carried the cookie tray and mugs into the kitchen. Delaney moved into the hallway, letting her thoughts clear. She felt something led her to the receiving room. A candle on the mantel and the candles in the windows were the only light. She entered the room, her eyes panning from end to end. She walked to the fireplace, immediately seeing the photograph of Freddy.

"Freddy, are you able to talk to me this evening?" Her voice dropped to a gentle tone, as if speaking to a small child. She sat the picture back on the mantle, turning towards the tree.

Austin and Carly stood in the kitchen doorway, quiet observers.

"Are you the boy at the Orphan House, Freddy Richards?" Delaney moved to the center of the room, closing her eyes. "Freddy, honey, what were you doing at the Pettigrew's house on the night of January 19th, 1799? Were you running away from the orphanage that night?" She opened her eyes, trying to see him, and then she closed her eyes again. "I see him hurrying down the empty street and nobody noticed him escape from the asylum. He pulls his ragged coat up to his chin, and his pants too short for his bony little legs. Poor mite is shivering as the sleet pelts down." Delaney continued describing what she saw in a whisper. "He walks towards King Street I think, although it looks different back then.

"How does she do this?" Austin leaned into Carly, whispering.

"She has this gift of intuition. Shh." Carly watched as Delaney turned and looked away through the centuries.

"Freddy, I can see you're coming to Celeste Pettigrew's house, aren't you? Why are coming here? Did Celeste know you were coming?" She moved toward the fireplace.

Austin and Carly tiptoed into the hallway, hoping Freddy would continue to speak to Delaney. Carly wished the digital voice recorder was still in the house.

"It's sleeting harder. The man who lives next door is coming onto the street. He doesn't see you. You continue walking down King Street." She opens her eyes, looking around the room for the boy's ghost.

"Delaney, is anyone else with Freddy?" Carly whispered.

"I can't tell, Carly. He's taking me down the street to this house. So dark, no street lights like today. It's sleeting heavier now, and it's so cold I can see the poor dear's breath." Delaney continued trying to talk with the spirit. "Freddy, can you tell me why you're going to the Pettigrew house? Why did you run away?"

Austin and Carly could hear the crying coming from somewhere in the house. It was a soft weeping at first, followed by a much louder sound. Delaney opened her eyes at the sound.

"Freddy, I can hear you crying. Are you afraid?" Delaney moved into the hallway.

"He sees the partially open window to this house's cellar and climbs inside and jumps down tracking wet footprints along the floor. It's dark, and he stops for a moment to let his eyes adjust. The cellar is cold, and his clothing wet and stiff from the frozen sleet," Delaney described. "Bless his heart, he's breathing heavy like he might be sick. I watch Freddy feeling his way to the stairs that would lead to the upper level. As he opens the door at the top of the stairs, he sees a glow coming from the room across the hallway."

"What does the kitchen look like?" Austin asked.

"It's a pantry of sorts with shelves on three sides. There are small glass jars on the shelves, and I can see barrels under the lowest shelf, maybe flour and rice." Delaney talked faster, "Freddy's listening for sounds in the room across the hallway. He sees the shadow of someone, now he's moving closer to the room."

Austin and Carly look at each other, afraid to say anything.

"Freddy, who do you see in the room?" Delaney turned to face the doorway. "Now he sees a man from the back so he must hide before being discovered. He crouches down, crawling along the wall, stopping to hide behind a large barrel-back chair. It's just like I saw before. I knew someone was in the room, but couldn't see him. Freddy's so small, he's completely hidden." Delaney's eyes look sad as she turns to face Austin and Carly.

"My perspective shifts from Freddy to being an observer. He watches a man who looks like Andrew Pettigrew place something inside the wall beside the fireplace." She moved to where Carly has placed a similar style of chair, near the spot where Freddy Richards hid 200 years ago. "Freddy, I know you want to see Celeste. Did she know you were comin' to the house that night? "

The group heard the crying became louder when Delaney continued to question the boy.

"Freddy? Where are you? I need you to help me." Delaney stretches out her arms. "I want to find you."

Carly and Austin listened as Delaney walked into the hallway, looking back to the receiving room.

"I hear footsteps coming into the pantry. Someone else came in through the opened window below. It looks like Benjamin Hastings coming into the hallway, but he can't see me and walks right through me. He surprises Andrew and wants money for Jacob Hinman." Delaney frowned as she watched.

Carly stood close to Austin, feeling a chill run the length of her spine and smelling the wood smoke from the fire long ago.

"I see Andrew Pettigrew taking the pistol from the safe. Oh no, Hastings rushes him, struggling to take the flint-lock." Delaney moved back, her body tense and her voice growing louder. "He overpowers Andrew...oh my, he's got the pistol and fires it point-blank. No!" Delaney screams into the room with only Austin and Carly as witnesses.

"He shot him point blank in the forehead." Delaney backs away, unsteady on her feet. Carly and Austin support her so she doesn't fall.

"With how pale she is, she could be in shock so let's monitor her," Austin said.

"There's smoke everywhere in the room. I see Ben going to the safe, shoving several money bags and coins into his pockets." Delaney's eyes were tearful.

Austin wrapped his arms around Carly, feeling the cold settle around them.

Delaney swayed, as she viewed the gruesome scene. "Oh no, Celeste is coming into the room, probably woken up by the gunshot. She looks so young and alive, in a long night gown, and her hair falls around her shoulders. Poor thing sees Hastings standing over the bleedin' body of her husband, and she screams. Now, she recognizes Freddy hiding behind the chair. She yells for him to run. Oh no, he fires the pistol again!" Delaney put her hand on her chest as if feeling the shot and folded to the floor. "Oh my lord, he shot Celeste in the heart." Delaney reaches out to the specters, while Carly and Austin watch in horror.

"Where's Freddy?" Carly rushed to her friend, she and Austin holding her arms to help her stand.

"So much blood...it's horrible...he's putting the pistol in Andrew's hand to make it look like suicide. But, he hears someone!" Delaney stood swaying, put a hand on the wall, and turned to the hallway.

In that moment, a rush of air passed through Carly and Austin.

"The scene disappeared just now, but I didn't see how it ended. Poor mite, little Freddy saw them murdered right in front of him. No wonder his ghost is too afraid to come back to this room. Carly, the locket you have, it's Celeste. I saw her and she was pretty, and petite with dark hair and eyes. Andrew wasn't a big man, certainly no match for Ben Hastings who appeared to be much heavier and stronger." She brought her hand to her nose. "I could smell Hastings' rank body odor when he came into the room. His chilling empty eyes looked right at me, but he didn't see me." Delaney tried to take a breath between sentences.

Austin helped her walk into the den and took her pulse, while Carly brought her a glass of water. Taking slow sips, Delaney tried to calm herself.

"Where did Freddy go? Did you see that?" Carly asked. They noticed the constant crying and banging of the spirits increased in volume.

"No, the smoke was so thick, I couldn't see where he went. Celeste saw him though, I'm sure."

"I wish we knew what Celeste and Andrew wanted to show us. She had something in her hand she wanted me to see that day she appeared in the nursery." Carly sat down beside her friend.

"I saw the same thing, when I saw them here. Do you think she and Andrew were going to indenture Freddy?" Delaney looked at Austin.

"I doubt we'll ever know. Maybe it's why they haven't left. We need to find Freddy, and they're trying to help us." Austin took his place on the loveseat across from them.

The couple realized until they find Freddy Richards, the Pettigrews and Benjamin Hastings wouldn't leave their home. Hastings was the common denominator.

"Do you think Ben killed Freddy, his only witness to the crime?" He raked his hand through his dark hair.

Delaney examined the enlarged photograph of Freddy and noted his sallow appearance. She told them she was sure it was the same child she saw hiding behind the chair. Carly agreed with her it was the same boy who sat beside her during the last investigation with Boyd and Tucker. The sounds of crying and banging continued.

"If you were Freddy, where would you have run?" Delaney turned to them. "Celeste screamed, 'run!' when she saw Freddy. When Hastings shot her, Freddy took his chance and ran from the room. The smoke was thick from the two musket shots, giving him a moment to escape. I saw Hastings turn in the direction Freddy had been hiding as if he heard or saw him." Delaney massaged her temples.

Carly replayed the scene in her mind: the first shot, the one that killed Andrew Pettigrew would have terrified little Freddy. Seeing Celeste come into the room, he probably knew the bad man would shoot her as well.

"If I were Freddy, I wouldn't have run out the front door because maybe he was afraid Hastings would have a clear shot. So, his best bet was to go back the way he entered which he was familiar with, back to the cellar and through the window where he crawled in." Carly looked at the photo in Delaney's hand.

"Makes sense he ran back down into the cellar. Maybe it's when he got disoriented in the dark and fell into the cistern." Austin sat up on the edge of the loveseat.

"Do you think it's how he died? I tend to think his body would have been visible in there, unless Ben put him in with something to weigh him down." Carly put the picture on the table, the constant crying and banging causing her to feel short of breath.

"Maybe the next owners decided to close the cistern and move it to the outdoors at that time, not knowing Freddy was inside." Delaney raised her voice over the clamor.

"How horrible! Poor little boy, no wonder he's terrified. He must have drowned, which would make sense. I feel like he choked; when I sense he is near or hear him crying, I feel the shortness of breath." Carly put her head on Austin's shoulder.

Delaney told them she sensed Freddy was still trying to communicate with them through the banging and crying, but it was Celeste and Andrew who wanted someone to find him. She felt Hastings was trying to prevent anyone from ever knowing Freddy Richards was his third victim. The reason the crying seemed to come from below, or within the very foundation, was because it could be where Freddy's young life ended two hundred years earlier. Carly and Austin agreed with her summary.

"Well, we have to know this final twist. I wish we knew what Celeste held in her hand. Maybe it's why Freddy was here in the first place." Carly tried taking deep breaths.

"I think I'll call Rich Trevenour again. Maybe he can recommend someone to come out with a jack hammer. We need to open up the floor and see what's inside the cistern." He put his hand on Carly's shoulder, worried her labored breathing signaled another episode.

"Are you okay, hon?" He moved his hand to her wrist, checking her pulse.

"I'm okay. The feeling of suffocation came on with the crying, but it's not as loud now." She took a deep breath, exhaling slowly.

"Good deal, I'll call Rich. If we're wrong, then we'll go to Plan B." Austin sat on the arm of the couch and patted Carly's back.

"And what would that be?" Delaney adjusted her glasses and wiped her forehead with a napkin.

"You'll have to get Celeste to tell you where he is," Austin said.

Chapter 24

Delaney's vision of the murders had occurred over several hours and they all had tried to relax and recover afterwards with small talk. However, it was getting late, and Austin had an early shift the following morning.

"Do you want to go to church with me at St. Michael's tomorrow?" Carly stood and stretched, waiting for Delaney to answer.

"Sorry, sweetie, I play the piano during the service this month, so I have to be at my church in North Ashley."

"It's fine, I feel the need to be in church tomorrow. Maybe I need divine intervention in solving this. Celeste was a Christian woman who did charity work with the orphans, plus she worshipped at St. Michael's." Carly smiled at her husband. "There's nowhere else to turn. I should've gone to God and the church first."

"I completely understand." Delaney touched her friend's hand. "I've prayed I can use my gift to help others, instead of trying to win the lottery. Clearly, I'm not doing that!" They laughed at her joke. "I think we need to solve this—Freddy was an innocent little boy."

Delaney hugged Austin and Carly before heading out the door. But, they saw her sit in her car for a few minutes and then she was back at the front door.

Carly opened the door. "Well, did you forget something?"

"No, I had a thought when I got in my car. If the owners removed the outside entrance, it would've made sense the cellar wasn't used for many years. Could the small brick structure in your back yard be where they moved the cistern? You know, the one capped with a cement pineapple on top?" Delaney stood shivering in the doorway.

"Hmm, don't know. I always thought it was a decorative planter, but we'll check it out tomorrow," Austin said.

"Alright, y'all, but I'll bet it was a cistern before city water came to Charleston. I'd say the original one is down in the cellar." She said goodnight for the second time and drove away.

Carly closed the door. She couldn't shake the feeling Benjamin Hastings wasn't going to allow them to find Freddy easily.

The next morning, the alarm rang early and interrupted Carly's dream about Freddy Richards. But she couldn't recall the details. Austin had left for the hospital hours before, so she showered to prepare to attend church at St. Michaels. After going downstairs, she noticed the house seemed colder, and she went into the receiving room and turned on the electric logs. Looking around the merrily decorated receiving room with its greenery and the Christmas tree, she gave thanks she hadn't observed the scene of the murders of Andrew and Celeste Pettigrew.

"We'll find you, little Freddy. Please, Lord, help us find this lost angel." Carly thought to herself, and flew up a prayer to heaven.

Leaving the room, she thought about what if Celeste and Andrew had been arranging to adopt Freddy, which would explain why he was in their home. They may never have their answer, as it seemed each time the mysterious paper was in view, time and space prevented it from both women's grasp.

Walking to historic St. Michael's that morning, she wondered if her prayer to find Freddy would be heard. Built in 1761, the stately church had withstood the years with grace. The dark carved woodwork, the intricate stained glass windows, and the soaring ceiling impressed her as she sat beside a young couple with small children nestled between them. She noticed the interior had retained much of its original appearance and was thankful the congregation had preserved it well. The sound of the large pipe organ behind the pulpit reverberated throughout the building, giving her chills. Carly felt uplifted after the encouraging sermon and many parishioners welcomed her after the service ended. She decided to return next Sunday, with Austin, if possible.

Another reason she'd attended church here included visiting Celeste's grave, and she walked down the stone path, searching the tall, simple headstones which stood at attention in neatly manicured family squares. After searching, she found the headstone carved with the name of Celeste Faysoux Pettigrew. Carly touched the now weathered letters, etched into the stone, closing her eyes as she did. "I'm so sorry about how you and Andrew died. But, I promise to find Freddy. Then maybe you can rest in peace, sweet Celeste."

The Sunday afternoon gave Carly time to finish her Christmas shopping before returning to a quiet house. The Christmas lights throughout the inside of her home made her homesick for the large farmhouse in which she grew up in rural Farlington, Kansas. Thoughts of her life before Charleston flooded her mind. When Austin met her at the gym where she worked during her college days, she expected no future in his flirting. He was older than she, and had recently divorced. Carly Evans, then twenty-one, had brains as well as looks and an infectious laugh which attracted the young medical resident. When she brought Austin home for Christmas that year, Curt and Paula Evans worried Austin, although clearly in love with Carly, might be on the rebound from his divorce and not the best match for their little girl. Regardless of her parents' concern, the two surprised everyone and married over that Christmas break. Without time for a honeymoon, they rented a moving van, driving all night to their condo in the suburbs of Denver. Now, almost ten years later, they were still happily married, but living 1000 miles away from her family. Carly missed her parents more than she thought she would. Now, in a twist, her focus had changed from wanting a child for her and Austin, to finding a child no one else had wanted.

Feeling tired from her afternoon excursion to the shopping mall, she carried a mug of warm cider into the receiving room. She covered up with an afghan and sat in the semi-darkness enjoying the memories of Christmases past. At first, she attributed the movement by the fireplace to her imagination. But, when she blinked her eyes, she saw someone was becoming more substantial. Celeste Pettigrew developed in a filmy apparition. The former lady of the house stood in front of the fireplace, her hand outstretched. Carly, mesmerized by the beseeching look in Celeste's eyes, couldn't break her gaze.

She rose from her chair, walking toward the ghost, but paused, not wanting her to disappear again. This time, Celeste led her from the room. As she floated into the hallway, Carly hurried to follow. However, when she reached the kitchen, Celeste disappeared. What remained was an iciness that made Carly feel distressed. She noticed the door to the cellar was open. As usual, the pitiful sound of a Freddy's weeping exuded from below. The sense of dread left her, and in its place, a feeling of heaviness settled in her chest. She knew Freddy was somewhere close, and she was closer to solving the mystery. Putting her fears aside, she started down the stairs. Descending the staircase, she gripped the rail, her legs shaking with each step. The air grew heavier, and she began taking in deeper breaths to draw in more oxygen.

The light bulb hanging from a single cord swayed back and forth like a pendulum. Her eyes began to adjust to the dim light and her nose picked up the musty smell of earth and moisture around her. She moved along the wall, fighting the urge to turn and run back up. The crying continued. The difficulty Carly felt with each breath caused her to feel lightheaded. She stopped for a moment to slow her breathing. Straining to hear where the cries were originating, she picked up another sound causing her to pause. Above her, she could hear slow steps walking across the kitchen towards the cellar door. She was trapped! She felt the temperature plunge colder around her, causing her to shiver and tremble.

The crying became louder, and she heard the footsteps began to descend the stairs. Carly tried to swallow, but her throat felt constricted, like she was chewing on cotton balls. Dropping to the floor, she sat with her head down hugging her knees, the fear of a confrontation with Hastings making her tremble. She hid her eyes, afraid of what was about to appear.

"Carly! What are you doing down here?" Austin rushed towards her.

Hearing Austin's voice, she found the strength to stand, wrapping her arms around him. "Oh thank heavens, it's you! I thought you were Ben Hastings." She buried her face in Austin's chest. "I heard footsteps above me, and it turned cold." She broke down sobbing.

"It's okay, honey. I called out when I came in the house, but I didn't see you anywhere. I almost closed the door until I heard you call my name." Austin held her close, gently caressing her hair and her back.

She wasn't sure what he thought he heard, but she wasn't going to question it. "Oh, sweetie, I saw Celeste tonight in the receiving room! She wanted me to come down here. Freddy was crying, and I couldn't breathe. I know he's down here!" She wiped her face with her sleeve. No sounds were evident now.

Austin looked around the room and crouched down where he'd found her curled up. "This is where the cistern was. Maybe he's here. We won't know until we uncap the cistern and see what's inside. I'll call Rich Trevenour tonight." He stood, helping her to her feet.

"Well, I'm just glad it was you. I'm not feeling well." Carly held onto his arm; her lightheaded feeling had changed to queasiness.

He helped her climb the narrow stairs, then turned off the light and locked the cellar door behind them. He walked her into the den, where she lay on the couch.

"Lie down, hon, I'll be right back. I'll get a cool washcloth for you." He bent over to kiss her forehead. He returned with a glass of water, a wet washrag, and a handful of oyster crackers.

"Oh, thanks. I need some water…" She didn't finish, as a wave of nausea overtook her and she was sick.

After a few minutes for her to get stabilized, Austin helped Carly upstairs to bed. After another bout with vomiting, she wanted to be left alone to sleep. He went downstairs to make a phone call.

After a few moments, he returned. "Don't worry, I called Rich. He's coming first thing tomorrow morning."

Chapter 25

Carly slept the rest of the evening and night, thankful her nausea passed.

"Hey sleepyhead, you probably slept eleven hours. Are you feeling better, hon? Do you feel like eating something?" Austin woke her up when he poked his head inside their bedroom and carried a tray into the room.

She sat up, taking the tray on her lap. "I do, actually. I think the uninterrupted sleep did me good. If there were any noises in the house last night, I couldn't have even heard them." She nibbled a bite of melon.

"Rich is coming over in a couple of hours. We're going to take the floor up where we think they had a cistern." Austin took a drink of his coffee. "I also talked to Delaney. She's coming over around nine."

"Okay, I'm feeling much better, and I'd like to be there too." She continued taking small bites of her food, not wanting it to come back up again.

Neither had thought about what would happen if the search revealed evidence of Freddy Richards. They would cross the bridge when they needed to, or if they even found a bridge.

Carly reviewed the minutes from the Charleston Orphan House listing all the workers and children. As she thought, Celeste's name came up as giving blankets, food, and clothing, in seven different sets of minutes from the years 1794-1799. She reviewed Andrew Pettigrew's will, "A sum of $2,000 to be bequeathed to the Charleston Orphan Asylum, to be used in the welfare, education, and care of the children of the Charleston Orphan Asylum, June 21st, 1790." The amount was generous for the time period after the American Revolution, making it apparent both Andrew and Celeste held a special interest in the orphans. She continued reading through her notes until the sound of the doorbell on the front door interrupted her.

"I'll get it, Austin." She walked into the entry hall.

Rich stood on the front piazza, his company truck parked on the street in front of the house.

"Good morning." Carly opened the door to the contractor and showed him into the house.

"Thanks for coming, Rich." Austin shook his hand. "If you want to pull your truck on through the gate, I'll open it up for you."

"Okay, thanks. I'd like to first take a look to see what I'll need to bring inside. Can I go on down to the cellar?" He removed his blue company baseball hat, then followed Austin into the cellar.

"Looks to me like this area is where I'll use the jack hammer. If you look close, you can see where the wall has a newer patch here. I'd say this was the original outside entrance and the general area where the rain pipe would have entered." Rich motioned with his hand at a particular location.

"That's what I was thinking. The floor seems higher at this one spot." Austin bent over, touching the stones which seemed to be different.

"Well, let's get started then. If you wanna open up the gate, I'll drive on into the driveway. I have a few more things to carry in." Rich followed Austin upstairs and went to his truck.

Carly decided to wait for Delaney and remained upstairs reading over the asylum minutes and the copied information. She watched Austin and Rich carry in a variety of chisels, along with a small jack hammer. Cutting through concrete and old stones must be a daunting job, she thought.

"I may need to call one of the guys who usually operate this one to come over and spell me. I haven't got the arms for it like I used to." Rich showed Austin the gas-powered jack hammer.

Rich also brought several earphones he suggested everyone wear during the job. He placed his on his head, then handed the extras to Austin. "If you, Carly, or anyone else is going to be down here, you gotta wear these due to OSHA requirements. Louder than thunder right on top of ya and not safe it ya don't."

Austin placed his earphone on his head and gave the extras to Carly. He descended to the cellar to watch the demolition of the stone floor section begin.

Carly could hear the loud clamor echoing throughout the house and wondered if it would bring out Hastings' evil ghost. She placed the earphones on and felt she looked ridiculous. Delaney arrived shortly and Carly welcomed her into the house with earphones.

"Hey! Early Christmas present…joking, but you have to wear these." Carly handed her the earphones and Delaney put them on as she entered.

"Oh my, it's loud enough to wake the dead!" Delaney shouted back, catching herself in the pun. "Sorry, Celeste, Andrew, and Freddy!"

Carly led Delaney up the stairway and into the hallway of the second floor. Speaking in a lower volume, she said, "Quieter up here, and we can go downstairs when Austin comes to get us. It might be awhile before Rich gets through the concrete and stone."

"Okay, that's best. We can talk up here." Delaney followed Carly down the hall, and the two removed their earphones and sat on a wooden bench decorated with woven pillows.

"Last night, I had an odd experience when I was thinkin' back to the other night. I saw Freddy when Ben shot the Pettigrews." Delaney moved closer to Carly to be heard.

"Well, I had quite an experience too—I saw Celeste." Carly leaned over to speak.

"I called to talk to you last night, Austin filled me in. Sorry you were sick. Please get yourself checked out, okay?" She patted Carly's knee.

"Yes, I'll be going in for a real checkup after Christmas, I promise." Carly held up her hand as if taking an oath.

"Good enough. I saw Freddy running from the receiving room after Celeste shouted to him and Hastings following him. Then I felt how hard it was for him to breathe, his heart pounding and trying to find a hiding place."

"I can't imagine how afraid he was." Carly looked down at her smooth hands.

"Freddy started down the stairs, trying to see, but it was dark. He missed the bottom two steps, falling on the stone floor below. I could hear Hastings footsteps above on the floor, starting to come down the steps."

Carly shuddered. She remembered the copper taste of fear, crouched on the floor. She was unable to catch a full breath, hearing the heavy footsteps coming down the stairs, which luckily turned out to be Austin. "I felt the same thing. Then Austin called my name." She felt queasy again.

"I couldn't see Freddy after that, as the cellar was dark. I know Ben Hastings was right behind him; he followed him down into the cellar. I'm sure of it." Delaney leaned back on the bench.

"I've been thinking about what could be under the floor. What are we going to do if his bones lie at the bottom of the cistern?" Carly's dark eyes looked like two brown orbs. "Let's go downstairs. I want to see how far they've gotten on the floor. I can't stand not knowing." Carly stood, and Delaney rose as well.

They donned their earphones and started walking to the kitchen, noticing the jackhammer sound wasn't as pronounced. The women continued down to the cellar, where Austin was taking small chunks of concrete away from the area where Rich was pounding. Carly and Delaney sat on the bottom step watching the men at work. After an hour, Rich had broken through the concrete and hit another obstacle.

"I'm finally through all the concrete and stone." Rich removed his earphones. "I think I'm down to the openin', but until I move out away and start breaking up the whole cap, I won't know for sure. I'm hoping it wasn't filled in with solid concrete."

"Do you think they would have filled the whole thing in, rather than dumping dirt or rocks in and capping it?" Austin took off his earphones and dusted his hands.

"Well, since it was the early 1800s, it's hard to say. I'm hoping they used ballast stones or rock." Rich wiped perspiration from his face with a blue bandana. The men started moving away the part of the floor loosened by the jack hammer.

"Rich, this is Delaney Warrick, our friend. I don't think I introduced you earlier." Austin ushered her over to where Rich stood.

"Pleased to meet ya, ma'am and apologize for being too dusty to shake your hand." Rich smiled up at her and showed her his dirty hands.

"Pleased to meet you, Rich, you're doing some good work here." Delaney stood over the cavity beginning to be exposed in the floor. She tried to envision the room the evening of the murders in 1799. She didn't hear the chatter of the others as she surveyed the room. She closed her eyes, waiting to see a vision or hear a sound. Nothing. Disappointed, Delaney walked back the step where Carly was sitting to wait and watch.

"Okay, back to work." Rich pulled his earphones back over his ears. Everyone donned their earphones for protection against the harsh noise.

After another hour of hammering and clearing, Austin asked if Carly would go out and get lunch for them.

"Sure, we'll be back in a jiffy. Are sub sandwiches okay?" She waved goodbye, and Delaney went upstairs.

While they drove down the narrow streets, Carly and Delaney discussed her upcoming trip to spend Christmas in Kansas. Delaney was expecting to have family and nieces and nephews visiting so she wouldn't be spending the holiday alone. She noted it would be a busy next couple of weeks getting her house ready for company but she felt glad to not be alone.

"When do you fly out for Kansas?" Delaney stared out the car window, looking at the Christmas decorations.

"I'm supposed to leave on the 23rd. Austin won't get to come this time." She adjusted the radio while waiting for the traffic light to turn green. "Since he's the new guy in neurosurgery, he'll be pulling all the hours over the holidays. It stinks."

She pulled into the parking lot of East Bay Deli. Twenty minutes later, they were walking back outside with bags of sandwiches and chips and Carly drove them back to the house.

Rich had left by the time they returned. Austin was sitting at the kitchen table finishing a conversation on his phone when they walked into the room. Carly unpacked the sandwiches and placed them on left-over Thanksgiving paper plates. Delaney brought out the pitcher of sweet tea from the fridge and filled three glasses.

"Okay, we're set. I'm sorry I missed Rich." She moved to the table.

"Yep, he had another job and didn't expect it to take this long. Thanks for getting lunch!" Austin finished his phone call and gave her a quick kiss on her cheek.

"Well, did I miss anything while we were gone?" She passed a napkin to Delaney.

"We finally got the cistern uncovered! It appears to be full of odds and ends. I'm hoping there are some antiques down in there. Look what I found." He placed an old spoon on the table.

"Wow, looks old. Where'd you find it?" She turned the spoon to check the mark, then passed it over to Delaney

"When I pulled some chunks of rock out of the way, I found this wedged between the side of the cistern rim and a rock. It's going to be some work cleaning the cistern out. I don't know how deep it goes." Austin took a bite of an Italian sub.

"It looks like silver, but it's hard to tell since it is covered in grime and tarnish." Delaney passed the spoon back to Carly.

After lunch, the trio went back downstairs to continue taking rock and debris out of the hole which was packed inside. The air still remained heavy with dust, and they wore surgical masks for protection. Delaney walked the length of the cellar once again. Walking along the outer wall directly under the front piazza, she stopped.

"What's wrong?"Carly noticed Delaney standing, her head cocked to one side.

Delaney held up her hand, and knelt down to the floor. "I hear someone or something. It sounds garbled, like someone is talking under water. I can't tell though. It's a different noise than anything I've heard." She clenched and relaxed her fists several times, a habit she'd developed when trying to concentrate.

"I don't hear anything." Austin stopped prying loose the stones and sat still.

"Do you think we are close to Freddy?" She stood next to the cistern opening.

Delaney sat on the stone floor, closing her eyes. Carly and Austin watched her in the yellow glow of incandescent light bathing the dark stone walls.

"He's here… oh my, he's crying." Delaney opened her eyes and closed them again. "I can't see; it's dark. And I hear the banging. I see a closed space. He's in the dark…so afraid. The banging is louder, and he is crying, screaming for someone." Delaney gasped, her voice becoming strained.

"I can't breathe, oh no! I'm feeling really light-headed." Carly tried to pull the surgical mask from her face.

"Delaney, I'm taking her upstairs. I'll be right back down." Austin pulled his wife to an upright position. The two walked upstairs, leaving Delaney in the cellar alone. "Are you okay, hon?" Austin helped Carly into the den, easing her onto the sofa.

"I'm better, but I swear, when I'm near Freddy I can't breathe." She closed her eyes and pulled her hair back.

"Lie still, I'll get you a cool cloth." He bent down and kissed her forehead.

Chapter 26

"Austin? Did you hear something?" Carly bolted up from her lying position. Austin didn't hear her because he was taking a call.

"That was the hospital. I have to go to do an emergency surgery." He leaned over to kiss her. Grabbing his badge and keys, he started for the door. "Tell Delaney I had to head out, sorry. Love you." She heard the door slam as he left.

Carly heard a definite scream from the cellar. She hurried to the kitchen and noticed the cellar door had closed. She pulled with all her might. "Delaney, are you okay?"Carly yelled. She put her ear to the door, trying to hear her friend below.

"Help! Please!" Delaney's voice barely carried upstairs.

"Hold on! I can't get the door open." Carly pulled again, and the door opened.

"Hurry! I'm afraid to move," Delaney said.

Carly flipped the light on. When she reached the bottom of the stairs, she spotted Delaney on all fours near the opening to the cistern.

"Here, let me help you. Are you okay?" She helped Delaney to her feet.

Delaney stood, brushing the gravel from her khakis. Squinting, her eyes took a moment to get used to the light. "Oh yes, I think so. I heard Freddy crying—it was dark, and he was afraid. The light went out and someone pushed me… I think it was that darn Benjamin Hastings." Delaney moved back from the cistern. "I could see through Freddy's eyes so he's trying to show me. He's inside something."

"Hastings is getting more violent towards us, and it isn't safe. Austin was called in, so it's just us here. Sounds like we must get this emptied and see what is at the bottom. I just can't rest until we know, but we'll wait for assistance." Carly bent down to the half filled cistern. "What's wrong, Delaney?" She watched as Delaney put her hands over her face.

"I can't see what I saw earlier. There's so many things coming to me, I can't make out who's showing me what!" She rubbed her eyes, opening them as Carly helped her upstairs.

"Are you hungry? You might feel better with some dinner, and we could go out," Carly offered.

"Yes, let's get out of here for now. I think we both need a break." Delaney collected her Aigner purse from the hall table. As Carly locked the door behind them, a man's laughter echoed throughout the house.

Rich Trevenour was unable to return until the following week, but he called and promised to send a couple of guys to finish cleaning out the cistern. On the evening of December twenty-first, Rich's son, Drake, and his friend, Aubry, came to the Tabor home to help clean out the cistern.

Carly greeted Drake and Aubry at the front door, and Austin took the boys down in the cellar to begin the hard job. While Carly sat on the steps, the three men began removing a hodge-podge of stone and discarded goods. On a blanket, Drake and Aubry placed a collection of kitchen items, including several broken bits of china plates, a few broken and whole small bottles, a rotten leather shoe, and a variety of crockery pieces. It appeared the cistern became a trash heap to collect items lying about or discarded to fill it up. Closer to the bottom, were large, smooth stones, which Drake told them were ballast stones, likely dating to the time when the home was built. Carly commented she'd read about how these large stones had filled the ships' holds to stabilize them when empty on the westbound voyage and then were thrown out when they arrived to fill the ship with trade goods from the colonies. Port cities, such as Charleston, would use these plentiful stones to pave streets or fill in a large hole.

When the men had cleared as far as possible from above ground, it became necessary for one to climb down into the cistern.

"Aubry, you're smaller, why don't you climb on down?" Drake moved back from the cistern and wiped his brow.

"Uh, no way, dude. I can't stand being in small spaces, and that would seriously freak me out." Aubry sat down near the opening and drank from a water bottle.

"Tell you what, if you two want to cut out, I'd understand. I think I can handle it from here." Austin smiled at the two, reaching into his billfold, giving each a twenty dollar bill. "If you charge more, just tell your dad what I owe, and I'll settle up."

Drake and Aubry at first refused, but after Austin insisted, took the money. "Thanks, Dr. Tabor. Sorry we couldn't get all the stones and stuff out for you. Looks like you're almost to the bottom." Aubry peered into the cistern.

"No problem. I can finish, and you've helped immensely." Austin led the boys upstairs. Carly thanked them. Austin showed them out of the house and returned to the kitchen to wash his hands and drink some water.

"You wanna come down in the cellar with me? Looks like I've a few more stones to move, and I'd like the company of my favorite person." As he slid his hand through his hair, a chip of concrete bounced off the table.

"Sure thing, hon. I've been on pins and needles all evening. I don't know how I feel about it now that we're ready to get to the bottom of this thing." She threw her empty bottle of water in the waste basket.

"Let's go, the sooner we get the spirits out of our house, the better we can sleep." He opened the door to the cellar and kissed her.

They descended the stairs—the cellar seemed hollow and cold. She shivered as she peered down into the cistern.

"Wow, the boys did a good job. I can't wait to clean those bottles and display them upstairs." She put the surgical mask over her mouth and nose, as he did.

He climbed down into the cistern, handing stones up in a large bucket to her leaning over to reach it. Even though they were heavy, she wanted to help in order to solve the mystery. He reached a portion of the floor of the cistern. Loading the rock, he was careful to check for small pieces of bone or anything that could be part of a skeleton.

"Do you see anything?" Carly looked deep down into the cistern.

"It's empty, nothing but brick and plaster." He sighed. "I'm surprised and disappointed, actually."

"Darn it, I was so sure poor Freddy was down there." She sat back on her heels, pulling the mask over her head.

"I think it's a relief we didn't find bones. Maybe Freddy got away. We don't know for sure that he died here." Austin climbed out, pulling the small ladder up with him.

"No, he's here. I know it. I want to keep looking."

"Do you think we can afford to pay Rich more for what may be a wild goose chase?" He pointed to the open cistern.

"I know, it sounds crazy. But I know he's down here. Delaney saw it, and Celeste brought me down here. Please, hon, I know Freddy's here." She put her hands on her hips.

"Okay, tell you what. Let's just get through Christmas since you're flying out day after tomorrow. We'll worry about it after the holidays." He took her hand, pulling her toward the stairs.

"Well, okay, I guess that makes sense. But as soon as I get back, I want to look in other places." She went with him, looking over her shoulder as they reached the stairs.

Delaney called before Carly turned in for the evening to hear of their progress. "Maybe we've been looking in the wrong area. I know he's down there, Carly. If I weren't before, I'm positive now. I feel certain that Freddy died in that cellar."

Several peaceful days passed with Carly wrapping presents for her family and concentrating on finishing the holiday décor in their lovely historic home. The night-time banging and crying stayed quieter, so they began to hope the spirits were calming down. She was unable to get a good night's sleep after the cistern proved empty, so getting out of town to Kansas to see family for a week would be a perfect break. Austin talked her into making an appointment with one of the doctors at the hospital for a check-up when she returned. With her faintness, nausea, and difficulty breathing, he told her he worried the spirits had begun to take a physical toll on her.

After several hours flight back to Kansas, Carly felt much better and began to sleep better. Seeing her parents and extended family acted like a balm for her soul. She was able to spend an afternoon alone with her mother, telling her everything they'd experienced. However, the revelations that Carly shared caused her mother's trepidation to increase more. Even though she was intrigued by the mystery of the murders and how Carly had uncovered the secrets buried in their home, she was concerned about their safety.

During the time Carly was in Kansas, she received text messages from Austin telling her the spirits had started again with the noises while he was alone. Each night, he awoke to a loud succession of banging and crying. On Christmas Eve, he shared that on two occasions he heard running down the cellar steps, only to find the door closed and locked. For his Christmas night, he worked the evening shift at the hospital. It was the first time Carly and Austin had not been in the same town on Christmas and she missed him, so she called, but her call went to voice mail. Later that evening, she smiled when she saw Austin's text message. "Merry Christmas, babe. I'm missing you like crazy. So are the Pettigrews, Ben, and Freddy. See you in two days! I love you. A." She replied, "Merry Christmas. I love and miss you. Only you! C."

Chapter 27

Over Christmas, Carly enjoyed spending time with her nieces and nephews, with the thought of having their own child in the back of her mind. Christmas evening, after her family retired for the night, she laid restless in bed, thinking about the miscarriage. Her pregnancy was a surprise, but both she and Austin welcomed a baby into their loving family. But, after carrying the baby into her 12th week, she suffered a miscarriage. Dr. Tabor, her father-in-law and an obstetrician, tried to reassure her of the unlikelihood of another miscarriage, but she grieved over the loss for over a year. When Austin was recruited for a better position at the hospital in Charleston, both felt it would be a good move. Perhaps they'd try again for a child, after settling in. Now, almost two years since the loss of the baby, she felt the desire again to try to get pregnant. However, lately her thoughts of having their own child had become replaced with thoughts of the child who haunted their home. Finding out what happened to Freddy had become an obsession.

After her family dispersed to their various homes in and around Kansas City, Carly and her parents had two days to spend together. At her parent's insistence, Carly shared all the mishaps and ongoing investigations with them.

"Carly, maybe you guys ought to put the house back on the market?" Curt straightened the crocheted doily on the arm of his recliner.

She couldn't understand why everyone suggested they sell their home. "Daddy, it's our home. We aren't selling!" She sighed, flipping her hair off her shoulders.

Her parents looked at one another, knowing their daughter wasn't one to give in or admit defeat.

"Well, will you promise to have a good check-up when you get home?" Paula reached over and put her hand under Carly's chin.

"You look thin, honey. I know you're over thirty, but you'll always be my little girl." Curt rubbed the stubble on his chin, and his voice cracked.

She smiled, knowing she'd lost weight since her parents' visit in August, although not intending to diet. "Austin already made me promise, Daddy. I'll be going in for a check-up as soon as I can get an appointment. I've actually felt more like my old self since I've been here, though. Please don't worry as we're close to solving the mystery and putting the spirits to rest."

On New Year's Eve, she and her parents enjoyed a quiet evening, sitting and eating popcorn in front of the fireplace in the family's living room. It wasn't the usual way she and Austin celebrated this holiday, but she enjoyed visiting them. Although she tried making it until midnight, she couldn't keep her eyes open.

She slept as sound as an innocent girl again in her old bed, and finally woke up, realizing she'd slept until noon. No noises to keep her awake improved her sleep quality. No one came to wake her, letting her sleep as long as she needed. Smelling bacon and coffee, she pulled her hair up in a ponytail and went downstairs. Paula Evans was cooking breakfast on the stove.

"Wow, late sleeper. You should have pulled the quilt off me like you used to!" She put her arms around her mother's shoulders.

"I figured you'd rather have breakfast instead of lunch. I have a plate of French toast and bacon on the table." Paula brought the coffee pot to the table, pouring a cup for her daughter. Within a few hours, Carly would be catching a four o'clock flight to Charleston.

Carly thought about Freddy Richards most of the flight home and knew they were close to finding him. Austin picked her up at nine o'clock, greeting her with a kiss. On the drive home, Carly chattered about her enjoyable Christmas in Kansas. Austin made a quick stop, picking up Chinese take-out he'd ordered ahead so they could enjoy their first meal together in awhile. Once home, he set the luggage down on the porch and unlocked the front door. Carly stepped inside carrying the bag of Chinese food. She felt the familiar anxiety overtake her as soon as she set foot inside. She took a breath, steeling herself and carried the bag to the kitchen, setting it on the table. After dinner, they took their glasses of wine into the den and sat watching the flames dance in the fireplace.

214

"Did you have any problems while I was away?" She took a sip of wine and slid her feet up onto the sofa. She purred while he rubbed the arches of her feet.

"Well, no problems, but I met Freddy." He continued to rub her feet, looking at the surprise on her face.

"Freddy? Where did you see him?" She sat up.

"The other night, after finishing surgery, I walked into the house and saw a small boy standing in the hallway. I saw the stairway visible through him." Austin rubbed a hand down his jeans clad pants leg. "He held the toy horse and ... well ... it scared the holy crap out of me." He took a big gulp of his red wine.

"What did you do?" Her eyes lit up like two balls of fire.

"Well, there we are, standing feet apart, but separated by two centuries. I called out, 'Freddy?'" Austin raked his hand through his hair. "He looked pale, and his eyes were dark, I don't remember seeing his iris or pupil...only dark holes. I moved toward him, but he turned and walked into the wall. I watched the toy horse from upstairs hit the floor with a thud. He was holding the real toy."

"I'll bet it scared the bejesus out of you! Why didn't you call me?" She socked him in the arm.

"I was in shock from what I'd seen. I called Delaney."

"Oh, okay." She cocked her head. "I guess I'm glad you thought to call her."

"She said she now knows where we can find Freddy."

"And where is it?" She raised an eyebrow.

"Down in the cellar, behind the stone wall." Austin settled back on the couch.

"I've wondered what was behind the wall since the first time I heard the banging down there. I assumed it had always been there." She placed her small feet back onto his lap.

"I called Rich the other night. He made a trip back to help me fill in the cistern, and said the load bearing braces must be behind the wall. He told me it would be a bear, but we could remove it." Austin kissed her on top of the head. "But, we'll do what we have to in order to solve this mystery and recover our sanity."

Carly smiled and was already thinking the wall would have to go.

The New Year began with a cold front settling over the low country. Although the time away had been good for her, she had not regained her energy.

She met Elise Ravanel for a lunch date that week at Jestine's. The two caught up on their lives since Thanksgiving, and Elise noticed Carly's pale complexion.

"Are you coming down with something, girl? You look a little pale since the last time I saw you." Elise grabbed her hand.

"Well, I've been under some stress lately, but I'm going for a check-up. Austin set up an appointment for me in two weeks." Carly took a sip of her water.

"So what's causing all your stress?" Elise pressed her friend for an answer.

"Let's just say we haven't rid the house of the strange noises and such…soon though." Carly took another drink, feeling nauseous.

Elise changed the subject, not wanting to pry. The two enjoyed a delicious lunch of she-crab soup and sandwiches, followed by a trip to a couple of shops in the historic district.

That evening, Delaney called to check on her. "I saw Boyd yesterday; we had lunch. He asked about the cistern and whether you found anything."

"Would he and Tucker want to come back?" Carly was beginning to think they'd never find Freddy's final resting place.

"Funny thing is, we went over the two investigations and the places seeming to hold the most activity. The receiving room and cellar are definitely places holding the spirits to the house. Something got me to thinking, though, that maybe all their high tech gadgets are getting in the way." Delaney's voice vibrated with laughter.

"Are we supposed to tear the house apart room by room?" Carly walked into the kitchen to start dinner.

Delaney continued, impervious to her snarky remark. "No, silly girl. I think it might be time to go 'old school'. I remember my Mammaw back in Tennessee talk about the old mountain ways. Her family came from the hills, and she talked about the remedies and ways they used to do things."

"So, what did she tell you to help in finding Freddy?" Carly listened, curious to see where the conversation was going.

"My great-great uncle used divining rods. He could find water in a desert with willow sticks." Delaney laughed.

"Oh yeah, I know what those are. Daddy asked our neighbor once to do his trick. He used two coat hangers to point to water when our well went bad, and we needed to have one dug to replace it. It was the neatest thing to watch."

"Okay, same premise. Instead of water, we're looking for a grave. I've seen it used to find unmarked graves back in the family cemetery in the town where I grew up." Delaney's voice sounded excited.

"Wow. I've never heard of anyone using them for such a purpose. How does it work?"

"They've used them for centuries, and the accuracy is amazing." Delaney explained how the willow sticks or divining rods worked as a precursor to modern ground penetrating radar. "I think it'd be worth a try to see if we can find a place in the floor where Hastings might have killed and buried little Freddy."

"You know we emptied the cistern? Nothing but odds and ends thrown in there." After a few more moments of conversation, Carly had another call coming in. "Hey, I have another call. Do you mind if I call you back in a bit?"

"Sure, we'll talk later. Think about the divining rods and let me know." Delaney said goodbye and hung up.

She answered the incoming call and heard someone ask "Hi, is Carly Tabor available?"

"This is Carly." She put her phone on her shoulder as she poured a glass of tea.

"Hi Carly, my name's Daria Foley. I'm the HR director for Channel 5 News. I have your resume here and wondered if you'd be able to come in for an interview later this week?"

"Oh, um, well…yes, well, I'm sure I could," Carly stammered.

"Great! How would Thursday work for you?"

"Yes, fine. For what position am I interviewing?" She sat down at the table, putting her glass on a coaster.

Daria went on to explain the station needed another reporter for special assignments, and her excellent investigative reporting in Denver caught their attention. She also mentioned the raving recommendation Carly's previous station manager gave. Carly hung up and couldn't wait to tell Austin about her interview set for the end of the week.

She packed all the Christmas decorations in the den into green and red plastic totes, to wait for Austin to put them in the attic. She noticed the familiar banging as she carried the smaller totes of ornaments up to the attic. The house assumed a chill, and she attributed it to the cold rain outside and kept working. By four o'clock, she was feeling exhausted from the marathon of packing up Christmas. She decided a short nap might help, since she wasn't expecting her husband to be home for a couple of hours.

Later, Carly woke to a noise and came downstairs to see Austin. "Sorry, I must've dozed off this afternoon. I didn't know you were home." She startled him from behind and reached up to kiss him.

But then he motioned for her to follow him, putting a finger to his lips. They crept towards the cellar door. "Just now, I watched Andrew Pettigrew walk through a wall, and I think I saw Freddy run past me right before you scared me half to death." He opened the door, listening to the sound below.

"The crying sounds different, almost like it's an echo. Do you hear the difference?" Austin turned to face her.

Her feeling of being lightheaded started to manifest again. "Oh, Austin…"

"Are you okay? You don't look well, hon."

She stood with her hands on the counter, trying to will herself to feel better. "It's the same feeling I always get when the crying starts. We have to find Freddy. He wants us to follow him."

"Are you sure you're all right then?" He rubbed his forehead.

She nodded, motioning for him to go downstairs. He picked up the flashlight and started down. The temperature was freezing as Carly and Austin reached the bottom of the stairs. The stillness was unnerving, the crying abruptly ceasing. Standing in the center of the room, she moved closer to Austin, feeling afraid.

"Are you okay?" He held her hand.

"It feels like I can't get enough air in my lungs, like before. I know it's only anxiety. But, I don't want to leave; let's follow Freddy and solve this." The two continued walking into the cellar.

Austin shone the flashlight along the stone wall. The beam moved to the window frame now standing open.

"That was one of the scariest things that happened down here." Carly shivered from the memory of the encounter with Hastings. "This must have been where Freddy crawled through from the street."

"If he chased Freddy down here in the dark, as Delaney saw it, where would he hide?" Austin shone the light all around the room. "The outside cellar entrance was closed, probably during the mid 1800s." Austin bent down, noticing the stone along the floor seemed capable of being dislodged. "I called Rich about coming over and helping me with this. I don't think we can do it without a jackhammer."

"If it was a larger room at one time, he could've found a place to hide in the dark. We won't know until we get rid of the wall." She walked to the center of the room. The mournful crying and banging grew louder.

"I need to go upstairs." She bolted toward the stairway. As her foot touched the second step up, the door above slammed shut with a force which shook the stairway. She screamed when she felt a force push her, knocking her back onto the floor. Thank goodness she hadn't been on the top of the stairs, she thought as she lay on the floor.

"Oh hon, are you okay? What on earth happened?" Austin reached over to help her to her feet.

"I think so. It felt like someone ran right through me. I'll be okay." She hugged him, and let Austin lead the way upstairs. When he got to the door, it opened without issue.

"Okay, I have to be at the hospital until late tomorrow, but I'm going to give Rich a call. Maybe he can schedule one of the crew to come over and get this wall down for us." Austin placed the flashlight back on the counter. "I can't allow this Hastings to keep pushing us around, so to speak. I'm getting worried for your safety, sweetheart."

"I'll be fine, it's only when we go nosing around down there that he gets mad. But, I think it's time we face the facts. The spirits aren't going away, and Ben Hastings is getting more physical and is trying to hurt us." She walked over to the counter, pouring a glass of wine.

Later in the evening, she called Delaney.

"Hey, sorry I didn't get a chance to call you back. We've had another encounter. Austin saw Hastings and Freddy, and the cellar door slammed shut again and I felt Hastings try to push me down the stairs. We were so close to finding the source of the crying," Carly said.

"Oh my goodness, are you okay? Things are escalating." Delaney's voice was serious.

"But, some good news, at least. I have an interview with Channel 5 this Thursday." Carly walked through the downstairs, turning off the lights as she went into the den.

"How exciting! You thought they forgot about you." Delaney answered.

"I'm excited, but everything with the Pettigrews and Freddy is wearing me out. I think I'm to a point where I'm glad Austin made the doctor appointment." Carly curled up on the couch, pulling a green fuzzy afghan around her.

"Me too. Keep me posted." Delaney said goodbye and to take care.

The morning of her interview, Austin stayed home so he could wish her good luck. Kissing her as she walked out for her appointment with the television station, he told her he'd hire her in a New York minute. Carly laughed and started up her car. She dabbed at her makeup in the car mirror, having to apply more makeup than usual to cover the dark circles underneath her eyes.

When she arrived at the television station, a young twenty-something male met her at the information desk.

"Good morning, I'm Carly Tabor. I have a nine o'clock appointment with Ms. Foley."

The young man, whose small lanyard and name tag read "Clayton" found her name on the schedule of appointments. "Of course, Ms. Tabor. If you'll follow me, I'll take you to Ms. Foley's office." Clayton led her from the reception area through a hallway not open to the public.

He moved to the side, leaving her to knock on the opened door. A petite, blonde woman in her early 30s, around Carly's age, looked up from her work.

"Come on in! May I call you Carly? I'm finishing up." She flipped a file folder across her desk, opening another one and glanced at its contents.

Her dark green eyes loomed bright like emeralds behind tortoise shell-framed glasses. Carly noticed her small fingers were accentuated with French nail tips and an impressive diamond wedding set on her left hand.

Carly spent the next forty-five minutes giving an overview of her work experience in television. Daria Foley seemed impressed with her experience given her age.

"Tell me about your experience in investigative reporting." Daria leaned on her elbow, listening.

"Well, I worked for five years as a news reporter. I worked on a couple of investigative reports, but nothing on a regular basis." She felt flushed, her throat as dry as a cotton ball. Carly emphasized her attention to detail and strong work ethic.

Daria closed her folder, folding her hands. Waiting for the interview to come to a close, Carly was surprised when Daria offered her a position with Channel 5 news.

"Carly, the position we have in mind is hosting a new segment airing once a month. You'll have a production team, but you'll write and host the program." She studied a chip on her perfect nails. "Of course, you'll select the stories, per approval of the station manager."

"Oh my goodness, I can't believe it! Well…I can start whenever you need me." Carly extended her hand and pumped Daria's small hand several times.

"Wonderful, you'll fit in so well! We'll contact you in a few days about coming in and getting your paperwork started. I'd like you to start at the end of the month. We're excited to have you on board! Welcome to the Channel 5 family." Daria smiled and showed her perfect white teeth.

Carly couldn't believe her luck as she drove home and whooped with excitement in the car. To get a job offered on her first interview was unbelievable and she couldn't wait to share the news with Austin. She walked into the quiet house because he'd left for the hospital. She warmed a cup of coffee in the microwave and made a quick call to her mother to share the exciting news of her job.

A half-hour later after chatting with her mother, she left a message to come home soon as she had a surprise on Austin's cell. It would be a few hours before he would be able to head home. She went upstairs to change out of her blue Talbot's suit and hose and pumps, putting on yoga pants and a University of Kansas sweatshirt. Pulling her hair in a ponytail, she went downstairs to warm up a bite for lunch. Putting a leftover bowl of soup into the microwave, she was startled by her phone and saw the number identified as the Historical Society.

"Carly, this is Tom Drummond, at the Historical Society. I found an item in the Orphan House minutes which may be of importance to you. This morning, I located a section of minutes listing children who were being adopted, not indentured." Tom Drummond's usual staid voice trembled with excitement.

"Oh, wonderful. Please, go on." Carly felt her stomach flutter.

"It states here Andrew and Celeste Pettigrew petitioned to adopt a male, Frederick Richards, aged eight, and a female, Emmaline Brochmeyer, age eleven months. The Pettigrew's were in the process of adopting two children. I printed the page for you."

"Oh, wow! Thank you for all the time you've put into searching for me. We thought the connection to the child and Celeste was the Orphan House."

"Glad to help a young researcher. I'll put it in an envelope at the reference desk. You can get it at your convenience."

How had they missed the adoption petition in their research? She took her soup over to sit at the table, feeling tired from the morning's interview. As she sipped tomato soup, she felt the familiar feeling of worry about Freddy creep back. How would she help find Freddy if she worked every day?

She texted Delaney, "I got the job! Will be starting the end of the month. I have BIG news on Freddy. C." She drank her coffee, reading the prompt answer from Delaney. "Congrats! I'm headed out to do a ghost tour...may need to add your house to my walk...will stop by to-morrow. Love, D."

Carly couldn't wait for Delaney's next visit. She planned to bring the divining rods. Maybe at last they could locate Freddy's final resting place and put all the ghosts to rest in peace.

Chapter 28

Carly heard the doorbell, expecting Delaney, she flung open the door. "Hey, Miss Delaney! Come on in." She gave Delaney a hug as she came into the hallway.

"Congrats on the job, hon." Delaney placed two coat hangers on the hall table.

Carly led her into the kitchen. She poured two glasses of tea, and both sat down at the table.

"Tell me what news you have on Freddy. I've been dying to know." Delaney took a long drink of sweet tea.

"You're not going to believe this. Tom Drummond found in the minutes where Andrew and Celeste Pettigrew petitioned the court to adopt two orphans, Frederick Richards, age eight and Emmaline Brockmeyer, only eleven months old." She grabbed Delaney's arm. "They were going to adopt two children, bless them."

"We were right. So it's why Freddy was here." Delaney slapped her knee. "Do you think Freddy knew he was going to be adopted?"

"We'll never know. But I'd bet money it's the paper Celeste and Andrew wanted to show us. It was the petition to adopt Freddy and the little girl." Carly twirled her ponytail.

"I don't know what to say. It's beyond amazing. Now we need to find him." Delaney walked into the hallway, bringing the two coat hangers to the table.

"Well, my goodness!" Carly took the L-shaped metal rods into her hand. "You bent two coat hangers to make this?"

"Yep, I improvised. We used them to locate Confederate graves in the cemetery back home."

"Let's go downstairs in the dark and you try them out. Austin should be here soon with Rich to use the jackhammer again." She held open the door, letting Delaney lead the way down into the cellar.

When they reached the bottom of the stairs, both women stood in the dark.

"This is what Freddy saw as he jumped onto the dirt floor. The window over there was cracked, but he didn't have time to search for something to climb onto and out to the street." Delaney reached up to turn on the lightbulb. They both jumped as the banging started. "Freddy climbed into something. I saw him; I heard him crying. He showed me that much." The banging started and grew louder.

"Freddy, we're here!" Carly moved toward the far end of the cellar, shouting over the noise.

"I hear him. It's as if he's talking into a cup. It's muffled, but he says it's dark." Delaney took out the divining rods and stood in the center of the room.

Rich and Austin came downstairs into the cellar. It was if a switch had turned the volume of the banging up a notch.

"What's this crying I hear?" Rich said, and sat the jackhammer down on the floor. The cellar turned ice cold. Delaney and Carly greeted the men but continued their investigation.

"Freddy Richards died in this house on the night of January 19, 1799. We know he's still here. He wants to be found." Delaney held the two rods out in front of her, positioning them between her index fingers and thumbs.

Rich shrugged at Austin and they moved over to the window where the hammering would begin. An unseen gust of wind blew into the cellar and ruffled everyone's hair.

"If I didn't see it, I wouldn't believe it." Rich gasped as gust of wind circled around them.

"Can you make Freddy understand we know he's here, and we're going to find him?" Carly shouted over the clamor and crying.

"He's enclosed. It's dark. There's no air in the space." Delaney turned, the rods moving away from one another. She moved to another location.

Carly understood the feeling, as she was experiencing a shortness of breath.

Delaney stood still, the two sticks moving towards the wall. Carly knelt on the floor next to the wall. "Andrew and Celeste are both here with us. We're close to Freddy." Delaney's head jerked around to stare behind them.

Rich tried talking over the noise, but resorted to shouting directions for Austin to shine the light on the area near the window. The mini jackhammer began the assault on the ancient wall. The icy wind continued to blow from an unseen force through a window long ago closed.

Carly became more anxious by the moment, feeling as if she might faint. Delaney turned, acknowledging the unseen guests. "Celeste and Andrew are imploring us to continue. I believe the icy wind is Benjamin Hastings." Delaney's strawberry blonde hair blew into her face.

Delaney closed her eyes, speaking to the direction of the window. "You have no hold over these souls, Benjamin Hastings. We know Freddy Richards is here. You're no longer allowed to remain in this house! Get out!" Delaney shouted.

As she commanded Hastings to leave, Rich Trevenour found a weakness in the mortar of the wall, and a large chunk fell at his feet. The window frame slammed back into the block, splitting the wood into two halves. The wind ceased to blow.

Austin jumped away, but not before a large splinter from the frame struck him above the eye. A crimson line appeared where the splinter struck his face. Bringing his hand to his face, he dabbed at the sticky trickle.

"Hey, I need to run up and wipe this off. The wood got me on the forehead." Austin yelled and ran up the stairs to tend the wound.

It was as if the spirit of Benjamin Hastings had been exorcised from the cellar. Delaney looked towards the now closed window.

"Rich, Andrew is showing me a small portion of the wall which is hollow behind the stone. You need to move down to the area in front of the cistern. It explains why I thought Freddy was here in the floor. They're saying this is the way to Freddy." Delaney's divining rods turned to the wall.

Rich looked at her, then at the wall where he was barely making a dent. He moved his equipment down to the far end of the cellar wall. Austin rejoined the group, a bandage covering the cut.

Carly remained sitting on the floor, now feeling more anxious. Austin bent down to hold her wrist. "Honey, your pulse is elevated. You might want to go upstairs until we get through the wall."

Willing herself to feel better, Carly didn't want to abandon her post beside the wall. Austin resumed his place beside Rich, taking turns with the mini-sledgehammer. Within an hour the two opened up a section of the stone wall, as Delaney had directed.

All noises stopped. A veil of stillness descended on the cellar. Delaney turned to see if the Pettigrews were still holding vigil, but only the shadows of Rich and Austin played on the wall behind her. "I can't hear Freddy anymore or the Pettigrews, but we'll find him." She put her arm around Carly.

Carly nodded, her attention focused on the men uncovering the wall.

The sound of Rich's voice broke the silence. "I think we can get through to the other side. We hit a pretty good opening."

Austin turned the shop light towards the hole in the wall. "I feel like Howard Carter. How about we shine this in first to see what is on the other side."

Carly and Delaney moved to the opening to see with the light. The opening was a three foot by three foot hole, enclosed roughly. A rush of warm air, accompanied by a dank odor, filled the small area. Immediately, the four sneezed from the dust assaulting their airways.

"There's cob webs everywhere. Looks like crates stacked against the back wall, and I see several barrels too." Rich surveyed the space, his light making an arc from floor to ceiling.

As soon as he said the word barrels, Carly moved passed Austin and crawled into the opening. "He's in one of those barrels. It's why he sounded muffled." She went on hands and knees through the opening to the other side.

"Carly, wait! Let me go first." Austin tried to move around her once through the opening. Before she could stand up, Delaney and Rich crawled into the tiny dark room as well. For the first time in over two centuries, the contents of this small forgotten space were about to share their secrets.

The beam from the spotlight illuminated the dark storage space. The stale odor was overwhelming, as the room had been closed since the 19th century. The floor was stone with large slabs of flagstone placed tight together. No windows were located along the walls, but three dusty shelves lined the back wall. Several stone crocks along with some wooden boxes stood on the shelves. Austin shone his light along the wall while Rich focused his light on the ceiling.

"It looks like the beams are still sound, I don't see any structural issues. Looks like the owner closed the room off for other reasons." He walked over to the shelves, examining the antique stoneware. Carly spotted the barrels lined up along the opposite wall, some stacked on top of others.

"Delaney, can you hear anything?" Carly asked as she approached the barrels.

Delaney moved as if entering hallowed ground. She put the diving rods down, bringing her hands to her chest. "Oh, Good God, I can see him! He's crouching, over by the barrel. He's clutching his knees with his arms. Poor mite…he's telling me he tried to be quiet, but he couldn't stop crying." She wiped her tears with her sleeve.

"Do you really see and hear people who're dead?" Rich whispered, after keeping his comments to himself through the evening, listening to all. Carly could tell he didn't want to believe in the paranormal, but Delaney gave him reason to believe.

"It's like I'm having a movie replay in my mind. Sometimes I experience a smell or a feeling the spirit wants to show or tell me." Delaney wiped her cheeks, keeping her attention on the ghost.

"We need to open the barrels. Rich, do you have a crowbar or hammer in the other room?" Carly moved towards the barrels, but Austin pulled her back by her arm.

"Hold on, let's shine the light over there first." Austin moved his light in the direction where Delaney saw Freddy.

Rich crawled back into the cellar where he had laid his tool belt. He brought his hammer and joined the others around the stacked barrels. All of them stood with heads bowed as if in mourning.

Rich pried the lid off the first wooden barrel. No contents left, save for a small collection of powder in the bottom. Austin put his finger into the mixture. "It looks like rice to me. Let's keep looking." He moved the barrel out of the way.

Carly looked at the remaining four barrels. Two had side plugs and the remaining two didn't have plugs, as the contents had long since evaporated or were empty. Rich and Austin worked on prying the lid from the next barrel as Carly held the light.

"Wait! There's another barrel over there." Delaney pulled Carly toward the back wall.

Hidden from view, an oak barrel sat in the corner beside the shelves in the darkest corner. Carly reverently touched the outside of the barrel. "Oh, this one has pegs on the side. It doesn't have plugs. It's air tight." She looked at Delaney, and then closed her eyes, tears streaming down her face.

"He's here!" Delaney looked back to the men. Rich and Austin stopped their work and walked back to where the women were now kneeling beside a larger barrel.

"Hurry, get the lid off!"

Carly bounced on her toes. Delaney explained Freddy's final moments. "Hastings heard Freddy crying over here in the corner. He found the barrel without a lid and put this one on top, knowing Freddy was hiding inside. " She touched the top of the barrel. "He put the lid down on precious little Freddy…" Delaney's voice was overcome with emotion. "He's crying." Delaney supported Carly and moved away from the barrel so it could be opened, both overcome with emotion.

Rich removed the lid while Austin shined the light inside.

"Oh man." Austin moved back as if an electrical charge sent a volt through his hands. He knelt on his knees and said a prayer.

Rich peered over his shoulder. "Well I'll be da…"

Carly walked back to the barrel. She saw the remains inside. "I'm going to be sick."

She sank to her knees. Austin crawled to his wife and put his arms around her as she wept for Freddy Richards.

"Freddy, you're safe now. Celeste and Andrew have been looking for you." Delaney spoke to the skeletal remains of the child.

"Can you see him?" Rich asked.

"Celeste is with him." Delaney wiped the tears streaming down her face. "Celeste is holding his hand. Andrew is holding out his hand to them. They were waiting for Freddy before they went to heaven." Delaney started to sob.

For several moments, all four wiped their eyes over what was left of Freddy found in the barrel. Austin sniffed, wiping his face on the hem of his shirt. He took another look into the contents of the barrel. "I need to call the police and report what we've found. Rich, if you want to leave, we'll understand."

Carly regained her composure and peered inside the barrel. A complete skeleton of a child lay against the side of the barrel. Along with it were tattered remnants of material still visible inside. "Oh, bless your little heart. I'm so sorry, Freddy."

"I never told another soul, but I saw a little boy the first time I came into this house. I did a walk-through before the crew started. But, I thought I was seeing things." Rich wiped his nose with his blue bandana.

"You mean you saw him before all the hammers went flying and the walls started banging, and you didn't tell us?" Carly turned to face him.

"I'm sorry, but I didn't believe it myself. But it was upstairs in the front room. He was sitting on the floor beside the fireplace; then he was gone." Rich sat on the floor, his knees shaking.

"It doesn't matter now. He wanted someone to find him, after all these years." Delaney put her arm around his shoulder, patting him.

Austin went upstairs to call the police. It was the right thing to do, even though they knew the police would have questions about how they found the skeleton.

Carly sat next to the barrel on the floor. She wasn't about to abandon Freddy yet. Delaney made a quick call to Boyd Hawley, sending a picture of the barrel to him.

After fifteen minutes, Carly heard the sound of Austin walking through the kitchen. Carly, Delaney, and Rich waited in reverent silence as Austin led the police down into the cellar.

Chapter 29

Sergeant Malone of the Charleston police followed Austin into the cellar. His large flashlight, gripped in his hand, flashed around the cellar. The sound of chatter on his radio broke the eerie silence.

"It's right through here." Austin ducked down and crawled through the hole in the stone wall.

Sergeant Malone radioed he was entering the cellar and followed Austin through the opening and stood, brushing off the dust from his dark blue uniform. "Has the opening always been in the wall there?" He noticed the tears Carly and Delaney had on their faces.

"No, we finished opening it up tonight. Then, we found the barrels." Austin shined his light on the barrel.

"You said there are bones inside? Did you or the ladies touch anything?" The officer took notes on a small notepad and walked over to the barrel.

"No, we called 911. We've been sitting here since we discovered the bones," Carly said and Delaney agreed.

Sergeant Malone put on latex gloves and scrutinized the lid next to the barrel. He shined the light inside, noting the skeletal remains. "Okay, I'm going to need to take your statements. I'll also need to call the coroner. I'd like to have you all upstairs, please, to secure the crime scene." He removed his cell phone and took a picture of the barrel and the lid.

Carly and Austin looked at each other in horror at the term "crime scene." Today was almost 215 years to the day Freddy Richards lost his life, along with Andrew and Celeste Pettigrew. Carly couldn't believe the irony.

Sergeant Malone called the county coroner while in the cellar securing the scene, and as the group waited upstairs in the kitchen, someone knocked on the door.

Carly saw the neighbor lady across the street watch through her window the activity of police and coroner vehicles at their home. When Carly caught sight of her from the window in the den, she shut the curtains. Busy body.

Sergeant Malone let the deputy coroner, Larry Deveroux, and a forensic anthropologist, Dr. Brooke Armstrong, into the home. Before they were escorted downstairs, Sergeant Malone excused Delaney Warrick and Rich Trevenour from the home.

"I have your statements, thanks. If I have any other questions, I'll be in touch." Sergeant Malone put his notebook in his pocket.

"We'll talk later." Delaney hugged Carly and told her not to worry about the investigation.

"Thanks, Rich. I'm sorry you got dragged into the drama. I can't thank you enough for helping us, though." Austin shook Rich's hand and walked him to the door.

Inside the Tabor house, Dr. Armstrong and Deputy Coroner Deveroux followed Carly down to the cellar. The sergeant stayed upstairs to interview Austin in the den. Larry Deveroux was a small, stout man, not much taller than Carly and appeared to be in his late fifties. His complexion was rutted with deep pits, probably from severe acne as a youth. He resembled Colombo in his large coat, minus the cigar. In contrast, Dr. Armstrong was tall, slender and in her early thirties. Her dark brown hair was pulled back into a sleek bun, and her navy wool pantsuit and silk camisole displayed professionalism and style. Carly hated to see her crawl through the small opening, getting dust on her neat attire.

"The barrel where we found the remains is over here." Carly led the pair to the opposite side of the room.

Deveroux began snapping photographs while Armstrong examined the outside of the barrel. "Has anyone touched anything?" she asked.

"My friend removed the lid on the barrel, and I believe my husband also touched the outer rim, but no one has touched the inside." Carly explained, moving away from the barrel.

"Thank you. Did you check the other barrels for remains after finding this one?" Armstrong looked up.

Carly felt like this was the beginning of many difficult questions. "Well, we were actually looking for this barrel. We opened all but two of them."

Deveroux looked at the doctor, then at Carly. "You mean you were looking for remains down here?"

"Actually, we've been looking for a while. This house was the scene of a triple homicide in 1799."

"Have you given this information to the police?" Deveroux asked. He continued to take photographs from every angle of the room. He then moved to the inside of the barrel to take more photographs.

Armstrong crouched down to examine the exterior of the barrel. The remaining barrels were still unopened, becoming part of the crime scene. Dr. Armstrong instructed Deveroux to be sure the barrels were photographed and sent to her office for examination. Apparently, she thought there might be more bodies.

"We gave him our statements as to how we came to find the barrel and the skeleton. Is there any way I could go with the child's remains? I feel like I owe it to him." Carly bit her lower lip.

Larry raised an eyebrow and faced Carly, who stood a distance away. "I'm sorry, it isn't allowed. Once we're through here, the coroner's office will take the remains."

Carly felt a wave of panic. What would become of Freddy? She couldn't let the coroner take him without knowing what they would do with his bones afterwards.

"If you folks will wait upstairs, we'll finish processing the scene and remove the barrels," Deveroux instructed.

Carly crawled back through the hole in the wall. For months she wanted the spirits in the house to leave. Now they were seemingly gone, but she felt no relief. Carly joined Austin and the police officer in the den.

"Mrs. Tabor, if I could have you answer a few more questions, I'll take this report back to the station," Malone asked.

"Mrs. Tabor, your husband told me about you and your friend, Ms. Warrick, finding information about a murder which happened in your home. Do you have a record of that?" Sergeant Malone asked.

The air felt thinner in the room, and Carly started to feel lightheaded. "Yes, I have the information. I'd be happy to show you the copies I obtained from the historical society. Tom Drummond, one of the employees, helped me locate the information." She found her files and showed him the information regarding the murders and the trial. Feeling she had no choice but to be completely honest, she also shared their research was all because of paranormal activity in the home. Austin cringed when she mentioned the connection to the paranormal, so Carly guessed he hadn't mentioned those details.

"I'll make a note." He looked down at his notepad. "In the meantime, I'll be filing the report of remains found in the home. From here out, the coroner's office will be handling the case."

Both Carly and Austin thanked the officer and walked him to the door. When his squad car pulled away, they let out their breath in a collective puff.

"You didn't have to tell him about the ghosts, Carly. I think he decided we have a screw loose when you mentioned the paranormal. Did you see his face?" Austin ran his hand through his hair.

"Well, how else could I explain it? Maybe I should've shown him the picture of Freddy beside Mom and me. He'd believe me then!" She argued back. "It would have come up at some point, so it's better to get it all out in the open from the beginning."

"Yeah, I guess you're right, but I hope it doesn't end up in the newspapers or I'll be the joke of the hospital." He wrapped his arms around his wife. "I'm glad it's over and we're safe and sound and can enjoy our dream house."

Within a half an hour, Dr. Armstrong came upstairs and brought a hand truck back from her van into the cellar to transport the barrels.

"Dr. Tabor, we'll be transporting the remains back to the coroner's office. I'm also taking the remaining two unopened barrels." Armstrong finished writing some notes on her clipboard.

"I know you and Mr. Deveroux think we are lunatics, but here's proof there's something paranormal going on here." Carly held out the photograph her mother had taken months earlier.

Dr. Armstrong looked at the photograph. "I know it must be awful to find remains in one's cellar, no matter how long they've been hidden there."

Carly watched her frown when she noticed the child, who appeared in shades of gray contrasting with the colorful clothing of the women.

Then, her expression changed to curiosity. "Well this *is* interesting. Was this taken here in the house?" Armstrong stared at the child in the photograph.

"Yes, it's upstairs in a bedroom. My father took the picture. We don't have children, so this was quite a shock. As you can see, he looks like an apparition." Carly pointed to the child.

Brooke Armstrong was a trained scientist, a forensic anthropologist, not a ghost hunter. Carly could see she was skeptical about her claims.

Austin walked over to join the two women, "I know you think we're nuts. I'm the last person to believe in this sort of thing, but we're living it. Others who've lived here have seen ghosts in this house. We feel this little boy was an orphan in the house at the time of the murders. We wanted to find him and to know his name." He put his arm around his wife.

To try to convince her, Carly showed her the paperwork from the Charleston Orphan House. As she was reading the information, Larry Deveroux came to the top of the cellar stairs.

"Dr. Armstrong? Are you up here?" He stuck his head into the kitchen.

"Yes, I'm coming. Sorry!" She almost dropped the papers at the sound of Larry Deveroux's voice.

"Is there some way we can know what you find after the examination?" Austin asked.

"You can call the office tomorrow. We should know more after we examine the remains back at the coroner's office." She placed her business card in Carly's hand. "I'm so sorry you've found something terrible like this in your house."

Within minutes, the two processed and photographed the scene. The barrel passed through the opening in the stone wall. After a couple of tense moments, Brooke Armstrong and Larry Deveroux carried the hand truck several times up the narrow cellar stairs. Carly watched as a shroud was placed over one barrel before it was taken from the house.

Carly and Austin walked out of the house and stood in the driveway as the barrel containing the remains of Freddy Richards was placed in the back of the coroner's van.

As soon as the van pulled onto the street, they walked back into the house. She collapsed into his arms, grieving for the child who wanted so badly to be found.

Austin and Carly made phone calls to their parents after taking some time to process and discuss what transpired earlier.

After that, Carly took a hot shower to relax and entered the bedroom when her cell phone started ringing. Looking at the display, she smiled. True to form, Delaney was calling to touch base with her.

"I'm sorry it's late. I can't get Freddy off my mind." Delaney's voice sounded worried.

"It's okay. Austin and I can't stop thinking about him either. Since the crying and banging had been our constant companions since moving into the house seven months ago, the house feels different." She told Delaney she suspected the stress from the spirit activity in her home caused her nausea, fatigue and other symptoms. "My goodness, I have a doctor's appointment tomorrow. All this stress has caused me to forget it." She took a breath.

"I have the number for the coroner's office, and tomorrow, after my doctor appointment, I'm going to call and talk to Dr. Armstrong about Freddy." Carly straightened her bed covers.

"Good luck tomorrow. Maybe tonight you'll get a good night's sleep. Lord knows you haven't gotten a good night's sleep for months," Delaney said.

"Thanks again for helping us, sweetie. You're a God-send." Carly felt a tear roll down her cheek.

"You're welcome. Oh, before I forget, I met up with Boyd tonight for dinner. He wanted to let you know he'd be in touch. He thought you might be interested in speaking at the Southern Paranormal Convention in June. He thinks your story is amazing," Delaney told her.

"Well, we'll see. I start work in a couple of weeks. I'll be keeping busy."

The two continued talking for a few moments more, then ended their conversation.

Austin stuck his head into the bedroom from the hallway. "Hon, I found this on the floor in the cellar. Did you bring it down there?" Austin held the small rocking horse.

"No, Freddy did. I guess we won't be finding it lying around the house after tonight." She took the horse, holding it close.

"It's all good, Carly. Now we can have our house back." He slid into bed beside her and snuggled her against his tall body.

Even though she felt safe, she couldn't fall asleep. She didn't feel like she could close the chapter on the Pettigrews and Freddy Richards yet.

Chapter 30

The following morning, Austin and Carly awoke rested after sleeping through the quietest night since they'd moved in. Although they were both saddened by finding Freddy, they agreed the spirits had stayed in the house to find Freddy, except for Hastings who tried to continue hiding him. Austin called Dr. Armstrong and talked with her, but only found her investigation was continuing slowly. She'd had trouble removing the bones from the barrel and did note the barrel seemed to date to the late 1700s as they'd indicated. Because of the apparent age of the crime scene, he also reported she would be consulting with Dr. Cameron Ross, an archeologist at the College of Charleston.

After kissing Austin goodbye, Carly left for her doctor's appointment, and he left for a long shift at the hospital.

Arriving a few minutes early for her appointment, she filled out several pages of insurance and patient history documents. Within a short time, a nurse called her back to the exam room and checked Carly's blood pressure and weight. She had to provide a urine specimen and had blood drawn before the doctor came in to examine her.

"Good morning, Mrs. Tabor. I'm Dr. Seig." Lynette Seig was older than Carly, but not by much. With her short black hair styled in a fashionable wedge cut, she wore grey slacks and a turquoise sweater, instead of the usual scrubs and lab coat.

"Good morning, Doctor." Carly adjusted the pink paper sheet.

Dr. Seig asked about the symptoms Carly was experiencing, and typed her notes on a lap top she brought into the room.

"When was your last period?" She continued typing Carly's answers.

Caught off guard, she didn't remember when her last cycle had been. With all the stress she'd been under, it was no wonder her periods were irregular. "Well, I remember having one a few months ago, but we've had a lot going on with moving into a house. It's been stressful." Carly felt her face flush.

After checking back over the notes the nurse had taken, Dr. Seig excused herself and left the room. Within a few moments, she returned with a smile on her face. "I have a diagnosis. Your fatigue, stomach upset, and light-headedness, Mrs. Tabor, all confirm you're pregnant. I'm guessing almost fourteen weeks. Have you felt any movement yet?" Dr. Seig washed her hands in the sink.

"I'm pregnant? I miscarried two years ago, and I didn't feel like I did with that pregnancy." Carly's mouth dropped open in disbelief.

"Well, your urine and blood tests confirmed my suspicions. I'd like to do an ultrasound today, and we can go ahead and do your annual exam. Congratulations!" She wrote the orders.

"So, umm, when am I due?" Carly felt the room spinning.

"Without knowing the exact date when your last period was, I'm thinking sometime around the middle of June. Let's do the ultrasound, and we'll know more after I've seen the results and completed your exam.

Carly watched the small screen as their longed-for baby performed acrobatics. She marveled at the perfection growing inside her.

"It's still a little too early to tell the sex, but it sure is active. I can't believe you haven't felt it yet." The technician moved the wand over her stomach.

I can't believe I'm pregnant!" Carly said, feeling tears pool in her eyes as she watched.

"Congratulations! I'll print out several pictures since I'm sure you'll want to pass these around." The technician left the room, returning with several photographs.

Dr. Seig confirmed the due date as June 25th, and wrote a prescription for prenatal vitamins for Carly. Still feeling shocked, Carly dressed and went back to the receptionist desk to schedule her first prenatal visit with the obstetrician Dr. Seig recommended visiting in a couple of weeks.

Carly left the office and went to the Neurosurgery wing of the hospital. She saw Dr. Hutchinson conferring at the nurse's station. When he saw her, he smiled as she approached.

"Hello, Carly. How are you? In the middle of a conference here, but good to see you." He said, then continued his discussion with the nurse.

Carly asked the nurse behind the desk if Austin was still in surgery.

"Let me check." She looked at the computer screen. "Looks like the surgery is still going on. Want me to have him call you when he's through, Mrs. Tabor?"

"That would be great. Just tell him I stopped by. Thanks." She drove home feeling elated, but still shocked she had no suspicions of her ailments indicating pregnancy.

In a matter of hours, Carly went from mourning the loss of a child who died two hundred years before, to experiencing the joy of seeing a new life she was carrying. The police had photographed the skeleton inside the barrel and the crime scene as they called it. Impatient to get Freddy's bones given a proper burial, she hoped Dr. Armstrong would finish her examination of his remains. However, in the meantime, she would grab a bite to eat. She was learning to not feel guilty about always feeling famished.

Later in the day, Austin walked into the nursery, finding Carly on the floor, holding something in her hand.

"I got your message today, hon. I didn't see you downstairs…I panicked thinking something happened." He continued talking, while she sat staring at a photograph in her hand.

"Hey, Carly? Your timer was beeping on the casserole. I put it on the counter." He walked further into the room. "Are you looking at the picture again?"

Carly turned to Austin, holding out a small black and white photograph. "No, this is a different picture. I think you should look at it." She looked up, tears pooling in her eyes.

For a moment, he frowned at the picture but then looked at Carly, a smile washing over his face. "Is this for real? Is this ours?" He sat down on the floor, holding the picture.

"I found out today! I'm pregnant! Fourteen weeks to be exact, and I had no idea. You're going to be a daddy!" She began laughing and crying at the time.

Austin took Carly into his arms, and the two wept tears of joy. What followed was a long evening of phone calls, emails and future planning. The casserole sat out for hours before being eaten.

<h1 style="text-align:center">Chapter 31</h1>

Carly and Delaney met for lunch the following day because she wanted to tell her good friend the news in person. After a few moments of crying and hugging, they talked about the new baby, followed by the latest update on Freddy. After lunch, they drove back to the Tabor's house where Delaney spent a few moments examining the receiving room, nursery, and cellar. She told Carly their house officially appeared to have been "ghost busted" and was spirit-free.

"What will become of Freddy now?" Delaney sat down on the couch in the den.

Carly shared they had been discussing what they would like to with the child's remains.

"We'd like to ask for his remains, if they will release him to us. Austin and I would like to purchase a plot in Magnolia Cemetery with the other orphans buried there. Freddy finally deserves a proper burial." Carly nibbled on a soda cracker.

Delaney recounted her conversation with Boyd Hawley. Carly's case was one the paranormal investigators would love to claim as having assisted to solve.

"Boyd wants to have a final meeting with you and Austin. I told him if you didn't mind, I'd like to have everyone over to my house. I think we should have a final meeting to bring Boyd and Tucker up to speed." Delaney looked at the photograph of Freddy on the mantel.

Carly agreed and knew she wouldn't have found Freddy without all of their help.

Looking at her watch, Delaney mentioned she still needed to run errands. "Congratulations, sweet girl. You're going to be a great little mama." She kissed Carly's cheek. "I've enjoyed getting to know you and Austin through all of this. I'm glad we've become friends."

Even though she was twenty years older than Carly, the two women grew closer in the past few months more than any other Charleston friends. "You're going to be an honorary Auntie for this baby. You're family to us." Carly hugged her again before showing her out of the house.

The rest of the afternoon, Carly tried not to think about Freddy, but her curiosity won, and she couldn't wait any longer.

Carly found Dr. Armstrong's business card and called her, getting connected right away. Dr. Armstrong explained the test results were complete. The formal report had been placed on the Coroner's desk, and the funeral director at Lattimer Mortuary was expected shortly to take the remains back to his establishment. Carly asked if she was at liberty to discuss the findings.

"I was able to come within a year or two of the age of the child. It appears to be a male child between the ages of seven and nine. From his teeth, it appears he was ill with a high fever sometime before his death," Brooke explained.

Carly felt this wasn't new information, but it was good to have it confirmed. She made notes as the doctor discussed the findings.

"Now it becomes a little harder to determine the age of the bones. Because they were so brittle, I concluded this boy died sometime around the year 1800. We're looking at a skeleton well over 200 years old. I had an archaeologist inspect the cloth found under the bones. The fibers were examined and are definitely 19th century, and carbon dating will likely place the cloth between one hundred fifty and two hundred years old."

Carly was amazed at how much information could be collected from a skeleton. She didn't want to interrupt, so she listened and gave an occasional 'hmm' during Dr. Armstrong's explanation.

"It's impossible to determine the manner or cause of death since we couldn't find any signs of blunt force trauma or fractures to the skull or body. There were no objects found inside the barrel which could have been a murder weapon. From looking at the inside portion of the barrel, interior scratches show the child may have been alive and trapped inside trying to get out. There are small scrapes on the inside staves consistent with finger nails digging into the wood, but I can't be certain. Whether the child died in the barrel or was killed and then placed in the barrel is another unknown. We will never know for sure. But it's my opinion this male child was a victim of homicide. As I was telling my colleague, it would be a horrible way to die, being stuffed inside a barrel to suffocate." Dr. Armstrong finished summarizing her report.

"Yes, it was horrible. It breaks my heart to know he's been down in the cellar, alone, over two hundred years." Carly's voice cracked. "My husband and I were hoping once all the forensic tests were completed, we could take possession of the remains. We'd like to have Freddy buried at Magnolia Cemetery."

Hearing Carly use a name for the child seemed to catch the doctor off-guard. "Well, the remains have been taken to Lattimer Mortuary on Calhoun Street. I don't think there would be a problem with you and your husband taking possession, since there is no next of kin. It's kind of you to do this. But, you called the child Freddy. I'd be interested in knowing how you figured out his possible name." Armstrong's voice showed her interest was piqued.

Carly knew she wouldn't believe her, but tried. "When I was doing research to find the victims' names of the couple murdered in my home, I found out the Pettigrews were planning to adopt a young boy and infant girl from the Orphan House. According to the minutes of the house, the boy, Freddy Richards, was reported to have run away the night the couple were murdered. During several paranormal investigations, we learned the boy came to the house, saw Benjamin Hastings murder the Pettigrews who were to adopt him, and tried to hide and run away. But, sadly, Hastings found the boy hiding in the barrel down in the cellar, and to cover up his crime, meanly sealed poor little Freddy Richards in the barrel."

"You have been doing quite a bit of sleuthing, Mrs. Tabor." Dr. Armstrong's voice didn't reveal if she believed her but she sounded curious. "Your case is one of the most interesting I've done in awhile."

After her conversation with Dr. Armstrong ended, Carly drove to Lattimer Mortuary. There, she met Vince Lattimer, owner and funeral director. She brought with her documentation stating she was the homeowner where the remains were found, as well as a typed statement she'd picked up from the coroner's office stating they found no reason the remains should not be released to the Tabors, as there are no relatives alive to claim the remains for burial.

Carly walked into the small sales area where coffins and urns were arranged around the room. The place was macabre, so she quickly chose a small white coffin with a baby blue satin drape and pillow. She made arrangements with Mr. Lattimer to have Freddy's remains interred, but she would have to contact Magnolia Cemetery to purchase a plot in the section where the Orphan House had long ago interred its dead.

Surprisingly, Carly phoned the cemetery and completed the arrangements, and they could have Freddy Richards laid to rest within two weeks.

In the following days, Carly was preoccupied with the start of her new job at Channel 5 News. Her evenings were spent in meetings with the production staff and discussing possible stories for upcoming segments. She found time to purchase a small blue and white checked baby quilt to be placed inside the coffin with Freddy.

On the morning of February 23rd, a small procession drove into the section of Magnolia Cemetery where many orphans already lay in eternal slumber. Austin, Boyd Hawley, and Delaney Warrick carried the small white coffin from the back of the funeral director's hearse. Carly followed the pallbearers, carrying a small arrangement of white roses. Tucker McGee and his wife, along with Rich Trevenour also attended the service. Carly read the Twenty-Third Psalm aloud; Delaney offered a prayer for Freddy Richards.

As each person walked away from the coffin, they gently placed a small white rose atop the lid.

Carly spent a moment at the grave before joining the rest of them. She patted her growing belly and felt a sense of closure for the Pettigrews and Freddy Richards. After she said her final goodbye, she leaned over to place a kiss on the tiny coffin. "You can rest now, little Freddy."

The group planned to meet for dinner later in the evening to celebrate the solving of the mystery at the Tabor house. The group of friends would forever be connected because of a tragic event which happened two hundred years before.

Carly walked back to the car where Austin stood holding the car door for her. "Would you mind if we stop by St. Michael's Church? I'd like to place a rose on Celeste's grave," she asked.

The procession of cars drove through the ornate gate at Magnolia Cemetery. No one noticed the funeral director locking the coffin after Carly had placed the small toy horse inside, now joined with its rightful owner.

Acknowledgements

It would not have been possible to write this book without the assistance and support of a host of individuals. Writing a novel involves hours of research. This novel required footwork that I was unable to do. Whether it was over the phone, in an email, or pounding the pavement, the following people were a god-send when I needed direction or information:

To my husband, Doug~ Thank you for your endless love and support.

Lisa Collins~ My resident tour guide to all things Charleston and the Low Country. Thank you for opening your home to me and giving me a greater appreciation for the Holy City.

Denny Collins~ Your artwork is amazing. You brought the house to life and captured the setting perfectly. Thank you for taking on the project.

Dr. Suzanne Abel~ I can't begin to thank you enough for your willingness to answer every forensic question I threw at you. It was a pleasure getting to work with you.

Harlan Greene~ Your help in locating information on the cemeteries and Orphan Asylum records was much appreciated. Thank you for pointing me in the right direction each time.

Thank you, Samuel Stewart, for answering my numerous questions through the College of Charleston Help Line.

To Mary Jo Fairchild, Linda Bennett, and Jeanine Branham~ Your help in answering my questions was much appreciated.

To Charlotte Hopps~ You're the first to meet my characters with all of their flaws. Thank you for your constant encouragement and support from the beginning.

To Darlene Hammond~ You were the inspiration for the character of Delaney Warrick. We share your gift.

To Brooke E. Armstrong~ A student with much promise. I believe you will accomplish great things.

About the Author:

Lori Roberts is a resident of Bedford, Indiana. She is married with three grown children and nine grandchildren. She has been an educator for 29 years and currently teaches 8th grade U.S. History. Lori has Bachelors of Science, Elementary Education and Middle School Social Studies degrees from Indiana University SE. She holds a Master of Arts Degree in Curriculum and Instruction from Nova Southeastern University.

Contact Lori Roberts at www.loriroberts.com